# BECOMING AUDREY HUTCHINS

## A NOVEL

This novel is dedicated to my family –
Lynne, James, Glyn, Lena, Nadine, Lily,
Oliver, and Sam and to my brother David
and sister Wendy.

I am deeply grateful to the Rivendell Retreat Centre which generously supported a writing retreat at the Penny Lou Cottage on Bowen Island, British Columbia in May 2023. This writing is much better for it.

Stephen Murgatroyd

Becoming Audrey Hutchins

ISBN: 978-1-716-837944

# Miss Audrey Hutchins

Audrey Hutchins is an elegant lady. Always carefully and stylishly dressed, ensuring that nothing inappropriate was revealed. Delicate make-up and a hint of gold in her ears, and a fine gold chain around her neck. Manicured nails and the same hairstyle daily – never a hair out of place. At five feet ten, she was what was once called "prim and proper." She spoke rarely but always correctly and usually in response to a question. She rarely initiated a conversation, especially with strangers. In her late thirties, obviously, from a well-to-do family, she was an enigma to others.

Her appearance at the concert was not a surprise. She had been coming to the Festival Hall since she was a teenager, always sitting in the same seat – dress circle, front row seat eleven. She always arrived and left alone. She read the program cover to cover and listened intently, never speaking to anyone before or after the concert or between compositions. She showed no more enthusiasm for Mozart or Brahms than for the more modern composers, like Kalevi Aho, Alexis French or John Adams. It was all music she seemed to appreciate in the same way that one appreciated delicate lace or a rare piece of porcelain.

At work, she was reliable, thorough, and always capable of all the assignments she was given. A chartered accountant with a penchant for forensic accounting, she was not only seen to be good at her work but one of those dependable souls who just got things done with no fuss. She would not tolerate mistakes, and the only time she had spoken more than a few short sentences to a colleague occurred when they had mistakenly entered expenses that were specifically disallowed by company policy. She had been in her position since she graduated from university with a first-class honour's degree in financial and forensic accounting and had secured her professional designation – some seventeen years ago.

No one knew much at all about her personal life. She lived alone in an apartment she had inherited from her aunt. It was in a highly sought-after neighbourhood surrounded by excellent restaurants, book and antique shops and cafes just off the Old Brompton Road in Knightsbridge, London. She was occasionally seen in some of them. She did not have a pet, nor did she speak much about any friends or family.

Her parents had both died when she was at university. As an only child, she inherited their estate, thought to be to be very valuable. The house she had grown up in sold for over eight million, and her father, a former venture capitalist, was thought to have been worth several million. Her mother, it was known, was a former bank executive who made shrewd investments. Audrey Hutchins never spoke about her own money. She was not short of it.

Other than classical music concerts, she was only occasionally seen outside her apartment. She did receive frequent deliveries of mail. Some of the packages were books she had ordered. Other items included magazines she subscribed to – The London Review of Books, The Gramophone, The New Statesman, Monocle and The Spectator. She did not subscribe to a newspaper or own a television. She also received a significant monthly delivery of compact discs and, according to a neighbour, played music constantly when she was home. Not too loud, but ever-present.

Each year she took two weeks' vacation. Always the first two weeks of May. She alternated her vacations between Paris and Amsterdam. She took the train to Paris, telling a colleague at work that she enjoyed the rhythm of the wheels – it put her in the mood for a change. She flew to Amsterdam, always staying at The Conservatorium Hotel on Van Baerlestraat near the Rijksmuseum. In Paris, she stayed at the Hotel George V. Expensive but central and close to concerts, museums, and cafes. She rarely talked to others about her vacations, though she once commented that she could "spend the rest of her days in the Van Gough Museum in Amsterdam or the Louvre in Paris."

Over the years, her colleagues had pieced together some aspects of her life. Growing up as an only child, she went to a private tutor rather than a public or private school. She was entered for five A levels, all of which she passed with distinction, securing her place at the London School of Economics at just seventeen. Graduating at the top of her class, no record could be found of her being involved in any social activities, clubs, or social events. Her parents had died during her second year at university, killed in a car crash in the Swiss Alps. She took two weeks' leave from the university to attend to family matters but returned to complete her degree as if nothing had happened.

After university, she started working on a work placement at Brooke and Walters, the accountants where she still works. She was appointed assistant accountant to chief accountant Michael Watters, who left just two years later. She succeeded him, despite being junior in both age and experience to many others who competed for the position. Explaining her appointment, the Chief Executive had made clear that she was an exceptional accountant and had made fourteen recommendations for improving the efficiency and profitability of the firm. All had been implemented, and she, single-handily, had been responsible for the largest bonuses ever paid to partners in the company's hundred-year history.

She was, it seemed, a dedicated and determined single woman with no interest in sex, adventure, or other passions except art, food, and music. She was both alone and aloof – qualities that the partners in the firm admired in their chief accountant.

Some of the single men in the office had approached her, suggesting lunch or dinner. She had been polite but firm when rejecting them. She clarified that she did not think social activities with colleagues were appropriate for someone in her position. Those that had asked once never asked again.

Each Friday, she ended her workday shortly after lunch. She had done so soon after her promotion to chief accountant. At three o'clock, she tidied her neat desktop, closed her files, and left the office. No one was sure where she went.

# Friday, 15<sup>th</sup> October 1998

Each Friday at four o'clock, Dr. Michelle May saw Miss Audrey Hutchins as her patient. She had been doing so for just over a year.

Miss Hutchins had been referred to her by her previous therapist, Dr. Sandy Fassbender, whose nickname amongst his therapist friends was Sandy Mindbender. He had said, at the time of the referral, that "he found this patient the most impenetrable he had ever encountered" and that she was one of the reasons he had finally decided to retire. Given that he was nearly ninety and had been working as a psychotherapist since his mid-twenties, this was a strong statement.

Michelle May liked Miss Hutchins and saw her arrival signalling the end of her working week. Despite being a lonely woman, Audrey Hutchins was a fascinating and intense person full of anxiety, bitterness, and anger. She always looked at Michelle May with hope tinged with fear. When she spoke, she did so in short sentences as if pulling them from a swirling well of phrases – each of which she had to "catch" and then "inspect" before she was ready to share.

At their first session, after some brief introductions, Audrey Hutchins shared a dream that she frequently had. In the dream, she was a young girl in Paris walking alone at night. As she passed an alleyway, she saw a baby crawling on all fours. The baby was not crying but seemed determined to get somewhere. Anxious not to upset the baby, she followed it intending to make sure that no harm came to it. The baby led her into a small apartment where several other babies sat in a circle. "Her" baby – the one she had followed – joined the circle. As it did so, the other babies looked attentively at their new friend. After a few moments, her baby spoke and apologized for being late. It then asked for news from each of them. As they each reported their news, they all listened attentively. When they had completed their news circle, her baby made a short statement about the need to keep their meeting secret and suggested that they make sure to keep an eye out for the evil woman who had kidnapped their friend. After a time, they all went their own way – crawling this way and that.

Her baby began the crawl back as it had come but stopped suddenly and looked straight at her. It said, "Don't worry, you are not the evil lady, but you will soon find your own circle, and all will be well." She thanked it and watched it crawl into darkness. It was then she always woke up.

Michelle May asked her what she made of the dream. Audrey Hutchins had no real explanation other than that these children are often much more observant than many adults think. Michelle May asked Audrey Hutchins what she had observed in her childhood that she did not think adults realized she knew. She was surprised by the answer.

"I observed that nothing good came of social encounters, sexual relations or dallying with the idea of friendship."

Asked to elaborate, Audrey Hutchins said that her father had an affair with a woman in London, which her mother knew about, and, as an act of revenge, her mother had several affairs with both men and women, none of which satisfied her and all of which intensified the bitterness she

6

felt toward her husband. Her father, realizing that his wife was acting in the way she was, stopped his affair and devoted more time and energy to his marriage. It made no difference. Her mother continued to engage in chance encounters and affairs, all of which ended in despair. Her father then decided that they needed mutual friends and began to hold regular soirees at home. These attempts to find friends and spend more time together failed. Her father then started travelling more with his wife, and it was during one of these trips that they were killed in a car accident on a windy road in Veneto on the Passo San Boldo in Italy, a notoriously treacherous drive.

Asked when she realized that her parent's marriage was failing, Audrey Hutchins said she was about six or seven. Asked what she felt about this realization, she said, "it is an inevitable consequence of trying to please others."

During a later session, Audrey Hutchins recounted her one attempt to form a relationship with another person.

"I was seventeen and in my first year at university. I met a woman called Eva Sundberg, and we seemed to have a similar, if bleak, outlook on life. We began having lunch together once a week and soon it was twice a week. She asked me if I liked boys, and I said, "I don't know I have never tried." This made her laugh. "Don't bother," she said, "it's not worth the effort". After a few weeks of lunching, we went to the cinema together one afternoon and had dinner at an Italian restaurant – a simple pasta with shrimp. She asked me if I wanted to go to bed with her, and I said yes, but it was a disaster. I had no clue what to do, and she was too impatient to teach me. I cried, and she threw me out. We didn't lunch together again."

It appeared that this was the only attempt at a "friends with benefits" relationship she had ever tried. Shortly after her parents were killed in the accident, she became much more inward-looking and gave up on the idea of friends, with or without benefits.

Michelle May asked Audrey Hutchins about sexual activity – what did she do to meet her sexual needs? She answered succinctly, "I suppressed them so long ago, so successfully, that it never occurs to me that this is a need. I would much rather listen to Haydn, Mozart, or Celine Dion."

Michelle May explored various themes with Audrey Hutchins, including her fear of failure, her anxieties about death and her prudence. All these themes were explored with calmness and objectivity, which Michelle May found rare in a patient. It was as if Audrey Hutchins was able to view herself as if she was observing a new species of plant or reviewing a new piece of music or offering insights into an entry in a ledger.

It was only when Michelle May asked how Audrey Hutchins saw her future that she saw raw emotion. Audrey Hutchins cried. Not gently but sobbed deeply from the pit of her stomach. "The future for me is the same as today and every day," she said after a few minutes.

Their sessions lasted fifty minutes. At their conclusion, Audrey Hutchins stood, straightened her often pleated skirt, adjusted her jacket, shook hands with Michelle May and thanked her. She left, as she had arrived, upright and determined, as if she had put her psychological needs behind her, at least for one more week.

# Saturday, 16th October

Michael Mearns sat at the table nearest the door, drinking a small cappuccino, nibbling at a Danish pastry, and reading The Daily Telegraph. He ignored the other customers coming and going from the Costa Coffee shop. He did, however, notice a story in his newspaper about the collapse of a building in the Dutch city of Apeldoorn, a city he had visited recently. The building was undergoing repairs when a crane collapsed onto it, collapsing the whole building. He felt a little strange. Not long ago, he had been in the Dutch town of Alphen on the Rijn, and a few days later, two cranes mounted on a barge had collapsed onto a bridge, destroying several buildings in the process, injuring some twenty people.

He drank some of his coffee and finished his Danish Pastry. As he did so, he noticed an elegant, middle-aged woman sitting at a table opposite him and looking, so it seemed, intently either at him or right through him. He smiled at her and received no response. He looked her over. Attractive, sophisticated, elegant, and aloof, which he found alluring. He was between women, his most recent having left him for a younger and more flamboyant man who worked in broadcasting. He was hoping to get a date with Angela Heston, who had just started working at the office, but she was playing hard to get. He needed some "action" soon, and maybe this woman opposite may be just what he needed to cheer up his lonely weekend.

She didn't seem interested in him. She was, it was now clear, looking right through him.

He finished his coffee, folded his newspaper, and went to her table.

"Excuse me," he began, "don't I know you from somewhere? A concert recently at the Wigmore Hall perhaps?". It was a long shot, but she looked like a concert-going type.

"I don't think so; I have not been to the Wigmore in some time," she replied.

"Perhaps it was the Barbican or Royal Albert Hall...I love to go", he tried valiantly.

"No, I do occasionally go to the Royal Albert Hall but have not been since a performance of Britten's War Requiem two years ago. I have a regular seat at the Festival Hall and will be there this evening for a performance of Sibelius's second symphony," she said.

"Must be the Festival Hall, then. I am not going tonight, have something else on, but I will no doubt see you there at some point in the future." He began to take his leave, but just before he reached the door, he turned and said to her, "There is an interesting duo performing at the Wigmore Hall this Sunday morning – Mozart, Schubert, Schulhoff and Mazzoli – piano and violin – perhaps I will see you there?"

She made no verbal response, merely held her head in a position which told him that she had heard him and, from her expression, was considering it. He left, writing off the encounter as a good but failed try.

As he walked down the street, he began to remove the image of the lonely middle-aged elegant woman sitting drinking a coffee in the Costa Coffee bar on Brampton Road in Knightsbridge. He was impressed with his memory of the event at the Wigmore Hall, having just seen an advertisement for it in the Daily Telegraph. He reminded himself to look up Schulhoff and Mazzoli before the end of the day – he had never heard of either of these composers.

## Sunday 17th October Wigmore Hall

She was not sure why she had decided to come to the concert. It was, she told herself, nothing to do with that annoying man in the coffee shop yesterday. She was here to listen to music and was intrigued by the program. She had decided to come while listening to the London Philharmonic play Sibelius last night at the Festival Hall. The conductor was the massive Finnish composer Leif Segerstam, who had composed over three hundred and forty-four symphonies, many of which were just little ditties lasting a few minutes. He did, however, know his Sibelius and the concert was wonderful – the best rendition of the second symphony she could recall. The Mozart Divertimento in B Flat and the Schubert Fantasy in C she knew, but she had not heard of either Missy Mazzoli or Erwin Schulhoff, though had a vague recollection of someone giving a talk about Schulhoff on Radio Three some six or so months ago. She looked forward to the concert at the Wigmore Hall.

She bought her ticket and went downstairs for a coffee and scone before the performance. The Wigmore Hall was a hive of activity, with many people pushing and shoving to find a seat in the small bistro. She had arrived early enough to ensure she had a seat at a table in the corner and could view the room. The attendees were largely elderly. A lot of walking sticks and grey hair. She smiled, knowing that at the end of the concert, there would be a rush for the sherry they always served – something she avoided since it was a cheap and nasty variety and nothing at all like quality sherry.

She looked out for the young man from the Costa coffee shop, intending to make sure she avoided him. She didn't see him, much to her relief. The last thing she wanted was any kind of connection or entanglement, especially with a brash young man who read the Daily Telegraph.

Ten minutes before the concert started, she sat at the end of the row in the aisle toward the centre of the left part of the hall. A good seat, which gave her a fine view of the piano and the hands that would move across it. Adam Golka, the Polish American pianist, had won the Tchaikovsky competition some years before was playing alongside Itamar Zorman, a handsome and talented Israeli violinist who had also won the Tchaikovsky competition in the same year.

The audience filed in, and the hall filled up gradually. The announcements were made, and the performers arrived on stage and got themselves ready. Given the audience, they politely spent time arranging themselves to permit the normal round of coughing and spluttering that act as a prelude to most concerts in London. The Mozart adagio was sublime – delicate yet commanding. She had heard it many times, usually played by a chamber orchestra, but string quartets have recorded adaptations. This was the first time she had heard it played on piano and violin.

Then the Mazzoli. The piece was called Vespers for Violin, and while there are some accompanying piano moments, the violin part calls for tremendous dexterity and focus. Zorman performed brilliantly, and Audrey Hutchins found herself transfixed by the music in a way which was rare for her. It is a short piece – around five minutes – but powerful and memorable. The applause was long and well deserved, with many on their feet shouting "Bravo!".

The Schulhoff second violin sonata was much more conventional, lyrical, and demanding. Itamar Zorman was truly showcased here, showing real versatility. Audrey was drawn to his finger movements – subtle, yet each shift of a finger produced remarkable nuances of sound. The piano part in this sonata is not easy and was done well. More standing, shouting and clapping at the end.

The Schubert D934 is not often performed, according to the program since it demands such careful and restrained violin playing. One well-known violinist described it as "unviolinistic" since there are steep technical challenges and a need not to overplay the emotions it often provokes. These performers knew what they were doing, and it was an emotional ride for all in the hall over the twenty-five minutes of the performance. As the audience rose to its feet, Audrey took her leave. Escaping before the sherry hoarding and coffee drinking.

Hailing a passing cab, she was home well before others in the audience had managed to scrounge a second sherry.

# Sunday 17th October, Evening

Later, in the quiet of her home after a small salad niçoise using quality tinned tuna from a fine Italian store, Audrey Hutchins rested in her favourite chair. At her side, a small glass of Pinot Gris and a novel. Playing quietly on her Mark Levinson music system – one of her extravagances – she listened to recordings of Mendelsohn's complete string quartets. And began reading A Certain Justice, a P D James novel.

Her thoughts ran back over the last few days – her quiet lunch of pistachio lamb chops at the Mantl on Brompton Road, followed by a walk to her favourite bookstore and an hour at the Saatchi Gallery. Then last nights and today's concerts, the cab home, a quick shower and then a late lunch at Mamounia Lounge and the walk home.

Apart from her encounter with the man at the coffee shop and the perfunctory conversations with waiters and serving staff, ticket office people, a cab driver as well as the hostess at the Wigmore Hall, she had not said much to anyone since her therapy session with Michelle May, which ended just before five in the evening on Friday. She found that pleasing. The less she had to do with people, the better.

Her thoughts turned to work. There was something in the air at the office – she had caught rumours of a possible merger with one of the big accounting companies and the idea that the owners might get a big payout. The business had been an independent accounting company for over one hundred and twenty-seven years, but it was getting tougher to survive as a small, boutique financial services company. So many new approaches to accounting, and so many new regulations changing all the time.

She had not ever really wanted to be an accountant, but her parents were both in finance, and they had done well at it. She drifted into it, as one does when it is not clear what options are available. She was, she knew, good at it. One of her Professors at university had suggested she study and go for a master's degree or a doctorate. She had decided not to. Nor had she ever regretted not pursuing her studies. She did not particularly like university life – too many people, too many intrigues, too much sex talk and too few intelligent, diligent, and focused people. She knew many of the students she met had no clue what they were doing there. She knew her task was simple – work, get a good degree, get a good job and don't get involved with other people.

She sometimes wondered whether, if she had given up accounting and taken up music or creative writing, what her parents would have thought of her. Just as she began considering these options, they were in the accident and gone from her life. She inherited the house, which was worth a lot of money and their significant savings. Even as she was adjusting to her new situation, her aunt – her mother's sister – died suddenly of a very rare disease – neuroendocrine cancer – and left her the apartment and a significant sum of money too.

She was unsure just how much money she had but knew it was around £18 million. At current interest rates, this was quickly gathering compound interest and, if she spent little or nothing, would be worth £46 million when she retired, though what she would do with it, she had no idea. She spent very little, given that she earned a good salary and had no rent to pay. She did not own a car or have to support children and their needs. Her luxuries – books, CDs, eating out, concerts and her two-week holidays – were hardly a drain on her resources.

Looking around her apartment – she did think of it as "hers" now, though this had taken some time to sink in – she realized how important it was to her. A safe place, a place she had always loved, a place she felt cared for her just as much as she cared for it.

Her aunt Catherine was a lively lady, unlike her mother – Catherine's sister. While Margaret had been the "snooty intellectual banker," Catherine was a commissioning editor for one of the big publishers based in London. She had found and signed up several Man-Booker prize winners and been successful not only in winning the rights to their books but in selling the film rights and translation rights. Her apartment in Montpelier Walk had a library and music room, two bedrooms, a decent-sized kitchen and dining space and a lounge.

Audrey Hutchins had changed little since she moved in. She had upgraded the sound system, added a pizza oven to the kitchen and made sure that the air conditioning in the apartment was upgraded. She had also changed the décor a little with the aim of giving the rooms a slighter lighter feel. New linens and mattresses on the beds, new covers for the sofas and comfortable chairs and a dedicated space for her growingly large collection of over four thousand compact discs.

She had heard that a similar apartment in her building had recently sold for some £24 million to some wealthy Russian oligarch. She doubted hers would fetch this kind of amount but would not be surprised if it was worth £10 million or so. Her aunt had inherited it from her mother, who had inherited it from her parents.

If the company was sold, she thought, would she leave and become a lady who lunches? Someone with no other people in her life, other than writers, composers, and performers whom she did not speak to but did feel close to? Would her encounters with others always be like those in the Costa coffee shop – brief, meaningless, and fleeting?

This thought led her to ask why she worked at all. She did not need the money. She worked largely alone and was, she knew, seen as aloof and isolated in her stylish but minimalist office. She was good at her job, but others could be hired who would do it just as well and probably be more engaged with others.

She had been hired as a personal favour in memory of her father by the Chief Executive, who the family had known for many years. The company had partnered with her father in executing a number of venture capital deals and in two initial public offerings, both of which had made the firm a lot of money.
Soon after she was hired, the Chief Executive – Brian Barton – had realized that she was an outstanding accountant. She knew how to ensure that the needed work was done accurately, efficiently and she was constantly advising him of subtle changes to the interpretation of regulations and tax laws which enabled the firm and their clients to improve their bottom lines. He

did know that she was not at all engaged in the social life of the office, but he rationalized that he paid her to be an accountant, not a gossip.

When she was appointed Chief Accountant, the Chief Executive also appointed Angela Dunstan to be Head of Human Resources. In a meeting between the three of them, he explained to them that he saw Audrey as overseeing all legal and technical aspects of the accounts they managed and Angela as managing the people side of the business. He felt he needed to add "this plays to your strengths - Angela is a people person and Audrey is a books and figures person".

The phrase had stuck with her for some time. "A books and figures person." He was quite right, though at the time, she was taken aback. She did not dislike people, just wanted little to do with them other when she needed to interact with them about a very specific thing. She was not interested in and had no patience for stories, jokes, tall tales, or fables. They were an accounting company, not script writers for Maisie Raine or Tales of the Unexpected.

In contrast, Angela was always checking on people, making sure they were happy. She loved organizing office lunches, parties for birthdays or baby showers for pregnant mothers who were about to take maternity leave. Audrey would attend briefly, say a few words to the person concerned, and be back at her desk in ten minutes or less. She knew people talked about her aloofness and distance, but she did not mind.

Most put her distance and apartness down to the sudden loss of her parents and her aunt while she was so young.

They did not know that their deaths did not change her behaviour, merely reinforced how she had always been. She was a solitary child, a loner at university and standoffish. Except for her brief encounter at university with the Eva Sundberg, she could not think of a relationship or friendship that mattered to her. Even that one relationship was so brief that it might more accurately be called "brusque."

She ended the Mendelsohn, finished her wine, and prepared for her nightly bath before bed. It was time for the weekend to end.

## Monday, 18th October

The meeting was called for ten o'clock, and the rumours were flying. The merger with one of the big five was "on." The merger was "off," and the company was sold to a foreign firm. The merger was "on," but lay-offs would occur – the new owners had the capacity to buy the firm to reduce competition and increase the size of their client list. None of the rumours reached Audrey Hutchins, who was working on the accounts of a company in Leeds which had been a client of the firm for over fifty years.

As the meeting began, Brian Barton explained that the business owners were getting on in years and had no heirs or immediate relatives to whom they could leave the business. They had decided to sell. They had asked KPMG to buy it for an agreed sum, which they agreed to do, and the sale was completed over the weekend. KPMG would formally own the business from the end of the month. They had asked one of their London managing partners,

Michael Mearns, to oversee the transition. Michael would be joining them at half past the hour.

Brian Barton wanted to assure everyone that the work would continue and that, while some may find themselves working on other businesses for KPMG, they had a guarantee that no one would be let go. However, a package was available for those wishing to leave – two months' full salary and pension for each year of service, calculated at the current pay rate. For those close to retirement, which a few were, "this may be an attractive proposition," he said.

A few questions were asked – would we still be working from this office (yes), would our pay remain the same or would we be working on a new pay scale (yes, the same), would there be more opportunities for promotion (very much so).

At precisely ten thirty, Michael Mearns arrived, and Audrey Hutchins was shocked to see him. This was the man from the Costa coffee shop who had suggested she might like to go the Wigmore Hall. He looked smarter – a suit and tie with a waistcoat and watch chain – but it was him. She could feel herself blush.

"Good morning, all," he began and, turning to face Audrey, "so nice to meet with you again," he said with a smile. She nodded, and everyone looked quite surprised that they had some connection, with one even laughing out loud at the idea that these two knew each other at all.

The rest of his time in the office was spent explaining why KPMG sought to grow its "footprint" in medium-sized enterprises across England – something Brooke and Walters had specialized in since its founding over a hundred years ago. He also explained that, in reviewing the operations of the company, his team had been impressed by the efficiency of the firm and its returns on capital and staff time. No major changes were anticipated, "at least for now," but one or two of you may want to explore other opportunities within the parent company.

He was asked if KPMG would keep the Brooke and Walters brand name, and he replied that it would, from the end of the month it would be known as "Brooke and Walters – A KPMG Company." He said it was now one of four such acquisitions KPMG had completed in the last fifteen months in England.

By eleven thirty, the meeting was over. Michael Mearns approached Audrey Hutchins in her office.

"So, did you get to the Wigmore Hall?" he asked.

"Yes, a good concert. Thank you for the suggestion," she responded.

"Couldn't make it myself, had to sort out some of the paperwork for this deal, though it was straightforward. Best profit and loss accounting I have seen for some time – which I understand was your work?".
"Yes, as Chief Accountant, I finalize all statements and reports which then go the owners."

"Well, made my job easier – especially assessing the EBITDA for the business, which is very strong."

"Yes, I am sure. Thank you," she said, feeling a little embarrassed at the unexpected praise.

"Look, I want you to know now that Brian Barton will leave the business. He is taking the package he no doubt told you about. Two others will be going too, so there will be some new blood coming over from Canada Square, our main London office in Canary Wharf. I assume you will stay on – Brian talks highly of you, and, having reviewed some of your work, I can see why."

"I am considering my options, Mr. Mearns. I tend not to rush into hasty decisions."

"Good, just like any sound accountant. Careful, cautious, and sometimes cunning."

"I understand that ownership formally transfers at the end of the month, thirteen days from now. I will be sure to inform you of my decision well before Halloween, Mr. Mearns", she said, intending that this end the conversation.

He left her office, satisfied that he had made a connection, surprised at her continued coldness and very clinical approach to the situation. He wondered how he could find a way into the soul of this woman and perhaps get past her undoubted fear of closeness to another person. He was intrigued and liked the sense of challenge.

## Later That Day

When Audrey Hutchins left work at precisely four-thirty, as she always did (except on Fridays), she thought she would walk a little to clear her mind. It was so full today of conflicting feelings. She wondered why she did this to herself – put herself "through the wringer as if she alone was responsible for all around her."

She walked a quarter of a mile to the Italian Centre Shop, which Teressa Spinelli had opened shortly after leaving school. Audrey knew Teressa as a child – her mother had been friends with her parents and had encouraged the young Teressa to think about being an entrepreneur.

The shop was full of delights – cheeses from across Europe, delicacies from Italy, wonderfully fresh pasta made locally and salamis and meats ready to be cut to the requirements of each customer. A place full of simple pleasures in cans, in boxes and on display, full of the aromas she recalled from her one visit to Florence in her final year of undergraduate studies.

She bought some fresh linguini, a creamy sauce and some clams and parsley and was set for a simple, quick meal. A nice bottle of white wine – a Vermentino – would help. This, too, was available in the store. She placed her purchases in a bag rolled up in her handbag, hailed a taxi and was in her apartment thirty minutes later.

She chose Angela Hewitt playing some of the Beethoven piano sonatas, put on her apron, and began to prepare her simple meal. The clams would be steamed in some white wine with cream and added to the drained pasta with a little of the salted pasta water and the parsley sprinkled on top. The whole "production" took less than twenty minutes, and she enjoyed the simple pleasure of preparing, cooking and then eating her meal – topped off with a glass of the dry Vermentino from Sicily.

She found some chocolate and made herself an espresso with her Nespresso machine – another of her additions to the kitchen and a godsend, especially in the mornings. No more grinding beans and waiting for the drips to end. Capsule in, coffee out.

As she listened to the compassionate piano playing of the Canadian Angela Hewitt, she began to turn over in her mind the options now facing her. Quit and spend her time pursuing her interests. Stay and adjust to the new realities of working for a global firm and fend off the seeming interest of her new manager, Mearns. Quit and try and find another position. Change career completely – go work for some non-profit or charitable organization which needed her expertise, but which would leave her alone and let her continue her peaceful existence as a dedicated but solitary worker.

Hewitt finished the Beethoven F Major Opus 54 – one of her favourite pieces. She fancied something different and soon found Paul Lewis's interpretation of the Haydn piano sonatas written just as the 1700s were coming to an end.

The trouble with her scenarios was that they assumed she had a life – passions, commitments, and activities which gave her satisfaction. But in fact, she had an existence – she knew that her "interests" were not so much passions, but activities to keep her occupied. Yes, she did feel deeply about the music she listened to – it touched her in a way that other activities did not, especially when she was at a live concert and could feel the tension between the instruments, the musicians, and the score and between the performers and the audience.

She enjoyed her simple cooking and good food. She enjoyed reading a novel, wandering around an art gallery, and looking to see what the artist saw and felt. She enjoyed her work, especially challenging issues which required her detailed technical understanding of the tax laws and financial regulations. She enjoyed digging into accounts and understanding their history – the forensic work. She was "satisfied", but never excited.

She didn't like gatherings where she was expected to engage and participate – people, chatter, gossip, innuendo. She didn't like being forced into conversations, which she feared Mr. Mearns would require her to do. The more she thought about it, the more likely it was that her life had again been changed for her without her consent, just as happened when her parents left her.

## Friday, 22nd October

She was, as always, punctual – something Dr. Michelle May liked about Ms. Audrey Hutchins – whatever else one might think about her, she was always on time for her Friday appointment.

As they sat, it was clear that something had happened to Audrey Hutchins that was bothering her. The doctor enquired and did not have to cajole a response.

"My world has changed completely. A new manager, new owners of the company I have worked at since I graduated from university and a subtle change in how we are expected to work. Worse, I think how we work will change in ways that I may find unacceptable. I am hurt and distressed by this, though I have worked hard all week not to show it."

The next several minutes were spent explaining the events of the week and the impact these were having on her routines. People she had worked with and trusted were leaving, "taking a package," as they called it. Others were looking at new opportunities. Her role could well change; though nothing specific has been said or explained, she made it clear.

When it came to describing Michael Mearns, she was blunt. "Brash, arrogant, determined and pushy" were her first words. Audrey missed the sarcasm of Dr. May's comment, "tell me what you really think, Audrey Hutchins!".

"I can see him wanting to spend ten to fifteen minutes a day just "chatting" for no apparent reason – distracting me. I also think he is very ambitious – he is a very young KPMG partner, and this acquisition is a steppingstone to bigger things for him. He has spent much time courting medium-sized businesses across Europe, especially in Holland. I can see me carrying much of his work, and he will get all the credit".
Dr May asked the obvious question "...and this makes you feel..."

"Used and abused, but then I have been used before."

For the next fifteen minutes or so, they used to explore these feelings and her understanding, with Audrey Hutchins saying more in this one session than she had done in the previous five.

"So, what are you planning to do? Stay, leave, change your work?" asked Dr. Michelle May.
At this, Audrey Hutchins began to sob with the tears coming from some deep place within her. "You will have to face up to the future, and most of us do so by facing up to the past, which I suspect you have not done," said Dr. May.

This statement seemed sharp and sudden and caught Audrey Hutchins by surprise. "What do you mean?"

"I mean only that whenever I ask you about the future, I get a powerful emotional reaction, but when I explore your past – your relationships, your upbringings, your relationship with your parents or your aunt – I get an unemotional, factual account devoid of any sense of concern or any sense of emotion. As a psychologist, I understand these dynamics – denial and distortion to protect your sense of who you are. You can't face the work of "becoming" because you have not yet faced up to "being" and "belonging.""

Audrey Hutchins stared at Dr. Michelle May as if she had uttered obscene remarks or recited a poem in an ancient but now forgotten language.

"Being, belonging – what on earth are you saying, Doctor. Are you suggesting, as I suspect you are, that I do not know who I am or how I became who I am and therefore am unable to determine whom I want to become – is this your thinking?"

"Basically, yes. I think you stopped asking questions about yourself and how you might behave when you saw what was happening to your parents and how their relationships were both self and mutually destructive. You spent time with your aunt – according to your notes, almost more time with her than with your mother or father – and found her more interesting and more engaging, but she was also very busy and not always available to you in an emotional and caring sense. You didn't go to school but instead were tutored privately by a succession of tutors, none of whom you appear to have liked. You never had a chance to explore who you were, so you played safe and retreated into routines which enabled you to survive and perform the tasks expected of you."

"You did well on academic subjects and found yourself in university shortly after your 17th birthday. There you immersed yourself in your studies, earning distinctions and accolades for your work – but all done at the expense of any social activities or relationships. You made one attempt at a relationship with a fellow student and it failed, and you have not even tried since. You discovered that the less you tried to contact others, to engage with them, to connect with them, the more they left you alone to be the lonely woman you had decided to become. Since this persona did not require much effort on your part – work, food, a few interests to stop you from sleeping for ten to fifteen hours a day – and you could survive. But it is hardly living life to the full, is it?".

"And what, if I may ask, would "living life to the full" involve?" asked a hesitant but determined Audrey Hutchins.

"You will have to discover your own path. For most exceptionally smart, attractive women, such as yourself, it is finding someone to share their life with — someone they can confide in, share moments of joy and pain, and explore the world together. For many women, it is finding something other than work to make commitments to and engage in a broader community of friendship. For some women, but not all, it involves having and bringing up children, though this seems less popular today than when I was younger. For many middle-aged people, it is having a group of friends to call on when they need company or help. You seem to have none of these things because you have chosen not to. And that is the key; your choices have made you who you are, and you are not sure that you are who you now want to be."

As these words were being spoken, the atmosphere in the room changed from one of tranquility and acceptance to one of tension.

"I see," Audrey Hutchins said after a long period of reflection. "So, if only everyone else had behaved differently toward me and me differently towards them, I would be a different person now — I think this captures what you are suggesting, Doctor May. I am not at all sure that this is in anyway helpful, but clearly, I will have to think about what you have said. It hurts me, I must say. But you have thought this way for some time and I need to reflect on whether this is wisdom or unwise thinking."

With that, the session ended, and Audrey Hutchins left the room. As she did so, Dr. Michelle May sat quietly and considered the situation she had created. Dr. Fassbender had, in sharing his case notes and discussing Audrey Hutchins with her, indicated that she was "a riddle, wrapped in a mystery inside an enigma" – Churchill's phrase about Stalin and the future of Russia. It seemed apt.

## Friday, 22$^{nd}$ October – Early Evening

Audrey Hutchins sat quietly at a table at the back of the restaurant. She had chosen the Margaux – expensive but quiet and always excellent. Beef bourguignon with creamy polenta with a side of haricot vert with lemon and shallots accompanied by a glass of Chablis Grand Cru. She needed a treat after the experience she had just been through.

She looked around her. She was the only woman eating alone. There were people at nine other tables – all couples or fours. Looking at each table, she saw smiles, grimaces and people engaged in serious conversations. She caught the odd phrase - "I don't believe it" and "well, he had it coming to him" and "the doctor said I had made a remarkable recovery" – and laughter from the table at the far end of the room.

As she ate, enjoying the rich and creamy taste of each mouthful, she asked herself questions about who she really was and what she wanted. Was this – sitting alone, enjoying wonderful food and wine, and speaking to hardly anyone each day – what her life would be forever? Was listening to music, going to concerts, art galleries, bookstores, and cooking "it"? Was there more to life than just "being there" and getting through a day?

At thirty-eight she had achieved a great deal at work and was more than comfortable in terms of money, a place to live and her life. She loved her apartment and her routines. She was safe, which is more than many women could say. Unlike her mother, she had not been let down by men or other women. Unlike her aunt, she was not suffering from a debilitating illness which would eventually kill her. She was safe.

If she simply quit her job, what would she do with herself? Would she volunteer somewhere? Look for another job – she was sure she would have excellent references. Would she just wander around Europe and visit art galleries, and museums and attend concerts? Why just Europe – what about Asia, and Australia? She had heard that New Zealand was nice.

If she stayed, how would she cope with all the fuss and bother of endless meetings – something she had been able to avoid in the past. She had been to some meetings but basically was there to answer specific technical questions – others did most of the show and tell and the long presentations with those PowerPoint slides (which she hated). She had once heard a colleague say, "Power corrupts, but PowerPoint corrupts absolutely!"
The nagging voice in her head – the voice she attributed to her mother – asked if being alone was a problem. She wondered why she was even asking the question. She had been alone even when she lived with her parents – they paid little attention to her, too busy making money, investing their money, having affairs, or shouting at each

other. She had her room and a small study room where she met her tutors. She did her study work and spent her time in her room listening to the radio – mainly BBC Radio By the age of nine, she had developed a real taste for baroque and classical music, though she could tolerate what some called "smooth jazz" – not the rough and tumble jazz. She hated anything that came close to rock or pop music and had no tolerance for the more modern music, except for Celine Dion. She was a woman, she told herself, of refined taste developed through careful listening.

She had been alone at university, living at home and commuting to lectures and seminars and working in the library. She spent more time at home in her room and in a study carrel at the university library than in the company of others. She did what she had to do and yet had been hugely successful. Except for her one attempt at connecting to another, which had been a disaster, she did remarkably well acting alone, aloof and distant from others. What mattered was the work.

It was the same at her job. What mattered was the work. She knew that many of her colleagues thought her odd, but she did not really care what they thought. No one had ever criticized her work or found fault with it. Work was not a social club. It is where we go to undertake tasks needed to get the job done.
What if she just accepted that her life was intended to be unsocial in the sense of not having a significant connection to others, but it was meaningful because of the pleasure she found in art, music, books, food and living in her own silky skin. What if she accepted there was nothing more to life than would be found in a continuation of the life she

was leading, with or without work, and with or without her weekly therapy session?

When the dessert arrived – lavender Crème Brule with a glass of Sauternes – she was less distressed and more comfortable being herself. It was amazing what a good meal could do. All she had to decide was whether to stay or leave work.

She walked home, feeling a little lightheaded. As she did so, she noticed a brand-new sports car parked near the entry to her apartment. A Porsche 911 Coupe, she read. She thought it would be difficult for any respectable woman to get in it without revealing more of her nature than was either polite or intended.

## Friday, 22<sup>nd</sup> October - Later

Settled in her favourite armchair, a glass of brandy by her side and the Czerny piano sonatas playing quietly, she began reading her novel. Denise Welsh was an interesting writer, she found. She writes what has been termed "false true crime" – seemingly historical accounts of true crime which are fiction. Very clever. She had read Gareth Slim when it first came out and had thoroughly enjoyed it, becoming quickly engaged in the storyline and the taciturn characters he had created. Now she was reading his earlier novels.
It was uncanny. While his main character is a man, she recognized many of his behaviours and attitudes as if they were hers. Her empathy for the character lead her to be shocked by some of his actions – covering up the death of a lady he tried to have a relationship with and failed. His actions when another woman disappears and connections

are made to his behaviour, even though her disappearance is not due to any action he took or may have taken.

Set in the small town of Saint-Louis in Alsace in north-eastern France, the novel captures the routines of life and its basic shapes and shadows. Little news happens each day, which is how life seems to be for her. Routines dominate the lives of all the characters, and it is only when these routines are disrupted that significant and real trouble occurs. This was a message, she felt. If she disrupted her own routines or others disrupted them, then trouble would occur.

Best to establish and own routines and not create conditions that others could disrupt.

## Monday, 25th October

She asked to see Mr. Mearns as soon as possible. He came to see her in her office at precisely nine thirty-seven.

"I have decided," she began, not looking directly at him but past him, as she had done in the Costa coffee shop on their first chance encounter, "to take the package and leave the service of Brooke and Walters. I have written my letter of resignation, which you will require. I understand that I will be paid two months' pay for each of the twenty years of service, all paid at my current salary rate, a total of £697,000 before tax."

For a moment, he said nothing. He just looked at her. "I am surprised, Miss Hutchins. Very surprised. I had hoped you would stay and help me build this business up. You are very competent and thorough, just what the back-office needs. We have plenty of people who can promote and sell, but we need solid people to do the focused, detailed quality work our clients pay for."

"I understand, Mr. Mearns. I do, but I have to think of my needs and myself at a time like this."

"Look, I understand that the money here is attractive...." she interrupted him.

"It's not about the money, it's about me and what I want for my life, and I have decided not to work here or indeed, at least for now, anywhere at all. I am going to take some time for myself perhaps for the first time in my life..." She left the idea hanging.

"I see, or at least I think I do," he responded. "Is there anything I could say or do to persuade you otherwise, Miss Hutchins, or is part of the "new you" - a determined and clear decision which cannot be revoked?"

"I think I have made myself clear, Mr. Mearns. I will spend my remaining time here ensuring that each file has appropriate documentation indicating what needs to be done and some notes with my observations about the client that whoever takes my place will find helpful. I also must file two sets of accountants with HMRC – files they requested for audit – they will come back clean. In twenty years, files I have been accountable for have been audited thirty-nine times, and not one has ever come back challenged."

"Quite the record, Miss. Hutchins – precisely why your work is so valued here and would be by KPMG should you change your mind."

"My mind is quite made up, Mr. Mearns. I have four days of leave due to me, so my last day would normally be today, but given that I need to handover files in good order and file with HMRC, perhaps you could add the four days to the payment I am to receive – it would be the easiest and cleanest way of handling the matter."

"Of course. You will be with us until this Friday?"

"That is correct. Friday will be my last day. I don't want any fuss. The others can be told after the fact that I, along with Mr. Barton and Mrs. Dunstan, have left the company. I am sure that KPMG has the bench strength to add capabilities to the firm."

"Indeed, we do, Miss. Hutchins, indeed we do. We don't know much about each other, but I was sincere in saying that I was looking forward to working with you. Mr. Barton spoke highly of you and having seen some of your skillful and insightful work, I can see why. Could we have lunch sometime after you have settled into your new life? I may have questions about clients or some concerns that need clarifying, but I would also like to know more about the history of the company than is evident from just reading the last ten years of annual reports and reviewing accounts. Could I call you – perhaps in mid or late November? KPMG's treat?"

"If you insist, but I am sure Mr. Barton could provide all the information you need."

"I will call you. But thank you for your service to the company and, frankly, for the refreshing directness of the conversation. I wish you all the best for whatever the future holds for you. Now, if you will excuse me, I have a ten-thirty at Canada House I need to get to."

With that he was gone.

She had done it. She had decided to begin her life again. A few days of sorting, closing, and tidying, and she would be able to determine her life as if it were a new beginning.

## Friday , 29<sup>th</sup> October

At precisely 3:50 pm, Audrey Hutchins arrived for her appointment with Dr. Michelle May and waited in the waiting room next to the doctor's study. She knew she had another patient with her, who would be just finishing. He or she (she suspected it was a "he" for some reason) would exit from the study's other door and leave by a separate entrance so that no one waiting to see the doctor would know whom she was seeing.

She used the few minutes to reflect on her time "in therapy." She started after her aunt died and had seen four different therapists. Hans Hoxter was the first — a very large, German-Jewish man who had once worked for the League of Nations and then for the Rothschilds. He had trained with the psychologists Jean Piaget, Melanie Klein, and John Bowlby, but his most significant learning was with Ernest Jones, who himself had been a student of Freud. To think, her first therapist was just one generation removed from Freud.

Not that it had helped. Hans had her talk about her parents, her aunt, her childhood, and her dreams. She did so diligently, but she did not feel any differently and almost forgot why she was in therapy. When he indicated that his health was failing and he would, if she did not object, refer her to someone else, she willingly agreed.

Her next therapist was John Rowan – another large man. Unlike Hans, John had been a humanistic therapist heavily influenced by Rollo May, Julian Silverman, and Danny Yuson. He encouraged her to express herself through music and art – sharing her experiences of listening to and "making music" (she played the flute badly) and commenting on art or making her own drawings. He also asked her to attend group therapy, which she did once and never went to again. This had angered him, but he said he understood. He said she was "a self apart" and "a self who lived within" – both phrases she liked.

She had found John helpful. But soon, all the sessions she had with him felt the same. She was not making progress. He told her she needed to be challenged and that a different approach would help. He suggested two options – a woman called Margaret Romanowsky or a man called Sandy Fassbender. She chose the latter.

Fassbender was, when she began working with him, an energetic and eager eighty-four-year-old who looked about forty. He described himself as Freudian with a soupçon of Carl Jung and a taste of Carl Rogers. They did a lot of dream work, and, at one time, he accused her of making up dreams to give them something to talk about. It was not true, and the accusation hurt. They had explored her attitudes towards men (she had no interest), women (she had no interest), sex (she had no interest). He once asked her what she felt the point of living was, and she had replied "to experience each day for oneself as if it was an intrigue." He had not asked her again.

He too had retired – she had, she reflected, "seen off" two and worn out one, Sandy Fassbender had referred her to Dr. Michelle May, who, as he thought of her name, appeared at the door and beckoned her in.

She sat in her usual place and, before Dr. May could say anything, Miss. Hutchins began.

"Dr. May, I need to share something with you. I have left my employment with Brooke and Walters and am not currently interested in working. I have decided to take time for myself. I have mentioned before that I have money, and I received a generous leaving package, so I do not have to work at all. I have also decided – and do not think this implies anything about the quality of your work – that I will also end therapy. I have been seeing one person or another ever since my aunt died and, while it has been helpful to me in some ways, I think ending work and therapy would be a good clean break from my past. I want to start, as they say, "anew."
"I see. I must say I am surprised, but pleased," said Dr. May.

"Pleased? Why is that?" asked Miss. Hutchins.

"I am not sure we were making progress about unleashing aspects of yourself or preparing yourself for your futures, and I think a break would be good for you. It will enable you to see what you are for yourself differently. Your work was, in my view, a shield, and without it you will have to explore other aspects of your life."

"Yes, well quite. I do want to thank you. I know I am not the most loquacious patient; I am sure. But I have found it useful to reflect after each of our sessions."

## Sunday, 31st October

Even as a child, Audrey Hutchins disliked Halloween. She didn't see the point. She didn't enjoy horror movies, dressing up in costume, or "trick or treating" (which she soon realized should be more aptly named "treat and more treats"). Her parents did not get involved either. Sometimes a wayward child dressed as some hideous character would knock at their door chanting "trick or treat" and her parents would give them an apple or an orange. This ensured that the child would not return. Once, her father, feeling a little devilish, gave a child a few carrots and the child, disgusted, threw them back at him. It made him smile.

On this day Audrey Hutchins had an early breakfast, a long bath and dressed elegantly but casually. It was her last official day as an employee. Tomorrow she would be "unemployed". She had decided to spend some time today reflecting on what this would mean, but first, she wanted to visit the Tate – one of her favourite places to spend time. She was especially keen to visit the exhibition exploring the early experimental works of the French sculptor Rodin. According to the brochure, the gallery had created a replica of Rodin's studio. It was populated with original pieces of his work "in progress," as well as offering an exhibition of some of his early finished work.

She loved visiting the Musée Rodin in Paris – one of her "go-to places" on her Paris vacations. In addition to some fascinating exhibits in the building, the Musée had a wonderful sculptor garden just off the Rue de Varenne and a very nice café.

She arrived at the Tate to find it relatively quiet. She spent some time in one or two of the public galleries before she entered the Rodin exhibition. It was all she had hoped it would be – inspiring, engaging, intriguing and insightful. She had not known until now just how excellent Rodin was as an artist – building small but incredibly meticulous models of things he had seen, including items he had drawn on his frequent visits to the British Museum. In his time, Rodin was a radical, but now he is simply regarded as one of the greatest sculptors of the modern era. Rodin, Barbara Hepworth, and Henry Moore were the sculptors who had excited her as a young curious art seeker.

Her father, on a visit to Bristol, had walked past an antique shop and had seen a small sculpture in a window. Not very large, but it was very well executed. He had gone into the shop and asked how much they wanted for it. The owner said £75, which he was not willing to pay. They bartered, and her father bought it for £45. He was quietly excited since he knew just what it was. It was an early version of Rodin's sculpture Despair and is now in the Victoria and Albert Museum. Her father's statuette is now valued at over £500,000. He had enjoyed the "chase" more than the ownership and had gifted the statuette to the V&A in exchange for a tax receipt for £100 – ever the businessman.

In the restaurant at the Tate, which had the best fish and chips in London, she chose a simple mushroom risotto and a pot of tea. She surveyed the scene. Thirty or forty people eating at tables, several young waiters and waitresses moving swiftly between tables. She must have walked past three or four hundred people in the galleries and in the Rodin exhibition, and, apart from the conversation involved in buying her ticket, she had said not a word to anyone. She wondered about them. Young couples holding hands and staring wistfully at a Picasso or Matisse, an elderly woman with a walker sat staring at a Kandinsky. What brought them here? What were they thinking? What did it mean to them?

She left a small tip and wandered into the Tate shop. She looked at books, cards, art supplies, a nice silk scarf and prints. She had several paintings in her home, including an abstract painting by Benode Behari Mukherjee, whose work was displayed here at the Tate. It was on the wall when she inherited the apartment. She remembered her aunt being given it by "an admirer" who had himself been given it by the artist himself on a visit to India. She didn't buy anything.

As she left the Tate, she remembered that not that far away was the Bankside Gallery, where the Royal Watercolour Society held exhibitions. She took a taxi to it and was surprised by the vibrancy of the exhibition. It featured the earliest works of now-famous artists. While the early paintings of Prince Charles were on display – a big draw for American visitors, no doubt – what caught her eye was the work of Georgia O'Keefe. She was an American artist based in Texas in the early 1900s and painted the vibrant Texas sky as abstract but distinct images. One in particular – Sunrise 1916 –caught her eye. Reds, pinks, a vibrant emerging yellow sun – it spoke to her of renewal, energy, and a new beginning. She bought a framed limited-edition print and was delighted. She would place it in her hallway as a symbol of the new self she now intended to become.

Pleased with herself, she took a cab home. She didn't fancy the hour and half walk home carrying her new picture.

At home, she carefully hung the picture in the hallway, positioning it so she would see it every time she left or entered the apartment.

She needed a drink and some music. A negroni – a mix of gin, vermouth, and Campari with a twist of orange peel and a hint of squeezed orange over ice – and a recording of Chopin Etudes was called for. The drink made, she sat in her favourite chair and listened. Jan Lisiecki's playing was stunning. A young Canadian with Polish ancestry, he was just twenty-six when he recorded this CD. It captures the tones and textures so well with his focused playing of these difficult pieces. It is so easy to go over the top with Chopin, but Lisiecki finds just the right balance between exuberance and caution. Remarkable.

Realizing that someone had done so much with their life from such a young age, she began to think of what she had done with her life. She was an accomplished and respected accountant. She was a capable person, living a life of art, music, and leisure when she was not working. She was financially secure – even wealthy. She was settled, stable and secure.

But now what? She had left her job and had no commitments to work or other people. No obligations, liabilities or duties. She was, again, alone. She had even severed her ties to therapy – her one hour a week when she had talked more than she did to another single person all week. If she was not purposeful and clear about what she would do with her time, she may just "drift" and become very maudlin, which she did not want.

She could take a break and go to Paris or Amsterdam for a recharge. She could travel to other parts of the world that she was curious about – Australia, South Africa, Dubai, New Zealand – and explore. She was free. She needed a plan.

But first, she needed an evening meal. Over the years she had taught herself to cook. She found both the shopping for ingredients, preparation, the cooking, and the eating pleasurable. It was a kind of meditation, a way of immersing oneself in an activity where you could enjoy the fruits of the work instantly. She opened the fridge to see what she could create. There was a small packet of shrimp, some crispy lettuce – a shrimp cocktail suggested itself. Then she spotted a pork tenderloin. She decided to stuff the tenderloin with herbs, breadcrumbs, garlic, and some dried figs and roast it together with a baked potato and some broccolini. Supper decided. She put on her apron and began the work needed to make her meal.

It was, though she thought so herself, delicious. The prawn cocktail took her back to her childhood – it was one of her mother's favourite dishes to order in a restaurant – and the pork was lovely. She had made a simple red wine and port reduction to go with it, and it tasted sublime.

Satisfied, she returned to the music and decided it was time for something more restful. She chose Scarlatti. She picked up a blank notebook and a fine fountain pen her father had bought himself when he made his first million pounds on a deal involving some technology stock. It was a Visconti limited edition – just five thousand of them were ever made – commemorating Leonardo de Vinci. She loved writing with it, not because it had once belonged to her father. It felt so "right" in her hand, and the ink flowed so beautifully.

She began to make a list of places she wanted to visit and explore:

- Barcelona – Picasso Museum, Sala Parés
- Madrid - Prado
- Dubai – Etihad Museum
- New York – Metropolitan Museum of Art, Museum of Modern Art, Whitney, Guggenheim, New Museum, Agora
- Washington – National Gallery of Art
- Toronto – Art Gallery of Ontario, Museum of Contemporary Art
- Vancouver – Museum of Anthropology, Vancouver Art Gallery
- Rome – Vatican Museum
- Florence – Uffizi

Then she made a list of the places she had heard were the best places to eat quality food cooked to perfection:

- Copenhagen – Noma, Geranium
- Barcelona – Disfrutar
- Singapore – Odette, Burnt Ends
- Madrid – Diver XO

If she went on a tour to various places with the aim of exploring art, music, food, and theatre, would that be a way to break with her past and start a new way of living? She didn't need money; she needed to occupy her time. While she did not especially enjoy flying – even at the front of the plane – she did like seeing new works of art and hearing some of the finest orchestras in the world. That thought triggered a new list: orchestras she would like to hear:

- Berlin Philharmonic
- Leipzig Gewandhaus Orchestra
- Royal Concertgebouw Orchestra
- Vienna Philharmonic
- Los Angeles Philharmonic

And some of the musicians she would like to hear:

- Martha Argerich – Piano
- Angela Hewitt – Piano
- Lang Lang – Piano
- Arsha Kaviani – Piano
- John Williams – Classical Guitar
- Itzhak Perlman – Violin
- Vikingur Olausson – Piano

- Mitsuko Uchida – Piano
- Ofra Harnoy – Cello
- Yo-Yo Ma – Cello
- Gilbert Tinetti - Piano

Tomorrow, she decided, she would start to plan her grand tour – concerts, art, food, and book festivals. She would immerse herself in those things that gave her the most pleasure and not think about the idea of "work" or of other people. She would be self-indulgent and enjoy herself.

Pleased, she poured herself a glass of Vin Santo and relaxed. She had a good day and now she had a plan.

## Friday, November 5th

It had taken her a week of almost full-time work, broken by the occasional trip to the shops or a restaurant for lunch or dinner. But now she had a detailed itinerary and plan for her grand tour. She would have to arrange for someone to keep an eye on the apartment and to come in and clean, but the concierge could make these arrangements. She would leave in a few days and travel first to Dubai, then come back through Europe. After a few weeks back at home, she would set off again for North America.

Dubai in November is, according to the guidebooks she had read at the Kensington Central Library, tolerable in November, with temperatures ranging from 20-31C. It was later in the year that things got ridiculously hot, sometimes getting into the low to mid 40Cs in July and occasionally as high as 55C. There was a major art exhibition of Middle Eastern Art and a side exhibition of East-Meets-West – Western artists responding to life in the Middle East, which she was hoping to visit. There were also some wonderful chamber concerts at the Madinat Theatre, and she had already arranged for tickets.

She had booked herself into the Dubai Ritz-Carlton for a week, staying in a studio room. It looked nice and near world-class shops, and fine dining as well as easy access to all attractions locally. She was flying first class on an Emirates flight, which someone at work had once told her was one of the best airlines in the world. She would soon find out. The flight left just after nine in the evening and arrived in Dubai at eight – a seven-hour flight.

November 5th, like Halloween, was another of those days she did not like. Guy Fawkes, she thought, had a lot to answer for. Later there would be fireworks from various bonfires and events across London. Party goers would be rowdy, so better not to go out. Why would anyone want to celebrate an attempt to blow up parliament and kill a lot of people? She couldn't imagine. After all, we don't have parties and events to celebrate Bloody Sunday or the bombings in London. We don't have a Lord Mountbatten blow-up day. It was, she knew, a Protestant versus Catholic thing – Fawkes was a Catholic. It did not make it any better or rational in her view. She tried to remember the verses of the story one of her tutors had taught her:

> Guy Fawkes, Guy Fawkes, 'twas his intent
> To blow up the King and the Parliament
> Three score barrels of powder below
> Poor old England to overthrow
> By God's providence, he was catch'd

With a dark lantern and burning match
Holler boys, holler boys, let the bells ring!

There were other lines, but she couldn't remember them.
She shivered at the thought of it. Her tutor at the time –
Martin Wall – had enjoyed reciting the whole thing.

Fawkes, on the gallows awaiting to be hung, drawn, and
quartered, had leapt off and broke his neck, dying
instantly. He hung anyway, and his body cut into quarters,
each piece being sent to a different part of Great Britain as
a way of warning other Catholics not to take on the
establishment. November 5th was declared a national
holiday, and hence the tradition began. It is no longer a
holiday, even though it is still "celebrated" nationwide.
She couldn't begin to imagine why.

She decided to have an early night and read her new novel
from the library – William Trevor's Felicia's Journey. She
had enjoyed some of his previous writing and this book
had been praised by several, including in the London
Review of Books. She has seen his play Family Voices at
the Royal Court. Harold Pinter directed it and played the
lead role alongside Michael Gambon and Julie Covington.
It resonated with her. It dealt with family dynamics, or
more accurately, the lack of them, and how the characters
relied on their inner lives to make sense of the world.

## November 8th and 9th

She arrived at the airport in good time – she had not been
to Heathrow for some time. She was surprised about how
attentive the staff at the check-in were. A young woman
accompanied her through the fast-track check-in, security

and passport control and took her to the Emirates first-class lounge. Such a luxurious place. She had a drink – a glass of champagne – and then was escorted to the flight by the same woman who had brought her to the lounge.

On the aircraft, she was shown into her private suite – each first-class passenger had their own "cabin" with a door that could be closed. The seat converted into a lie-flat bed. Her seat had air conditioning, a large screen, and a small drinks cabinet. She did not have to interact or engage with other passengers, which was a relief.

She had dressed casually in comfortable clothes – slacks, a blouse and sweater, sneakers, and compression socks which her doctor had recommended she wear on long-haul flights. Her underwear was also comfy – a sports bra and "big panties" that let her move without elastic reminding her to sit up.

The light meal was salmon en croûte with stir-fried vegetables and a cheesecake dessert. All lovely, especially nice with the glass of Chablis. She settled down to watch a movie – since she did not have a television, this was a special treat. She chose Elizabeth, newly released, with Cate Blanchett, Geoffrey Rush, and Joseph Fiennes. She thought Blanchett was very good and carried this movie. John Gielgud, who she had seen many times in the theatre, had a wonderful cameo role as the Pope.

After the movie, she settled down to read her novel – finishing the William Trevor – and then she planned to get some sleep.

Her personal steward – Aza – checked in to make sure she was comfortable and adjusted the seat to turn it into the lay flat bed. She slept very well, being woken two hours before landing by the attentive Aza.

The "big" meal was a fresh tuna salad followed by duck breast with steamed vegetables and a gleaming orange sauce. For dessert, she chose a selection of cheeses and fruits.

The landing was smooth, and she was met on leaving the aircraft by another young lady, who escorted her through the airport, passport control and security and to a waiting chauffeured car. In no time – just twenty-five minutes – she was checking in at the hotel and was being shown into her apartment suite. Modern, luxurious, and as quiet as one could hope for.

She bathed, dressed in a skirt and blouse with a green cardigan and took a walk around the nearby shopping complex known as the Bur Jurman – luxurious fashion, high end watches, shoes, perfumes as well as more "ordinary" stores. It was a moderately large place with some three hundred retailers. It was surprisingly busy. Handsome men in their spotless, flowing dishdashi, women in burqas looking very elegant, showing the occasional glimpse of wonderfully designed long dresses underneath. Other women in western clothes. The Bur Juman was a place to be seen.

She bought a beautiful scarf – silk print in varying shades of blue – and a gold necklace with matching earrings from the part of the mall known as the souk. When she returned to her suite, she found that the staff had turned down her bed, placed a bowl of fresh fruit and some cheese and biscuits on the desk and left her a note welcoming her. She began to feel a little special. She slept the sleep of dreams.

## November 10<sup>th</sup>

The Majilis Gallery is just five and a half miles from the Ritz Carlton. Her driver had her there just as it opened at 11am. The first impression Audrey Hutchins had of this space was of vibrant colour, rich textures of paint and wonderful shapes. She fell in love with the abstract work of Mohamed El Masry, an Egyptian artist who had four works on display. She was tempted to buy one of them but decided to think about it. They wanted US$7,000 for each – which seemed reasonable – but she had to consider where she might hang them. She wasn't sure she had the wall space. She did buy a small sculpture by Tamer Ragab – a brown bronze mounted on a plinth of ash. He too was Egyptian. She arranged for it to be shipped to her and, after a light lunch in a nearby café, she was driven back to her hotel.

After a rest – what her mother used to call a "napette" – she showered and dressed in an elegant silk suit for the concert. The Tokyo String Quartet was performing at the studio at the Madinat Theatre. She had seen them at the Wigmore Hall and had been most impressed by their mastery of difficult music. The viola player – Kazuhdie Isomura – was stunningly good as was the lead violinist, Peter Oundjian. The quartet had won many awards and prizes, and she had a recording of them playing the Schuman string quartets, which she played often. It is widely regarded as one of the finest recordings of these works.

The concert was truly wonderful. Two Beethoven string quartets, Barber's Dover Beach and a piece by Phillip Glass – his fourth string quartet. The audience demanded and got an encore, and they chose to play the final movement of the Mendelsohn quartet in D major – a piece she adored. She could feel engaged in the music, and she felt truly alive. It was as if the concert and her visit to the gallery had confirmed her decision to leave work and spend her time doing what she loved.

Back at her hotel and in bed she found herself quickly drifting to sleep. She dreamt of the sea, with dolphins following a boat she was being carried on to an island where the sand was pure white, and there were palm trees.

## November 11<sup>th</sup>

She wandered around the Al Ghurair Centre – a very elegant shopping mall. With over two hundred shops and more than twenty places to eat and enjoy food, all without alcohol, a visitor is spoilt for choice. She looked in at the Montblanc store, at watches and pens, explored jewelry and clothing stores and found a nice bracelet in Al Anwaar Golden Jewelers, which she bought together with a matching pair of earrings.

Pleased with her purchase, she sat and watched the fish in the aquarium. What such a thing was doing in a mall was a surprise to her, but here it was.

Suddenly hungry, she wanted something to eat. The hotel concierge had advised her to try Le Gourmet on the second floor. She found it, asked for a quiet table and sat. She ordered the sea bass with roasted vegetables and a soft drink. She did not have long to wait. Cooked perfectly in a light creamy fish sauce, the fish was delectable, and she truly enjoyed the experience.

She watched fascinated, as two women in burkas sat and ordered their meal. She had seen many women dressed in traditional Muslim clothes in the mall and handsome men in their dish dash. But how were they going to eat? She soon found out. They cut their food into small bites and lifted the veil of their burkas ever so slightly and guided the food on a fork into their mouth. They did this without any spillage or stains on their clothes, which was almost like a hand ballet to watch. One of the women glanced over at her and she felt embarrassed. She could not tell whether the woman was smiling, upset or angry. She left soon after.

She found on this same floor the most wonderful bookstore - Borders. A very large selection of books – novels, cookbooks, textbooks, guidebooks, books about photography, fashion, and photo-books about the Emirates – as well as a selection of fountain pens, drawing materials and stationery.

To commemorate her visit to Dubai, she bought an expensive fountain pen – a Visconti Homo Sapiens Dark Age. Her father had a small collection of fountain pens – one was a Parker 51 used by the Queen at the opening of a particular charity he was associated with. He also owned a wonderful Koh-I-Noor Omega Marbled Pearl pen which he bought himself after making his second million pounds. She liked writing with a fountain pen – she had used a standard Lamy at the office and had around a dozen pens of various makes, which she added to the collection she had inherited from her father. She used them to keep notes about music, novels, or interesting ideas she encountered in her "daybook" – something she had done since she was around twelve. She asked for the pen to be filled.

She returned to her room and decided to enjoy a glass of wine. Calling her steward, he quickly produced a bottle of Pinot Gris, which he opened and poured an appropriate measure into a very chilled glass, placing the open bottle on ice in an ice tub and leaving the cork. She found the classical music station on the radio and found herself caught up in a live performance of Bach's Mass in B Minor. Two more glasses of wine later, she was ready for bed.

## November 14th

Her last few days in Dubai had been busy. She had taken an architectural tour, looking at some fascinating buildings and designs from the outside and the inside. She also went to the Jumeirah Mosque. She had eaten at both Al and Al Hallab – two outstanding restaurants. She had been on a short cruise and eaten some of the best buffet food she had ever eaten and had been to a stunning garden in the grounds of a very English house in Dubai – a memorable experience.

But she had had enough of being a tourist. She needed some substance for her life, and she was realizing that doing nothing but being busy doing nothing was hard work. She needed purpose and a challenge of some sort.

55

She packed her bag and arranged for her driver to take her to her flight to Berlin later – her next stop on this journey. She was flying KLM and the flight left at some dreadfully late time – just before 1 AM. She bathed, set her alarm, and slept. Waking about forty-five minutes before leaving for the airport, she felt remarkably refreshed.

The flight took just over ten hours, delayed from landing by a storm in Berlin. The flight landed shortly after nine-thirty in the morning, Berlin time. A driver was waiting for her near the luggage carrousel, took her bags and drove her to the Hotel Adlon Kempinski near the Brandenburg gate - highly recommended by all the guidebooks she had consulted as amongst the best hotels in Germany. She had booked a premium suite and was delighted when, upon entering, she heard some Beethoven being played quietly on the radio.

She showered, dressed for sleep, and slept solidly until just after noon. She had not been able to sleep on the flight from Dubai, even though KLM's business class had lay-flat beds, and she had her earplugs. She had opted for reading instead, having no interest in the movies available for viewing on the large screen at her seat.

She had been reading The God of Small Things by Arundhati Roy. She couldn't put it down. It was a powerful, compelling story of love, madness, hope, joy, frustration, and anger written in a fascinating style. No wonder it had won the Booker Prize – it deserved to. She made a note to look for and buy her next novel.

After a light lunch at the restaurant at the hotel, she was driven to the KW Institute for Contemporary Art where the first ever Biennale for Contemporary Art was being held, with a plan that it be held every two years. She understood that a featured artist this year would be Christine Safatly from Beirut, whose work she had seen exhibited in London. She soon found the eight items Christine had entered in the exhibition and was stunned by their simplicity on the other side of complexity – combining textures, shifting lines and different materials, she had created stunning visual pieces.

There were some four hundred pieces to see, which took over three hours. She was exhausted, both physically and mentally, by the time she had finished. It was four o'clock. She took a taxi back to her hotel and ran a bath.

After another light meal, she was back in a taxi enroute to the Philharmonie for a concert she had been looking forward to. Vladimir Ashkenazy playing the Rachmaninov third piano concerto with the Berlin Philharmonic and Eugene Ormandy. There was a Brahms overture and a piece by Harrison Birtwistle, the English composer whom Simon Rattle seemed to be a fan of. Once Ashkenazy started playing, everyone was enraptured by both his touch and the tempo he and Ricardo Muti had chosen for this performance – it was fast, but also brought out the best of both the orchestra and the soloist.

Exhausted, she returned to her hotel room and slept the deepest sleep she had had in years.

## November 15th

At a late breakfast, at least for her, she asked for a copy of The Guardian – her English newspaper of choice. She was interested in any news from London. Since she rarely watched television – she did not have one at home – and had been so busy as a tourist, she had given very little thought to what was going on in the world. After all, she was now a free spirit – able to do whatever she wanted.

With an egg white cheese souffle with a side of tomatoes, coffee, and an orange juice she began to explore the news. So many political bickerings, entertainers suing each other for libel, footballers asking for millions and the release of so many dreadful films, if the critics were to be believed, she found little of interest to explore in the paper.

When she looked up, a middle-aged gentleman was approaching her table. Tall, elegant, and dressed immaculately in a pin-striped suit with waistcoat, he smiled as he neared.

> "Miss Hutchins, I believe?" he said as he arrived at her side.
>
> "Why yes, but you have me at a disadvantage. I am afraid I do not recognize you."
>
> "Oh, no you shouldn't. We have not met. It's just that you and I are the only English people staying in this hotel at the moment and I felt obliged to introduce myself. I am Sir John Aston. I have been coming here for years – used to be the "away from home" for a lot of us - used to be half full of English people, hence the little library at the back of the bar – books left by Brits who no longer needed them".

"Well, Sir John Aston, I am pleased to meet you. I do hope you enjoy your visit to Berlin".

"Yes. Quite. Did you enjoy Ashkenazy last evening – the Rachmaninov?"

"Well, yes," she responded cautiously, unsure how this man knew she had been at the concert. Did everyone know her business?

"Oh, don't panic. I am not keeping you under surveillance. I saw you return with a program for the concert under your arm as I was checking in last evening. Do have a wonderful day, Miss Hutchins."

"How did you know my name?" she asked just as he was about to leave.

"I asked after you at reception as I was checking in."

With that, he was gone. This two-minute conversation left her feeling a little strange. After all, she had never before encountered a stranger who knew so much about her and conveyed the fact that he did in such a short time. Who was Sir John Aston? She was curious.

Glancing at the newspaper while sipping at the very strong coffee, she noted that there was very little news. Some new scandal involving a politician, a homosexual man, and a dog which she knew nothing at all about and some trouble with printer unions. But nothing remarkable.

Later that day, at the Schinkel Pavilion, she saw some strange art by a Swiss artist called HR Giger, a late surrealist and imagineer – which is how he is described in the notes that accompany the exhibition of oil paintings, ink drawings and seven sculptures. She found some of the work disturbing, especially Der Tod, which shows some kind of devilish creature with a large lion-like mane devouring a naked woman. "Really," she thought.

As she was about to leave, there was Sir Jon Aston.

"Ah, Miss Hutchins. What a coincidence!", he exclaimed.

"Is it really, Sir John? Too coincidental for my liking!", she said in riposte as she walked hurriedly away.

Back at the hotel, found an old copy of Who's Who in the small library near the bar – next to a copy of Wisden – the cricket bible. She looked up "Sir John Aston". What she saw surprised her:

Aston, Sir John (59). Sir John Aston was recognized as a legitimate descendant of Aston of Tixhall – a baronet created in 1611. He is the fourteenth generation of Aston's to hold this title. A graduate of Cambridge (Economics) and Oxford (English literature), he has served as a senior official in the Foreign and Commonwealth Office, later seconded to the Prime Minister's Office in Downing Street, serving in an unnamed portfolio. He is an authority on the economic consequences of currency disruption and on the poetry of A. E. Houseman, whom he studied for his master's degree at Oxford (Merton). Sir John Aston is married to Angela Waterston (48), whom he married in 1971. He has no heirs.

She could find no further biographical information. But she found this brief description interesting.

Back in her room, she took out her new Dubai pen and her daybook and began to write out a description of Sir John:

- App 5 feet 10 inches, clean shaven and upright – very straight.
- Walks brusquely and attentively.
- Immaculately dressed in what looks to be a tailored suit rather than one off the hanger at Marks and Spencer.
- An Oxford tie (possibly Merton) – mauve with a stripe with a matching pocket handkerchief.
- Matching fine leather belt and shoes rather than braces.
- A crisp pressed white shirt.
- Carries a small leather briefcase, clearly old with a solid reinforced handle – shows a great deal of wear.

Then she wrote down the three questions that were troubling her:

1. Why is he intent on connecting and speaking with me?
2. What is he doing in this hotel and in Germany?
3. Should I be concerned about the attention he seems to be giving me?

She poured herself a gin and tonic from the drinks cabinet discretely placed in her room and put in two cubes of ice from the ice bucket which room service provided each afternoon.

After dinner – trout in a bearnaise sauce with sauteed potato and green beans – and a glass of Chablis, she returned to her room and found the classical music on the radio. A performance of some fascinating Danish chamber music by the composer Emil Sjogren, who she had never heard of. The violin sonatas were both mournful and lyrical and seemed to catch her mood perfectly.

As she listened, she opened her new novel bought today on her return from her visit to the art gallery at an international bookstore on Schlutersrasse called Taschen, which was as interesting as the art gallery with a wonderfully tiled floor and rich collection of books, especially related to art and photography. Titled Whispers by an American author new to her – Dean Koontz. She did not normally like suspense or murder mystery but was intrigued by the cover notes for this one. The novel is a story about a woman who keeps being attacked by a person she believed to be already dead. Written in 1980, the book explores the nuances of memory and meaning. She found it interesting.

She fell asleep in her chair – something that rarely happened and which she found very frustrating. It meant she would not get a good night's sleep, even after a bath and stiff brandy.

In her dream later, she was walking in Berlin – just strolling and exploring the wonderful Kurfürstendamm shops, stopping in a café for a light lunch and cup of tea, and then exploring the side streets and the luxury brand shops – and from time to time would catch Sir John Alton following her or she would see his image in a shop window. She wondered why he was following her.

## November 16<sup>th</sup>

Her last full day in Berlin and a lunchtime concert was the only thing she planned to do. She had a restless night, not helped by her dream of being followed wherever she went. She woke late for her – just after eight. Bathed, dressed, and went down for a late breakfast.

She decided to have what the British think of as "continental" breakfast – whole wheat and rye bread with a selection of salami, cheeses, meats and tomato with a boiled egg and some strong coffee and a glass of orange juice. She took her time.

There were just three other guests in the dining room – a young couple she had not seen before and a solitary, very dignified gentleman with a very large handlebar moustache. He was reading the Frankfurter Allgemeine Zeitung – the very popular German newspaper. He was dressed unusually for Germany, at least in her mind – a heavy tweed suit with plus-four trousers and long green woolen socks, and what looked like a light check Tattersall shirt and woolen tie. It was as if he was ready to go out on the Scottish moors and shoot game.

He was German – as could be clearly heard when he spoke to the waiter and ordered his eggs and bratwurst for breakfast. But he dressed like an English Lord. She was curious.

When the waiter came to fill her coffee cup, she asked quietly who he was. The waiter, a wonderful corpulent and elderly man with exquisite manners, said quietly, "That gentleman, my good lady, is Siegfried Prince of Castell-Rudenhausen, who has breakfast here each Tuesday before his meeting upstairs with a young man whom none of us will ever speak of," he winked, poured her coffee, and left her to contemplate the information.

She had another slice of bread with Emmentaler, sipped her orange juice and observed her new subject. She thought he was about seventy. She noticed three things. He wore a massive diamond ring with what looked to have twenty diamonds on his left pinky finger. His pocket handkerchief was a brilliant yellow silk which made his hunting outfit look just a tad more social. Third, he had very effeminate mannerisms – when he drank from his coffee cup, his ringed pinkie finger was extended; his gestures to the waiter exaggerated; and his laugh somewhat high pitched. She was fascinated.

When he left, paying with cash for his meal, he didn't just leave the room. He strode with purpose and a sense of presence. Everyone who saw him looked. He was a character.

She finished her breakfast and returned to her room, already cleaned by the efficient cleaning and room staff. She checked the weather forecast, helpfully provided in a daily bulletin left beside the bed. Cloudy, but no rain. She read some more of her novel and looked at her map to calculate how long it would take her to walk to the concert hall.

At around ten forty-five she left the hotel and walked to the concert hall at Isoldestrasse – part of the Universitaet der Kunste. A baroque concert played on authentic instruments with music by Corelli, Lully, and Buxtehude. A variety of performers, some students at the university, but one was to be a Cellist who she had seen reviewed following a performance at the Wigmore Hall – Natalia Gutman, who had been a student of Rostropovich.

She arrived just a few minutes before the doors opened but was soon sitting on a comfortable chair with a clear view of the performance area. She made herself comfortable and began reviewing the program notes which she had been handed at the door. Though the substantial material was in German, the organizers had provided a short paragraph in English for each of the pieces to be performed.

Gutman had been providing a masterclass to cello students in Berlin for the last three days and this performance was the "capstone" of this work. Others had been working in a similar way with students working on different instruments – Elizabeth Wallfisch (violin) and Piers Lane (piano and harpsichord) at the same time.

It turned out to be a wonderful concert – full of fun pieces, richness, and nuances which she had not heard before in the more familiar pieces. The Lully music – he wrote mainly opera for Louis XIV – was the most surprising. The students, aided by Gutman and Wallfisch, had taken some of the music he had written for the theatre and created an orchestral suite called Moliere, since much of his theatre music was written to accompany Moliere's plays. Wonderfully rich and occasionally amusing.

The concert finished at one thirty. She found an excellent restaurant near the photography museum and sat at a table at the back of the room. A young waitress placed a menu, a glass of sparkling water and a red rose on her table. Looking back at the waitress with a questioning look, she smiled and said, "To make you feel happy!". They both smiled.

She chose a middle eastern salad of beans and herbs followed by an oven roasted cauliflower steak, something she had never heard of and was surprised about just how delicious it was. For dessert, she had a rich chocolate and tahini mousse. All the menu items were new to her – she felt a little bold, even risqué eating a fully vegetarian meal – but the wine she chose helped her truly enjoy it – a glass of Nordheimer Vögelein.

She took a taxi back to her hotel and took to her bed for an afternoon nap, reveling in the pleasures of the day.

She woke just after four, took a bath and dressed for dinner, which she decided she would have in the hotel. Rather than take the elevator – something that would not have been out of place in the Victoria & Albert Museum – she walked down the five flights of stairs to the dining room. She sat at a table near the back of the restaurant and was surprised to see the same waiter that served her breakfast still providing service. She asked for a negroni while she explored the menu.

She chose a lamb loin with courgetti, lovage, asparagus and a potato terrine followed by a custard nutmeg tart with vanilla ice cream. As for wine, she chose to drink a Bordeaux from Chateau Guiraud.

As she waited, she took out of her purse her daybook and what she had now christened her "Dubai pen". She made notes about the concerts and artworks she had seen, adding to her notes from Dubai. On reflection, she had most thoroughly enjoyed her little lunchtime concert today over the concert by Ashkenazy. Indeed, she started to think that the big orchestral pieces involving so many sounds and complexities were becoming less attractive as she got older. She found the chamber pieces more intimate and intriguing.

As she looked up, negroni in hand, she saw Sir John Alton approaching.

> "Miss Hutchins, I do hope you had a good day. I don't want to interrupt your meal, but I just wanted to say that I have enjoyed our occasional encounters. It is comforting to know that there is at least one other English person here. As I mentioned, there used to be many of us, especially during the immediate period after the end of the Cold War. But now, just you and me. I do hope your stay was pleasant and that you enjoy wherever your travels take you."

He smiled, as she responded.

> "Well, that is kind of you Sir John. I must admit, I was concerned that you were – what is the modern

word they use – "stalking" me, but I do thank you. I hope you have achieved whatever you were hoping to do on this visit to Berlin."

"Oh yes," he responded, "I have had the most productive meetings and managed to get to the Museum of Photography this afternoon – I always try and catch the latest exhibition there. Do have a wonderful meal. I'll bid you goodbye."

and with that, he was gone.

What an interesting encounter, she thought just as her lamb arrived. She made a note in her daybook to look up more about Sir John on her return to London – she was sure she would be able to find more information at her local library.

The lamb was perfectly cooked – just slightly pink, with a wonderful mint and rhubarb compote and a lamb jus. The vegetables, each a small portion, were excellent accompaniments and the wine a real complementary taste. It was one of the best meals she had ever eaten. It got even better when the nutmeg and custard tart arrived – a sublime, delicate and remarkably traditional English dish with simple yet luscious flavours.

She had a second glass of wine and began to think about the next leg of her journey.

## November 17th

Florence was a place she had read a lot about. She had, in her mid-twenties, been fascinated by stories of Medici and the Dukes of Florence. She had devoured histories borrowed from the local library and had been to the National Film Theatre to see documentary portrays of Lorenzo de' Medici, patron of the arts. She also recalled seeing an opera about his life, possibly by Leoncavallo if she remembered correctly – I Medici she thought it was called. She did remember that Placido Domingo was the star tenor in the production she saw at Glyndebourne.

Her Lufthansa flight, which required a change in Munich, left just before ten, though boarding was at nine fifteen. Her business class seat was by the window and her seat companion was a woman from London who worked for the BBC in radio.

Chatting before take-off, sipping the Prosecco thoughtfully provided by their steward, Hans, she told her that she was going to Florence to "scout" for an upcoming live broadcast of a concert due to go out three months from now. She was a sound engineer and they needed to appraise just what equipment they would need to bring or have their Italian partners provide. The concert was to be played at the Cattedrale di Santa Maria del Fiore. While this sounds like a wonderful venue, it is a sound engineer's worst nightmare. It is the third largest church in the world – cavernous and very tall. While stunning to look at and pleasant to be in, broadcasting from here will be difficult, she explained. The BBC were producing this documentary in partnership with American and Italian broadcasters – an added part of the "nightmare", according to her companion.

The orchestra was a French orchestra which specialized in baroque music, and they were to play music from the

Renaissance, including pieces by Dufay, Binchois, Issacs and a rare performance of Les Elements by Jean-Fery Rebel. She had not heard of some of these composers. Her seat companion explained that they were all writing for the court of Medici. While Rebel was French, he composed in the Italian style made popular by the Medici composers.

Their conversation was interrupted by the landing in Munich and the departure of some passengers and the arrival of others. To ease the disruption, the growingly friendly Hans had provided more Prosecco.

It is a short hop from Munich to Florence – just over an hour. By one o'clock she was checking into her hotel – the Hotel Balestri, just a short distance from the Uffizi Gallery and the Pitti Palace and a slightly longer walk to the Cathedral. Check-in was smooth and very efficient. A handsome young man took her luggage to her room and showed her the use of the shower, almost suggesting that they try it together. She smiled ruefully, placed a few lire in his hand and said: "thank you".

The room was luxurious – a studio with two large sofas, a wonderful armoire and a balcony overlooking the river Arno. The bed was the largest King-sized bed she had ever seen. There was a drinks cabinet, fresh ice in an ice bucket and some snacks in case she felt a pang of hunger.
She unpacked, hanging her three carefully chosen dresses and three skirts and four blouses in the wardrobe and then the remaining clothes in the armoire. She equipped the bathroom with her toiletries and creams. Undressed and showered, she put on a pair of slacks and a blouse and a warm cardigan and put her feet in what her mother used

to call "sensible" shoes. She wanted a walk and some lunch.

She wandered into the Ristorante Braceria Auditore on the Piazza del Grano, very close to Uffizi and the Galileo Museum. As she entered, she was greeted by the head waiter Giuliano, who seated her at a table by a window. She decided on a seafood risotto which when it came, was stunning. Beautifully fresh prawns, scallops, and pieces of octopus in perfectly cooked, creamy rice. She had a glass of crisp Vermentino and was thoroughly delighted with the experience. She decided to try the Lemon and Rosemary Panna Cotta and was amazed at the lightness of this simple but tasty dish.

As she finished her meal, enjoying her coffee and a glass of Grappa which Giuliano served even though she had not asked for one, she looked up and was stunned to see Sir John Alton approaching her table.

> "Well, Miss Hutchins. What a pleasant surprise. We meet again!"

> "Sir John, I am amazed to see you here. Now I am convinced you are following me!"

> "What? Oh, not at all. Not at all. I have business in Rome later this week and thought I would pop up to Florence and visit the Uffizi while I am in town. One of the perks of my work – going to museums, galleries, and concerts. Rather like you, though I suspect you are not between work assignments as I am?" He looked at her quizzically as he began to seat himself at her table.

"No, Sir John, I am recently retired and am spending some of my time exploring galleries I have always wanted to see and going to concerts that interest me."

"Yes, I understand. So sorry. I am rude; you don't mind me joining you – I see you have finished your meal. The food here is excellent, and they have a wonderful wine list."

"No, do make yourself at home. I will not be staying long, as you rightly observed I have finished my meal."

"I have already eaten, but I will join you in a grappa". He gestured to Giuliano to bring two more grappas.

"You are not trying to get me tipsy are you, Sir John?" she asked lightly but with a hint of seriousness.

"Wouldn't dream of it, Miss. Hutchins. Not my style."

They chatted about nothing in particular, and they left the restaurant together. Just as they were about to part and go their separate ways, Sir John asked if he could tempt her to have dinner with him this evening. He was staying at the Four Seasons and would be happy for her to join him at, say seven. She found herself agreeing.

She arrived promptly at seven and was escorted to Il Palagio, the elegant and palatial dining room. There she found Sir John, dressed in an immaculate white suite, blue shirt, and red tie with a red pocket square in his jacket top pocket. He looked like a movie star.

They continued chatting, perusing the extensive menu, and sipping a Prosecco. She ordered linguine morelli with blond shrimp, citrus and asparagus to be followed by a fish dish - pesce nero cotto nell'acqua di Vongole, peperone dolce e verdure verdi di stagione. Sir John went for baccala, followed by a steak in a pepper sauce with linguine. He ordered a white wine to accompany her meal - a glass of Quintodecimo - and a glass of red for his – a Vajra.

> "Well, this strikes me as intriguing. We keep meeting as if by chance, but I suspect there is something you are not telling me, Sir John. Time to spill the beans?"

> "You are part right, Miss Hutchins, or can I call you Audrey? Such a lovely name – not much in use today, but I like it. I did meet you by chance in Berlin at the hotel and, given the nature of my work, made inquiries back in London about you. I know you have recently left employment as a highly regarded accountant with real insight into how money flows within an organization. I know that you graduated not only top of your class with a specialization in forensic accounting, but also one of the top ten graduates in finance of the last fifty years. I know that your parents died during your first years at university, and your aunt died shortly afterwards. I know that, by today's standards, you are a wealthy woman. Somewhat reclusive,

passionate about music and art. I also know, both from my researchers and from my observations, that you have very good taste."

"Well. So, you have been investigating me. Am I under "suspicion?"

"Not at all. Quite the contrary. We'd like to offer you an opportunity to work for us, on contract, not permanently. On a particular project," said Sir John looking at her intently.

"And who is we?", she asked.

"Well, let me just say I work for the Government of Great Britain in a special capacity."

"Intriguing. And what would this work involve?"

"Looking at the money trail of three very wealthy people who, like you, travel a lot, enjoy music – especially opera and large concerts – and art. They are very wealthy, but we are concerned about both where their wealth is coming from and what they are doing with some of it."

"I am not a practising forensic accountant, which is a most specialized skill," she said quickly, "though I do have some academic qualifications in that sphere."

"I understand, and we are working with a team of forensic accountants, but I am interested in someone with a different take who has proven diligence and a keen eye."

"I had planned not to work again, but to spend my life traveling, exploring the world of art and music and going to places I have read about and am interested in."

"Like Dubai?", he said with a smile.

"Oh, so you have checked my itinerary. I am not sure I like all this poking around into my movements and background."

"I am afraid, given my work, it is very necessary. You shouldn't worry, Audrey. My assistant, Riya – a very smart lady – says you are the nearest thing to a saint she has come across since she began working for me several years ago! Your previous employer, Brian Barton I believe he is called, said you were the best accountant he had ever hired, and he praised not only your skill but your ability to stand above it all with a "cold and watchful eye" – just what we're looking for."

"Mr. Barton said that of me; how interesting. What would I have to do, Sir John?"
"Ah, well I think you will like this. We want you to assist us in developing a greatly enhanced money laundering policy, which Gordon Brown – our leader in waiting – wants to encourage the EU to adopt. Things are getting worse on this file, and the new Mafia, known as the 'Ndrangheta based in Calabria, London, Sydney, and Ontario, have found

new and creative ways of turning "dirty money" into clean money, sometimes using their connections with the Vatican to do so.

We have key targets in mind. You will review the information we provide and suggest what other information we may need, and we will make sure we build a comprehensive picture of the financial transactions that accompany this person's movements and those of his wife.

There are two more individuals we are interested in, both British subjects. Since each has a passion for art, ballet, opera, and classical music, you will be able to pursue your passions while working for Her Majesty's Government. We will, of course, pay some expenses, but not all of those you incur, given your preference for five star hotels and two and three Michelin star dining.

At no time will you be in danger, come into direct contact with our targets or interact with them. Your work will involve you using your considerable accounting knowledge to identify patterns and routines which would be the methods we need to control, regulate and, hopefully, stamp out. How does this sound?"
"I take it that the "us" we are talking about here is MI6 – our international spy agency, home of James Bond?"

"I couldn't confirm or deny the suggestion, Audrey. What I can say is that your country will be generous in supporting your interests".

"How substantial is the scale of money laundering, do you think Sir John?"

"Well, we have been looking very closely at Deutsche Bank and our estimate of their involvement with the 'Ndrangheta and Russian crime groups is in the excess of three billion US dollar region. We are also reasonably sure that Banco di Roma is involved with both the Sicilian mafia and their cousins in Calabria. In terms of British banks and financial institutions, both NatWest and Equitable Life are being investigated as we speak. A Building Society, which I can't name, is also close to prosecution. Our American cousins are keeping a watchful eye on a bank in Washington DC and the Bank of New York. Action has already been taken on a Mexican bank – Banamex – and is being taken now on a well-established bank in New York – the Republic National Bank."

"How is the Vatican involved?" asked Audrey.

"As we understand it, through several different ways, most of which revolve around the Vatican bank – technically the Institute for Religious Works. The National Crime Squad arrested and took to trial a very nasty man called Vincenzo Di Marco, who headed up 'Ndragheta operations in London. He got twenty years just three months ago and has been talking ever since. According to him, the various Mafia organizations front as real estate and construction organizations. The Vatican buys or commissions buildings and the criminals use genuine Vatican money, mixed with money from drugs, human trafficking, prostitution, and other "rackets" so as to flow dirty cash with clean cash seamlessly."

"I thought the EU and our own government had enacted legislation. Is the issue now that the laws and regulations are being flaunted or that they are inadequate?" she asked.

"Indeed, you are quite right. Last year Britain passed the Proceeds of Crime Act, which reinforced some provisions of the Criminal Justice Act of 1994. The EU also just adopted their third money laundering directive – building on the 1991 and 1995 directives. But these are not enough. Gordon Brown is very keen to introduce British regulations for money laundering "which will be the toughest in the world" and for the EU to use these as a basis for new regulations and laws. He wants this to be a part of his legacy as "Britain's best Finance Minister", according to Tony Blair."

They attended to their food, which was delicious – every mouthful a taste of perfection. The wine too was a wonderful accompaniment. They chatted about music – he was a big opera fan and had been a board member of the Royal Opera Company. He also loved Gilbert & Sullivan and was surprised that she did not.

As the coffee and grappa arrived, he looked at her quizzically.

"Who are these people you are so interested in?", she asked.

"I cannot tell you that unless you agree to join us and sign the Official Secrets Act", he said seriously. "I'll just say that they give the superficial impression of being decent and sincere, but in fact they are not all nice people, and we need to understand just how they operate. We have, unbeknown to them, access to their bank accounts in Germany, Italy, Switzerland, Barbados, and Cyprus, but we know they are still hiding money. We are worried about where some of this money is going and who is benefiting".

"When do I need to tell you of my decision?" she asked, folding her napkin, indicating she was staging her departure.

"I leave Florence the day after tomorrow and travel to Rome to meet with officials at both the Vatican bank and the Direzione Investigativia Antimafia. It would be good to know your decision before I do so."

"I will connect with you here before you leave. But now I must take my leave of you. I have a lot to think about".

"Of course, and, just for the record, whatever you decide Miss Hutchins, I have truly enjoyed meeting you". He said as he stood to hold her chair as she took her leave.

She took a taxi back to her hotel, even though it was just a twenty-five-minute walk. She felt after the wine and grappa a little unsteady on her feet, though she also found the feeling very pleasant.

In the bath in her suite at the hotel, she thought about her encounter with Sir John and his investigation of her. A part of her was upset – was her life so transparent that a woman in London could retrace her movements, chat with her former employer, and develop a "file" on her? Part of her was flattered to be considered an "expert", someone whose skills could serve her country and who was thought of, by the same woman in London, as a "Saint."

She thought carefully. She would be on a contract. She would sign the Official Secrets Act, which bound her for life. She would not be in danger, she assumed. The British Government would subsidize her travel and accommodations and her concert-going. They would, presumably, also pay her a fee. She could pursue her interests at someone else's expense, at least recovering some of her costs. She was quite sure that a very frugal Scottish finance minister would not be paying for her five-star hotel room.

She drained the bath, dried herself and put on her night wear – a simple silk smock. Within a few minutes she fell asleep. She dreamt that night of the babies meeting again – a dream she had not had for months – but this time the baby who spoke to her at the end said, "be careful – the world is never as it seems".

## November 18<sup>th</sup>

The Uffizi Galleries contain some wonderful works of art by Raphael, Botticelli, Ferrari, de Vinci, and others. Her favourite was a painting called Cousin Argia painted by Giovanni Fattori, created around 1861 by a more modern painter (he died in 1908). Her gaze captivates and intrigues and Audrey Hutchins saw something of herself in this painting. It is a deeply psychological portrait – something Fattori explored again and again in his career.

She also loved to sit and stroll in the Gardino di Boboli – beautifully maintained and manicured gardens. Today, as she sat near the grand fountain, a string quartet quietly played quartets from Haydn's Opus 17 – she loved their playing of the twenty-first quartet, one of her all-time favourites. It seemed to fit the occasion.

As she listened, she thought of Sir John's "offer" or, more accurately, "direct request." What did she have to lose? She was, as she realized in Dubai, drifting. While pleasant – great food, wonderful music and art, stunning walks and vistas and great hotels, what was so important in her life that prevented her from saying "yes?". She could think of no reasonable excuse other than "I don't want to," which was never, in her view, good enough as a reason to say no.

The string quartet moved on to Haydn's seventeenth quartet, which was also so beautiful, especially the third movement adagio. So delicate, like some of the flowers all around her.

On her way out she bought a small card of a stunning group of citrus fruits grown in the garden. It came with an envelope. She wrote a short note on the card: "Miss. Audrey Hutchins says yes" and placed it inside the envelope with the card. She addressed the envelope to "Sir John Alton at the Four Seasons Hotel, Florence." On her return to her hotel for her "napette," she asked the concierge to arrange for this note to be delivered as soon as possible. She also clarified that she did not want to be disturbed for the next two hours.

When she awoke, there was a note under her door. Sir John was to join her for breakfast the next morning at her hotel. She took dinner in her room – a tuna niçoise with a glass of light Pinot Gris – and listened to a concert on the radio – Beethoven piano trios.

## November 19<sup>th</sup>

What to wear? She had no doubt Sir John would be wearing his David Niven like white suite, blue shirt, red tie and matching handkerchief and beautifully hand-crafted brown leather shoes and matching belt. She chose a very light, flower-patterned knee length dress which came with a large bow to be tied at the left side and high heels and added the jewelry she had bought in Dubai. She decided not to wear tights – even though it was November and not especially warm. She could always change later. She applied a light foundation and lipstick and looked at herself in the mirror.

"What was she doing?" she asked herself. Was she trying to look younger than she was? Was she trying to attract Sir John – heaven forbid! Was she trying to make herself look and feel younger? She did look "nice." She also felt a tad excited.

Going down in the elevator to breakfast, a middle-aged man who joined her on the floor below her own greeted her with a wink. What did that mean?

Entering the restaurant, she saw that Sir John was indeed dressed in his summer whites and was standing to greet her. He beamed when he saw her, showing his appreciation for the effort she had made and his seeming surprise.

> "Well, so very nice to see you and to see you looking so elegant, if I may be so bold", he began as she seated herself with his help.

> "Thank you, Sir John. We both look like we are ready for summer, yet we both know that it is more likely to rain today and unlikely for the temperature to be much above 15 degrees centigrade."

> "Quite. But it makes us feel better and, hopefully, younger too".

They ordered breakfast – in both cases a selection of pastries, some bread and cheese accompanied by strong black coffee and orange juice – and chatted about the hotel and its ambience.

> "Thank you for your note and for your agreement to join us," he began. "I will not brief you now – we will do that when you return to London after your brief visit to Amsterdam, which I understand is your next port of call?"

"Correct, I leave in two days and will spend just two nights at my usual hotel in Amsterdam and attend two concerts at the Concertgebouw for which I have already arranged for tickets and will be back in London on the 23rd. I will need a day or so to attend to the mail and issues at home, and then I can be at your disposal".

"I will return to London on the 25th, via Rome and Paris. We should meet on the 27th. I too, have matters to deal with on my return. My associate, Riya, will contact you and arrange to meet. We could meet at 1030, and then I could take you for lunch at Claridge's – they do a wonderful Dorset crab or, if you prefer, Duck croquettes in the Fumoir room."

"What did I need to know before we meet?" she asked.

"Riya will send you a copy of both the Official Secrets Act and a basic contractual agreement for you to review before we meet. She will also send you a sample itinerary of the three men we are interested in, based on the last six months of our surveillance of them. When you look at these, remember we will be looking at them one at a time unless they are in the same place at the same time, which has not yet happened. These documents won't tell you who they are; we can only share that information once you have signed the Act. What they will suggest is the kind of trips you may be asked to take.

A strong focus is on liaison with colleagues in the EU – something I have been doing solo since 1997. You could help with that too. If we convince the French, Germans, Italians, and the Dutch then everyone else will fall into line."

"Will I be working for MI6?" she asked, not at all sure he would be willing to answer.

"You will be working for Her Majesty's Government is all I am willing to say," he replied, looking at her directly, sending a signal not to pursue this angle of inquiry.

"Will I be in any danger?" she asked.

"Not for a second. You will go about your business just as you have done on this present journey, Miss Hutchins. Still, during the day you will be provided with documents and information which we will ask you to review as a matter of urgency and provide an analysis. That's it. No guns, shooting, car chases or fist fights, though there may be the occasional cry of anguish at the volume of information which arrives at your hotel door!", he said trying to lighten the mood.

"Couldn't all this be done from London?", she asked.

"No. Some of the documents and materials must be viewed "in situ" or close by and returned within a very short period. We could, I suppose, photograph them, and review them later, but time is often of the essence. I assure you; we do need your help, and we do need it in various places."

They continued to chat and, and thirty minutes later, he was gone leaving her alone at the table with her thoughts. She took out her Dubai pen and her daybook and turned to a new page. She wrote in underlined capital letters: "BECOMING A CIVIL SERVANT!" - and made a list of her thoughts and feelings:

- o Anxious and nervous, like a teenager about to go on her first date.
- o Excited and enthusiastic, like a cricketer close to making his first century.
- o Curious about just how all this will work and how my knowledge and skills will be used.
- o Hesitant about giving up some of the newfound control over my life to a third party, also known as Her Majesty's Government (I really do think its MI6).
- o Keen to know more about Sir John – the first fascinating man I have ever spent time with and the only man I have had dinner and breakfast with! Talked to him more in a few days than to any colleague at work over the course of a year!
- o Inquiring about who I will be "investigating" and why – who are these three mysterious people, and why is HMG so interested in them? What are they doing to raise the concerns of governments?
- o Ready for the challenge – a phrase I never thought I would say or write!

o   Hopeful that I will be able to go to some interesting places, concerts, and art galleries – all at the expense of HMG! It could be a dream come true!!

She changed out of her flower print dress. Put on warm tights – almost woolly – and a pair of slacks and her sensible shoes, a warm shirt, and a warm woolen jacket. She felt more like Miss Hutchins and less like Miss Moneypenny. What had she been thinking?

She returned to the Uffizi. This time she focused on Renaissance art and sculptures. No one should spend more than a few hours in a gallery or museum – it becomes too overwhelming otherwise. She had once overheard an American tourist say that they had seen all the treasures of Europe in a week. She doubted it very much.

That evening she went to a concert at the Sala Vanni on Piazza del Carmine. A choral event – the choir singing Rachmaninov's Vespers was something she had not heard for quite some time. The next night the same choir, with a small orchestra, performed Pergolesi Stabat Mater with a wonderful, coloured countertenor from the United States called Derek Lee Ragin – simply wonderful. She had seen him earlier in the year at a performance of Handel's opera Tamerlano at the Royal Opera House and had thought at the time she would love to hear him sing a more sedate piece.

## November 21st

The Conservatorium in Amsterdam was one of those hotels where she felt almost at home. The receptionist, Daan, had been there for over two decades and recognized her as she approached. Check-in was seamless and quick, and in five minutes, she was in her favourite room – one she had stayed in more than a dozen times. She had been helped to her room by Johanna – a woman in her late thirties – whom she knew to oversee all matters of room service and room cleaning. They chatted for a few minutes, Johanna making sure that everything was just as it should be which, of course, it was.

She unpacked, hung her dresses in the mahogany wardrobe and her underwear, stockings, tights, and cardigans in the armoire. She ran a bath and sank herself in its deep enclave. Bubbles everywhere. She felt like a Princess.

The first of the two concerts she was to attend at the Concertgebouw featured the Bruckner third symphony, which Bruckner dedicated to Wagner – a heroic, demanding and yet deeply moving piece. It is supposed to have been Mahler's favourite Bruckner symphony. There are several versions of this symphony – Bruckner could not stop fiddling with it. The performance will be by the Orchestre Metropolitan from Quebec with their dynamic young conductor Yannick Nézet-Séguin.

The second concert on the following night was by a different orchestra, the Halle Orchestra based in Manchester and conducted by Kent Nagano of the "big hair", as The Guardian's music critic is fond of saying. The program is to include a short new piece by John Adams and then Vaughn Williams' pastoral symphony – his third. She loved this music – one of her go to recordings was with the London Symphony under Andre Previn with Heather Harper singing the soprano part. It would be magic.

As she contemplated these concerts, she also planned her limited time and her visits to the wonderful Portrait Gallery of the 17th Century and the Moco Museum – both places she had only occasionally visited. She didn't really have time for the Van Gough or the Rijksmuseum.

## November 23rd

The short flight from Amsterdam to London was on time, and the scheduled driver met her at the airport by arrangement. She was back in her apartment by noon. The apartment was spotless. The cleaning company the building concierge had arranged had done a wonderful job. Her mail, not very substantial, was neatly placed in three piles on the hall table: bills, advertisements and brochures and personal mail.

She unpacked and placed her clothes in three piles – "dry cleaning," "washing" and "to be put away" and placed her suitcase in its "home" at home. She was done travelling, at least for a while or until her new arrangements were settled. Who knew, she may be packing again in a few days.

She went through her mail, wrote out cheques for her bills – subscription renewals and a bill for a furniture repair she had arranged before her journeying began – and settled in to look at her personal correspondence.

A letter from a former colleague asking her for a reference was the first. Really, why did Michael Minter think she would be willing to provide any statement about his work which she had hardly oversaw? But she would.

A letter from her financial advisor reminding her to decide about a potential real estate investment they had discussed. She would say no. The less complicated her life was, the better. She always remembered her father saying that while real estate often produced the best long-term returns, it always, without exception, produced the most short-term pain.

## November 25<sup>th</sup>

A package was delivered. "Confidential" on the envelope. She had to sign for it. Inside was a short, hand-written note from Riya Akter, personal assistant to Sir John Alton, Cabinet Office, 10 Downing Street. It simply said, "For your information. Please confirm your attendance at this office on 10:30 on 27<sup>th</sup> November, followed by lunch with Sir John. Our office is on the 6<sup>th</sup> Floor (620), 110 Southwark Street, just behind the old Bankside Power Station, which is soon to become the Tate Modern. The name on the office door is Abloom Landscaping Ltd.

She scanned the Official Secrets Act 1989. It is not a long document but makes clear not only the penalties for disclosing information deemed confidential and top secret but also how revealing information is a breach of the act. Keeping confidence is part of the professional duty of an accountant, almost like a Catholic priest and what they hear in confession. She would have no difficulty in signing this act. She had spent her life not disclosing the financial arrangements and deceits of others.

The other documents were a draft contract for service in which the basis for her work was laid out, together with the basis for compensation, her reporting line to Sir John and some conditions she had to meet over and above the signing of the Official Secrets Act. Key amongst these was that she was not to have any direct contact with the individuals "targeted" for investigation. She wouldn't find this difficult. Her entire life had been about avoiding contact with others. The exceptions had been those she had to interact with because of her employment, her therapist and those that provided services to her.

She went for a walk and collected her dry cleaning and some groceries and food for a simple supper – a breast of chicken stuffed with ricotta and shrouded in pancetta with green beans and a light cream and white wine sauce. Her visit to the wine store was more fruitful – there, she found a bottle of Vermentino-Chardonnay from Tuscany, which she put in the fridge to chill.

Her music of choice after her afternoon nap was Bruckner's String Quintet, beautifully crafted and played wonderfully well by the Raphael Ensemble. She decided to read Hotel du Lac again – the prize-winning novel by Anita Brookner, which had struck a real chord with her when she first read it in 1984. Brookner had never married, had a wonderfully rich life as a Professor at Cambridge and seemed, like herself, to be a woman of a solitary character yet with some specific passions. In Brookner's case, it was art and literature. In her case it was music, art, and food.

## November 26th

At precisely 10:30, she arrived at the offices of Abloom Landscaping Ltd. She wore a pleated grey-green woollen skirt, matching stockings, brown leather brogues, a cream blouse and a jacket that matched the skirt. When she saw herself in the mirror, she was reminded of the wonderfully dressed Siegfried Prince of Castell-Rudenhausen, whom she had seen at breakfast in Berlin. She thought she would make the perfectly dressed companion.

Riya was expecting her. A stunningly beautiful woman in her mid-thirties with long, fulsome, flowing black hair dressed in a dark blazer, white blouse and slacks that matched the blazer with short heeled black pump shoes, she was beaming.

> "Miss Hutchins, I presume. I am Riya – Sir John has spoken so kindly of you. I have been looking forward to meeting you. Please, take a seat. Sir John is on the telephone now, but I am sure he will not be long."

> "Nice to meet you too, Riya. Such an unusual name – Indian?"

> "Bangladeshi, though I was born in Bradford, studied at Oxford and in Rome, and live in London and have never been to what my parents call "home." I am a Yorkshire lady through and through!" she laughed, "though you would never guess from my accent."

She was right. She spoke almost too perfectly received English, like an announcer on the BBC from the 1960s.

"How long have you been working here, Riya?" she asked.

"Oh, three years and six months since the unit was first established. They wanted someone who could speak several languages, who understood financial transactions and had strong skills in discretion. Somehow, I fit the bill. My degree from Oxford is in statistics, but I had been my father's bookkeeper for his real estate business since I was sixteen and knew a lot about loans, valuations, cash flow and transactions."

"...and she is also good at anticipating the likely moves of those we are keeping an eye on," added Sir John who had appeared in the reception area from his office in the corner of the suite. "Nice to see you again Miss. Hutchins. Shall we?", he said gesturing for her to join him in the office.

The corner office was large and, though the building was modern, Sir John's office felt more like a private room at Raffles or the Devonshire Club. Oak panels, a very old desk and chair, plush and comfy leather seats, and a settee. On the wall were two paintings. One was The Burning of the House of Commons – a copy of the Constable painting she assumed, and the other was a copy of another Constable – Old Sarum.

"Welcome to my little den, Miss Hutchins. I see you admire the Constables – copies I am afraid.

Couldn't afford the insurance on the originals, even if the Victoria and Albert would lend them to me. But I do love the feel of these. Please take a seat."

They dealt with formalities – contracts, the Official Secrets Act, access arrangements to Riya and himself and how, if she ever needed to, she would explain her relationship to a Landscaping company in London. She signed what needed to be signed.

"Now, to explain what we are up to. For the last two years we have been concerned about the laundering of money by a small group of influential people. We think, but cannot yet prove, that this group is moving millions each week from drugs, sex trafficking and gambling into legitimate businesses by means of some clever banking and trading arrangements. Several governments are wanting to introduce new measures to stop or, more likely, inhibit this. But it is difficult to do until we know more about the specific methods being used.

What makes this more urgent is the emergence of a more rapid means of money transfer and new technologies – this thing called the internet is taking off in financial circles and makes it easier to move money around. Some of the boffins suggest that, as soon as 2000, most financial transactions will be done via the internet, though just what this means, I have no clue."

"I see. Just what is it that I would do?"

"We – that is Her Majesty's Government and several other government agencies in other countries – want to bring a small number of those laundering money to justice and use their prosecution to create the conditions in which governments feel compelled to act. More specifically, in my view, we need new banking regulations and new international arrangements to reduce the ability of these people to abuse our financial institutions. What we need you to do, Miss. Hutchins is to look closely at certain transactions our target individuals are engaged in, study their banking arrangements – we will arrange for you to have secure but time-limited access to their bank records – and identify not just suspicious transactions but patterns of transactions and the methods they are using to turn "dirty" money into "clean" money."

"And this requires me to do this work when travelling? It can't be done from here?" she asked again, knowing that he had already answered this question.

"Some of it can be done from here, certainly. But some of the methods we are using to access the information we need, including the bank information, require us to be near where the "action" is – we have limited time access to some of the information. Rather like Cinderella at the ball, we lose all access to the information at a certain time."
"So, I travel according to the schedule you provide. Am given information to study, complete my

analysis and review, then return the information to the person who provided it and carry on as if nothing had happened?"

"Precisely, Miss Hutchins. I know it sounds odd. But when I tell you more, I think you may understand."

"Then do tell me more, Sir John."

"We are looking in depth at three people. One is an Italian banker – the head of Banca Sella di Bari, Giuseppe Valin. We think he may be the next Roberto Calvi – you remember the Italian banker found hanging underneath Blackfriars bridge in 1982? Calvi was Chair of the Banco Ambrosiano which had gone bust, owing around $1.5 billion, some of which was laundered through the Vatican bank. We think our man is following the same path. He has close ties to several Cardinals who, in turn, have roles to play in the financial affairs of the Vatican. We don't want to see Valin murdered, as Calvi certainly was. But we do need to keep an eye on him. Valin's wife has more recently also become a person of interest."

"The second," he continued, "is a former British cabinet minister and now a Euro MEP, Michael Major – you may recall he was Minister of Labour in John Major's government – he was not related. He was "let go" after he lost his seat in 1992. He inherited quite a sum of money from his father, and, within a few years, the sum had more than tripled. He seems to live a lifestyle that is way beyond the means of an MEP, and yet his finances continue to grow more rapidly than most successful businessmen or investors could achieve. We are suspicious. He too has links to the Vatican".

"Our third person of interest is also a British citizen. A seemingly successful businessman – Sir Andrew Rabkin. He is in the media business. Newspapers, magazines, books, and pamphlets. He came from nowhere and now runs one of the most important newspapers in Britain. Some suggest he's been funded by Russian intelligence. Others think he is a Mossad agent working for Israel. We think he is a fraudster. He is laundering black money, raiding pension funds, using funds from one account to fund another and then vice versa. He has an ego the size of a small planet. As far as we can tell, he had no Vatican connections – the only one of the three who does not. But he does have some connection to the other two. He does know and has met Michael Major several times. He was also seen recently in the company of Valin and his wife at a performance in Turin – they both love the Opera."

"What an interesting cast of characters, Sir John. Can I ask, what scale of money laundering are we talking about among just these three?"

"Good question, Miss. Hutchins. We suspect, that is Riya and I and our colleagues across Europe, are talking between eight and twelve billion pounds a year."

"Good grief," she said, visibly surprised. "I had not realized the scale of the challenge you are working on Sir John."

"Quite! Neither had we until we started digging. Remember, these characters are not the only figures engaged in this kind of skullduggery. There are many more like them – we are probably talking a trillion pounds a year. The whole thing is made more complicated by certain countries banking and financial systems which seem to be designed to be tax-havens and places where dirty money can be parked almost without trace – Panama, Cyprus, Cayman Islands, Bermuda, and a few others."

He paused. She crossed her legs and sat with her hands together in her lap and was deep in thought. After a few minutes, they chatted some more, and Sir John provided more information about each of the individuals. Most revealing was that all were using the bank Valin headed and that this bank had significant ties to the Vatican bank and financial system. Also of interest was that the three of them often attended the same events, not necessarily connecting at them. All three seemed to appreciate classical music, opera, and ballet. All three seemed to be interested in good food. All three had good taste in hotels.

"What about women? Are they all married?"

"They are, indeed, Miss Hutchins, though I must say that two of them seem to treat their marriage more of a necessity than a constraint. Both Major and Rabkin will be seen in the company of very attractive, much younger women at dinner and a

subsequent breakfast if you understand my meaning. Valin seems devoted to his wife, but then again, she is a force of nature and comes from a strong, shall we say, enforcement background."
"You mean Mafia?"

"I do indeed. She is the daughter of Victor Amuso of the Lucchese crime family from New York – one of the five Italian-American crime families originally from Sicily. I don't think you mess with these people and having seen her in action at her husband's side during Milan fashion week and later at the Opera, I would not want to mess with her. I thought my own ex-wife was difficult, but she was not vicious!"

The car had arrived to take them to lunch at Claridge's, as Sir John had promised. The car took thirty minutes, and they arrived to find an almost full dining room. The maître d'hôtel guided them to their table and handed them a menu. After an enjoyable meal with wine pairings, Sir John suggested she plan a trip to Rome for the second week of February. There was to be a major arts festival, and he knew that two of the three "targets" would be there. Riya would help plan and make needed arrangements.

With that he was gone. She looked around the room and saw a well-known Shakespearian actor at lunch with another actor better known for his ability to impersonate others. Further down the room was a novelist she had long admired, chatting with a woman with whom she appeared to be very friendly.

She returned to her apartment. Took out her daybook and made notes of the conversation, adding questions she wanted to explore. After a nap, she needed a walk to clear her head.

After a walk to the local library, she looked up any material she could find on Sir Andrew Rabkin, Michael Major, and Giuseppe Valin. For good measure, she also looked up Sir John Aston. Much to her surprise, she found a book Sir John Aston had written about A. E. Houseman's poetry entitled A New Form of Being English – The Poetry of A. E. Houseman. In her quick scan, he seemed to be suggesting that his two volumes of poetry shaped the way English people saw England and themselves within it and gave them a language and phrases that helped shape an English identity.

She found a lot of information about two targets, as one might expect when looking at prominent politicians like Michael Major and Sir Andrew Rabkin. It seems that Rabkin was not his original name, just one he adopted after the second world war and established himself using that name, later made legitimate. As for Michael Major, no one seemed to like him. One writer declared him "amongst the least competent cabinet Minister since the second world war," and another wrote that "he did for Conservatives what an eccentric pack of dogs does for fox hunting," which, though the phrase sounded contrived, told her that the writer thought he was inept. She found nothing on Giuseppe Valin.

She returned home, made a light salad with chicken and croutons and a simple oil and balsamic vinegar dressing, and started listening to the Delius string quartet followed by the three Schuman piano trios – all accompanied by a glass of Armagnac – the Darroze forty-year-old. She thought she could enjoy being a civil servant on contract.

## December 1998

Throughout December, she went about her normal business. Walking, visiting galleries, and attending concerts, lunches, dinners, and bookshops.

The most enjoyable concert was a performance of Mozart's Great Mass in C Major at the Festival Hall, with Elliot Gardiner conducting the English Baroque Soloists and a wonderful group of soloists with the Monteverdi Choir. So moving. So powerful. So memorable.

She had a terrific meal at the Mirabelle, where Marco Pierre White recently began his tenure as chef patron. Sea bass with fennel and garlic mashed potato followed by a Tarte Tatin - all very French. A light Chablis was a perfect accompaniment.

Her book of the month, which she devoured, was the story of an eccentric professor of mathematics at Princeton, a man called John Nash – Sylvia Naser's A Beautiful Mind. She loved the book for its compassionate account of madness and its understanding of how different kinds of people are needed to make the world work. She strongly identified with John Nash and thought that, in some ways, her journey could have been very similar.

She managed to avoid the growing hoop-la over a book about a school for witches and wizards which the new author of the moment – Joanne Kathleen Rowling – seemed to be doing well with. She had never understood the attraction to this genre which so many people seemed to like.

Christmas, as always, was spent listening to the radio, selections from her music collection and dining out, though this was becoming more difficult. The nearer to Christmas, the fewer tables for a walk-in diner were available, especially for a single person. She found herself cooking and meal-making for herself at home more often.

She spent the "dead time" between Christmas and New Year planning a trip in January. She would do something she had always wanted to do and go to New York for a few days in early January before she was due to go to Rome "on assignment" for Sir John.

She met with him twice in December, both times for lunch, and he provided some more information about the targeted three. Valin was becoming more active in the European financial scene, with more bank-to-bank agreements with French, German and Irish banks. He had not yet been able to reach an agreement with a British bank but was known to be in discussion with two – the Bank of Scotland and Coutts.

Sir Andrew Rabkin had completed two more book publishing acquisitions – textbook publishers in both cases – using stock in his parent company as the lure for the sale. He had also created four new corporations, which both Riya and Sir John thought were "shells" – set up to pass money through – rather than actual businesses.

Michael Major was travelling in Latin America, visiting Chile, Paraguay, and Argentina. "Likely up to no good!".

We think he may pop into Panama before he comes home. He has also bought a house in Provence, and his wife and two teenage daughters will be there over Christmas.

He had wished her well for the season and said he was off to Spain, where he had a "small place" which he found restful and far away from the British tourists. It was a house in Almeria on the Mediterranean coast. He said it would be warm, dry, and not at all busy. Since his divorce – he did not have offspring – he preferred to be away for Christmas and "be alone, away, all on my own." She understood perfectly.

## January 1999

She had decided to fly to New York in style. Concorde was again flying between London and New York following the lifting of a ban imposed because of alleged noise from take-off and landing. She booked a seat and arranged to stay at The Langham. Her travel agent said the 5th Avenue hotel executive suite was the perfect place for her – everything she needed.

She flew on the 18th of January. The journey time was 3 hours and eleven minutes, twenty-five minutes faster than usual, but not the fastest time for this journey. On the flight, she spotted Henry Kissinger, Nixon's former Secretary of State and one of the ugliest men ever to hold office. Also on board was Joan Collins, whose movie The Clandestine Marriage she had seen in the cinema. If she remembered correctly, it also had Nigel Hawthorne and Timothy Spall. Not an especially memorable film.

She looked at the magazine she had picked up in the first-class lounge – a copy of National Geographic. It was focused on making sense of the coming millennium, which she thought was a little premature. She enjoyed the service – very pleasant poached salmon with asparagus and a nice cheesecake and crisp, chilled white wine.

She was met at the airport by a driver sent by the Langham Hotel, and just fifty minutes after landing, she was shown to her room. Spacious, with a full kitchen and very modern appliances, she was more than pleased with her surroundings. From the window, she could see mid-town Manhattan and quite a lot of the activity on 5th Avenue. She would explore later, but first, a bath and a rest.

She slept longer than intended – close to two and a half hours. She dressed quickly in tweeds with a decent pair of brogue shoes and a coat and went for a walk. A quick look at Tiffany's and a much longer walk around the department store Bergdorf and Goodman housed in what was once a Vanderbilt family mansion. Eight floors of very fine clothes and shopping. She was tempted by many things she saw, especially a fine fountain pen that would be her keepsake from this visit – a rare Wahl Oxford Black and Pearl with a 22-karat gold medium nib – just $550, but a masterpiece. She would think about it.

She spent so much time in Bergdorf and Goodman that her day was running out on her. She needed to eat and then change for her concert at Carnegie Hall. The Berlin Philharmonic was playing Mahler's seventh symphony with Claudio Abbado conducting. She had not always liked Mahler – so demanding of the audience and so deeply

Germanic, full of tension, angst, passion, and bluster. Still, she had grown to admire his work, even borrowing the musical scores from the library so she could listen to a recording and read the score at home.

She dined at the hotel, changing into a more suitable dress for the evening. Ai Fiori, the hotels restaurant, was an elegant and modern space with a fine Italian French menu. She chose the Long Island duck breast stuffed with chicken liver mousse served with a potato terrine, cabbage, and a lovely pistachio gravy. For a wine pairing, she opted for a Brunello from Tuscany. She skipped dessert and instead had a cheese selection with coffee. One of the cheeses – Mad River Blue from Vermont – was the nicest blue cheese she had ever tasted.

The concert was remarkable. Abbado seemed to have the orchestra at his fingertips, and they played brilliantly for all eighty minutes the Mahler takes to play. There was not a second in which she felt distracted or disengaged. The final movement – a rondo with variations – is full of references to works by others, like Wagner and Lehar, but is powerful and moving. As the program notes suggest, the symphony represents a journey from dusk till dawn, and Audrey Hutchins could see herself embarking on this journey.

Back at the hotel, she stopped by the bar for a nightcap – that mixture of American bourbon, Angostura bitters and red Vermouth known as a Manhattan. She had never had one and wanted to try. She enjoyed it and, sitting at the bar, had a second.

As it was being made, a young man to her left asked if she was new in town. She replied that she was. He warned her about the dangers of being a woman in New York and suggested that she needed a patron or a male escort. She thanked him for his thoughtfulness but said that she was a solitary person who had no intention of putting herself in harm's way. He smiled and wished her a safe stay in New York and was gone. Her second Manhattan finished, she returned to her room and prepared herself for a night's sleep.

Two nights later, having walked to a variety of "must-see shops" and having returned to Bergdorf and Goodman to buy the fountain pen, she was back at Carnegie Hall. This time a performance of the Brahms German Requiem. Kurt Masur conducted the New York Philharmonic and the Westminster Symphonic Choir with soprano Sylvia McNair and baritone Håkan Hagegård. This is the same team who recorded this work on a recording released just three years before – a recording she owned. She recollected a comment about this Requiem from the curmudgeon George Bernard Shaw who said something like, "A first-class undertaker could have written it"!

In her daybook, writing with her new Black Pearl pen, she noted that this performance was "rich in texture, substance and meaning – it moved my heart and soul in ways many other performances of choral music have not. Masur brought out the implicit humanism of Brahms and his care for mankind".

Two days later, she was back on Concorde on the return flight and soon back in her apartment.

A letter awaited her from Sir John Aston:

Dear Miss Hutchins:

We need you in Rome from 12-20th of February. You are booked to stay at the Roma Fori Imperiali for the duration of your stay – all meals and expenses paid. Your airline tickets are included in this envelope.

On the 12th, we will meet for cocktails at seven on the rooftop bar – please wear a suitable cocktail wear which takes account of the likely temperature (around 18C). Also, make sure you have a notebook and pen with you. You may need to take notes during our dinner. Riya will join us.

Our focus for this visit is the links between our protagonists, especially our Italian and the Vatican. More when we meet. Please read the attached briefing document before we meet.

I do hope you had a wonderful time in New York and onboard Concorde – a great achievement of British engineering.

John Aston.

Attached were her airline tickets and a one-page note about the ways in which the Roberto Calvi scandal had exposed the money laundering through the Vatican bank and the role played by Cardinal Paul Marcinkus.

Marcinkus had been President of the Vatican Bank between 1971 and 1989, appointed by Pope Paul VI and retained by John Paul II, even though he had no background in finance, accounting, or banking. He was accused of being part of the Banco Ambrosiano money laundering scheme but refused ever to discuss the matter or answer prosecutors' questions. He continued to use his Vatican diplomatic immunity even after the Vatican paid our $244 million to creditors of Calvi's bank – money taken from pension funds which created further problems for the Vatican. Earlier, the Vatican Bank had lost around $10 million in a scandal involving a Sicilian banker called Michele Sindona and the Franklin National Bank in the US and the Italian Banca Privata Italiana. He was closely connected to the Gambino crime family and Pope Paul VI. Sindona was found guilty not only of fraud and money laundering but also of murder. He was murdered while in prison.

An arrest order for Cardinal Marcinkus was issued by the Italian government, but he again claimed diplomatic immunity and was supported in doing so by the Italian courts. He told a fellow Cardinal that "I may be a lousy banker, but at least I am not in jail!". He retired in 1990 and moved back to the United States where he was from – Sun City, Arizona, where he lived until he died from natural causes, celebrating mass each day, despite increasing frailty.

Giuseppe Vali is on a similar path to that taken by Roberto Calvi, with strong links to the Legion of Christ and Regnum Christi – organizations founded by Marcial Maciel Delgado – a Mexican priest and particular favourite of Pope John Paul II and his Secretary of State, Cardinal Sodano. We suspect that there is a substantial worldwide money laundering operation involving the Vatican, aided by

Delgado. We are narrowing our focus on Vali and his transactions.

She found all this fascinating but was still very unclear on what work she was being asked to do or how any of this related to current concerns about money laundering. Still, if Sir John was willing to fly her to Rome and put her up in one of the smartest hotels in the city, she was not going to argue.

It all made her think. For years she had worked as a thorough, diligent accountant and had undertaken several audits. She had detected some questionable activities but never fraud or outright corrupt money laundering. What she found interesting was the danger and risk people like Vali would take for money.

Risk-taking was not part of her makeup. Her entire life had been about owning control of situations, relationships, and sensations. The idea of being in danger, possibly life-threatening, was something beyond her understanding. Why would anyone risk everything for the sake of money, especially if they already had a lot of it?

## February 12th

The most convenient British Airways flight left London at ten-forty, arriving in Rome at two-twenty – a flight just short of three hours. Her seat companion was a priest who was delighted to have been upgraded to business class on his first flight to Rome and first visit to the Vatican. He was being interviewed for a position in the Vatican apostolic archive. He was, he explained, an expert book restorer and a qualified librarian who had come to the priesthood in his late twenties.

He explained to her that the Vatican apostolic archive is massive – eighty-five kilometres of shelving - about fifty-three miles. No one had counted how many books and documents were housed there, but a selective collection of archives relating to specific papacies contained over thirty-five thousand documents and books. The archives were available to certain scholars, and if he correctly understood the position he was applying for, it would be his job to facilitate the work of these scholars while ensuring that the access rules were maintained together with the preservation of the materials.

He was excited, and she found the whole subject of the archive fascinating. She asked whether the application for a marriage annulment made by Henry VIII to Pope Clement VII was the kind of document to be found in the archives. He told her it was. Cardinal Farina, who oversees both the archive and the Vatican library, had recently displayed some materials from this time in an exhibition. Also included was a letter to Clement VII from Mary, Queen of Scots, saying she was dedicating her life to the defence of the Catholic church and would be fighting Henry VIII's reformation.

The aircraft's crew served a simple meal – cod with braised vegetables followed by cheese and biscuits. Nothing to write home about.
A driver sent by the hotel met her at the baggage carousel as she collected her solitary though large suitcase. Forty-five minutes later, having driven past the Colosseum, she

arrived in her room at the Roma Fori Imperiali. A five-star hotel, her suite was spacious and luxurious.

After a quick shower, she took a taxi to the Villa Borghese, where she joined the gallery tour. The statues are simply exquisite, especially the Bernini statue of the Rape of Proserpina and that of Apollo. She was close to tears when she looked at the canvasses of Caravaggio, Titian, and Raphael. Exhausted by the experience, she took a quick taxi back to the hotel and had an afternoon nap before her appointment with Sir John and Riya.

## Later That Evening

She arrived, as requested at seven on the elegant and heated roof-top bar, to find Sir John Aston in his warm winter suit of dark charcoal and Riya in a pants-suit and cardigan, looking like a model from Vogue. They both looked pleased to see her. She asked for a Manhattan and took in the view. From this place, she could see all sorts of parts of Rome, including the rooftop of the Vatican, the Temple of Antonio Faustina, the Foro di Augusta and the Lupa Capitolina with its She-Woolfe's head.

Riya had studied in Rome and took her around the roof and explained the sights. Sir John quietly sipped his gin and tonic and looked over some papers. As they sat back down, he looked at both seriously and began a short statement.

> "Well we are going to have to do a lot of work in the next few days. We have people to see, documents and materials to review, some of them secret and available to us only for a short time –

friends inside the Vatican are helping as are some of the people we know in Government, but not officially. They are sure, as we are, that something unpleasant is happening and that significant attempts are being made to cover this all up at the highest levels in government and in the Vatican – and I mean the highest levels."

"You mean some senior people know about money laundering and are complicit?" asked Miss Hutchins.

"Worse. Money laundering is only a part of what we understand to be happening, aided, and abetted by Giuseppe Valin and his associates. We can talk more over dinner. We will be joined by one of our close informants, Monsignor Jacques Lepone, who works in the office of the Vatican Secretary of State, Cardinal Sodano. He is a "friendly", but we need to protect his identity in all that we do. We are therefore eating in a private dining room here at the hotel. He will be sharing some documents that we must review and return early tomorrow."

"This sounds very intriguing", said Audrey Hutchins.

"It is actually very disturbing," said Sir John.

They chatted as they finished their drinks and wandered downstairs to the private dining room made available to them on the second floor of the hotel.

The meal began with a charcuterie board of excellent Italian meats and cheeses, olives, tiny tomatoes, grapes, almonds, walnuts and some thinly sliced crisp bread. Audrey Hutchins had not seen this before and was fascinated. She explored the tastes and small bites, as did Riya. Sir John just had a few pieces of cheese and some bread.

The first course was a calamari fritter – squid, perfectly lightly fried, in a very delicate tomato sauce. Another first for her. The second course was a delicate linguine con vongole – fresh clams in a white wine sauce with linguini pasta. Some beautiful white wine from Venice – a Soave – went beautifully well with both courses. For dessert, a stunningly light white and dark chocolate cake served with yogurt ice cream.

As the coffee arrived, so did their guest. An elderly man in a full, red-trimmed cassock with purple slashes, and gold rimless glasses entered. They all stood.

> "Please, please – carry on, and I will join you for coffee and a piece of that lovely-looking torta. It looks very much like what my Nona used to make – rich, yet light – always delicious. My doctor says I have to watch my diet, but eating sensibly followed by prayer seems to be working!". He smiled as he walked around the table, firmly shaking the hand of each of them as they introduced themselves to him. He may be getting on in years, thought Audrey Hutchins, but he is still strong.

After a pause while the waiter brought coffees and a slice of the cake for the Monsignor, Sir John opened the more formal part of the evening.

> "Monsignor, we are most grateful for your time and your presence. I know this is not easy for you but, as we agreed when we met briefly yesterday, the matters we need to deal with are both serious and dangerous and threaten not only the Church but also the stability of the Italian banking system and therefore the whole of the European currency, which is now in place as of the first of January this year. As I explained, the three of us represent a kind of British expeditionary force tasked by the Prime Minister Tony Blair with the protection of our banking and financial system. We understand you have some relevant information for us which you will share in total confidence in this room".

The Monsignor looked at each of the three intently, and then began:

> "Indeed, I do. But I need to make clear that I am acting alone and directly against the instructions of not only Secretary of State Cardinal Angelo Sodano, to whom I report, but also to His Holiness Pope John Paul II, who has been informed of the issues that concern us here but wishes it to be kept secret. I cannot, in conscience, agree. You will see why. I would be grateful if no written record of our gathering here is kept. I will leave a file folder for your review. I need this to be returned by courier no later than ten tomorrow morning."

I advise you to brace yourselves. This is not a pretty story. In 1941, a young Mexican man formed an organization he called the Legion of Christ. He saw it as a kind of beginning of a mission – a starting point for a renewal of Catholic commitments first in Mexico, then in other parts of Latin America and then around the world. This man became a priest a few years later, in 1944, and has been seen by many as a Saint-like person – focused, serious, and committed. His name is Marcial Maciel Degollado. Remember that name. He is the villain of this story – at least one of them.

The Legion was meant to be a training ground for priests and other religious roles – he founded schools, seminaries, and related institutions. Yet rumours soon began about how this seemingly saintly man abused boys and young men. About his drug abuse. About his living arrangements with women. In 1956, he was put under investigation by the Vatican – he was suspended from any role connected with the Legion or his parish church. He was cleared through the direct intervention of Pope John XXIII and his then Secretary of State, Cardinal Dominic Tardini. That was in 1959. I suspect money was involved in "buying" his forgiveness. A large amount of money. Probably some property too. Tardini now lives in a real palace.

In response, Maciel (which is how he asked to be referred to) in 1959, with the Legion already proving to be a great success, created a layperson's organization called Regnum Christi which soon caught on and became almost a cult within the church. Maciel cultivated some key members of this fast-growing community, securing significant donations of cash, shares, equities of other kinds and real estate. He seems to have been selling pardons or access to eternal grace – something the church gave up on after Luther's reformation.

These two organizations - the Legion and Regnum - got very large. Our best estimate – you will soon appreciate that records and accounts are somewhat "murky" – are that there are seventy-thousand members of Regnum Christi, over two and a half thousand seminarians, eight hundred priests working for or directly with the Legion, including four fully approved and consecrated Bishops. We can also attest, and these numbers are verified, that the Legion is operating fifteen universities; fifty seminaries or similar institutions; around forty-five schools for disadvantaged young people, mainly secondary schools; one hundred and twenty-five religious houses and monasteries; two hundred educational and outreach centres; and that the Legion supports over one thousand two hundred houses of worship – churches, oratories, and chapels. It is a big business.

In addition – yes, there is more – there are some four hundred and twenty-seven charitable organizations or trusts directly associated with either Regnum Christi or the Legion or both.

Through these organizations and operations, the Legion owns a vast number of properties. It has significant landholdings in Latin America, the United States, Spain, Rome and in other parts of the world. In Rome alone, the Legion owns sixty-eight properties. The Legion also funded the restoration and expansion of the building in which Cardinal Sodano, Secretary of State, now lives. It also paid for a private house in the name of Monsignor Stanislav Dziwisz, personal secretary to the Holy Father, even though he does not yet use it.

I have evidence, seen also by others, that Maciel is not only a pedophile who abuses young boys – eight seminarians have filed formal complaints with the appropriate Catholic authorities – but also that he is living with at least one woman, possibly two and up to five, and that he has fathered at least three children. Remember, he is committed to vows of celibacy, poverty and obedience and is a priest.

I also have signed witness statements that he practices sadism with young men. I see this man, who to outsiders appears a saint, to be deeply wicked and awful. Corrupt to the core and not adverse to corrupting and then abusing others.

But there is yet more. He presents himself as living life simply. Yet he owns several properties in Mexico, Spain and Rome. He owns a Lamborghini, a Ferrari, and a Bentley. He has significant sums of money in bank accounts only he has access to – our intelligence from one Swiss bank and a friendly soul in Panama – suggests that his personal wealth is more than $100 million US dollars. The Legion has assets are, in total, more than $35 billion US dollars.

When Maciel travels, he does not stay in locations owned by the Legion or Regnum Christi. No, he stays in luxurious hotels like this one and often is not alone. When he travels, he pays in cash. On his most recent visit here, I witnessed him handing Dziwisz a large envelope stuffed with brand new Euros - around €75,000. He also, on behalf of a benefactor, gave Sodano €50,000 on this same trip.

On a flight back to Mexico from Rome, he was stopped at the airport by security. They checked his luggage and found over €1 million in various currencies. However, he made one call and, following that call, was allowed to continue on his journey, securing an apology from the Minister of the Interior.

One of his followers here – a member of the Regnum Christi – is Giuseppe Valin. A banker and money mover with ties to the Vatican, most especially to Dziwisz and, through him, directly to Pope John Paul II and Sodano. I fear that Maciel is protected at the highest levels. Indeed, I overheard Sodano say to Dziwisz that "it is better that eight innocent men suffer than millions lose their faith." He was speaking of the formal complaint recently filed against Maciel filed by seminarians. We are in deep trouble, and it disturbs my conscience and hurts my soul".

He stopped. Clearly shaken by his long and detailed statement, as were all in the room. The silence and tension were palpable.

Riya was the first to speak.

> "Monsignor, I can't begin to imagine the pain this causes you, and we all thank you for your directness and clarity. What role do you understand Valin to play with the Legion, Regnum Christi or the Vatican itself?"

> "Ah yes, good question Miss Riya" replied the Monsignor. "I understand he is of significant interest to you three. Giuseppe Valin is both an officer in Italy for Regnum Christi and its banker. He also acts as a banker for some of the Legion's funds. However, they do not bank with just one bank in any jurisdiction – they always place money in different places to minimize risk and maximize confusion for any investigators.

> Each week, Valin reports to Alessandro Bianchi, the Legions finance director for Italy. Valin details new donations – equities, land, cash, endowments – and payments made. For example, to fund the Legion's university here in Rome at via Aurelia – they train priests. In a typical month, I am given to understand; they secure new funds of around €5 million and spend less than half of that. The balance is moved to other locations worldwide where it is needed.

Some of the donations are made in cash – it could well be money from crime or nefarious activities. In exchange, the "donor" may receive certain privileges or property. In one case, a donor was given a property on the outskirts of Venice which he was then able to sell for twice the amount he had donated.

Valin looks like a banker. Walks like a banker and, for part of each day, he is a banker. But for the other part of each day, he is a conspirator and corrupt financier, of this, I am sure. You will see information in the folder I have provided that he has an offer on the table for the Vatican to invest in property in London and New York for a few hundred million euros which the Papal Nuncio can use but also be rent earning, gaining in value every day. He's floating the idea that property values grow between 12% and 15% each year in these cities – we lower our costs of diplomatic services while all the time building up equity. Through a company he has connections in London, he will do the deal in exchange for a commission – around €15 million. Cardinal Sodano is keen. I am less keen – I understand the proposition, but I am doubtful that the "deal" will be as profitable or as "clean" as Valin makes it sound. The details and observations are in this folder". He placed a file folder on the table, taken from the leather valet case he had brought.

Audrey Hutchins asked him a question:

> "You mentioned the cash sums used as gifts to various persons in authority within the Vatican – what happens to this cash? It sounds like these are what we accountants might think of as "off-the-books cash" that can then be used to buy goods and services which appear legitimate since the person purchasing them with cash is a senior officer of the Vatican. For example, if the Pope's secretary uses cash to buy a shirt and a pair of shoes, that cash would have been used for a legitimate purpose, even though the cash may originally have come from some illegitimate drug deal or other nefarious activity?"

> "Exactly, Miss Hutchins," replied the Monsignor. "When I look at the lifestyle of my superior, Secretary of State Cardinal Sodano, I can see that he must be receiving substantial funds from somewhere every week. We in the Curia live on a monthly stipend. Since Sodano is the most senior Cardinal, he receives around €5,250 each month – which he probably spends in a week. What he has to do in exchange for the money someone is paying concerns me. He is not alone. Many other cardinals are also living a life which does not "fit" with their monthly salary or their vow of poverty."

> "One of the people supplying funds to these cardinals, you seem to be suggesting, is Valin acting on behalf of the Legion or its lay-organization Regnum Christi?" asked Miss Hutchins.

"Exactly correct Miss Hutchins. It's a web of deceit which has entangled the church at a senior level."

Sir John, sensing that it was time to end the conversation – the Monsignor looked very tired after this significant disclosure – brought the meeting to a close, at least for their friendly priest.

"I thank you for your candour, Monsignor. I can assure you that the three of us understand the pain it must cause you to share these "secrets" with us and the distress it must cause you when you think of the church and its mission. We will review the file and guarantee its return by courier no later than ten tomorrow. "

They all stood. The Monsignor shook each of their hands and then left. They all let out an exhausted sigh. Sir John gave the folder to Miss Hutchins and asked her to review it overnight and suggested breakfast at seven the next morning so that she could share her observations and that he and Riya could look over the file. They each left, returning to their own rooms.

Back in her room, Audrey Hutchins sat and reviewed the file. In it, the Monsignor had listed payments made that he was aware of by Valin to various people in the Vatican and what had happened to the money subsequently. An idea began to form in her mind about moving money, some illegitimate in terms of source, into the banking system and out again. She saw three phases. The first phase was using a" front" like the Legion to donate money which the Legion then placed in a legitimate, regulated bank. She called this "placement." The next step she called "layering and moving" – the bank account holder used the funds to move it to other places, buy property or goods or services. The third step was to secure gains on the use of the money – a return on the investment, either in terms of sales, sales of goods and services or exchange of money for a new opportunity. She called this "integration."

The proposal to involve the Vatican in buying a building in London involved all these stages, she could see by the information in the file. The basic idea was simple. The Vatican wanted to buy a luxurious building in Chelsea, London, worth over €400 million. The idea was to buy the building – clean up the property and sell it for a profit. Valin proposed that he be paid €15 million to close the deal, oversee the refurbishment and then arrange the sale.

The papers showed that a year before the Vatican was seeking to buy the building, it had been sold to Valin's bank for €150 million. He was trying to secure a fee for arranging the sale of a building he already owned through the bank and, at the same time, secure a profit on the sale of €250 million. If he had bought the building with Legion money secured from a Mafia source, some of the profit would be returned to that source, and the Vatican would be complicit.

She was tired. She ran a bath, put on her silk nightgown, and went to bed. Her dream was of dancing cardinals and Mafia shootouts in the halls of the Vatican. She did not sleep well.

## February 13th

At breakfast, she shared her observations with Sir John and Riya and passed the file to Riya, who would review it and arrange for its safe return to the Monsignor.

Sir John made two observations. First, he liked and trusted the Monsignor and found his directness and openness both refreshing and, at the same time, very chilling. The Vatican and its most senior prelates were corrupted. Second, through Monsignor, we can look at one slice of the transactions of Valin – it was just a part of his money laundering. They needed to find others.

This was a good observation, thought Audrey Hutchins. While the Vatican was an intriguing angle, it was not the only angle. Valin had other irons in the fire.

>"Perhaps by exploring the Vatican angle, we can uncover other aspects of Valin's work and activity', she suggested.

>"Exactly – I think we can use this as a template for looking at other activities, especially as they involve the Legion or other entities," said Riya. "We may be able to connect the dots between placement, layering and moving and integration if we are to use Miss. Hutchins terms", she added.

>"Why don't we divide and explore?" said Sir John. "Miss. Hutchins, you explore other aspects of the work of Valin's bank, and Riya will look at the Vatican in more depth. I have arranged for you, Miss. Hutchins, to spend time in the Bank of Italy's

supervisory authority for banks where you will meet and work today with Tommaso Bellucci – a trusted colleague – I went to university with his father and have known Tommaso for many years. He has been looking at Valin. You will be free this evening. We will meet here tomorrow at eight." He passed her a piece of paper with the address of the office she was to visit and a telephone number for Mr. Bellucci.

With that, breakfast was over.

She returned to her room, found a classical music station on the radio, and began listening to some of Beethoven's piano sonatas – a recorded concert with Alfred Brendel. She opened her daybook, and with her New York Wahl pen, she made some notes:

Ways to Launder Money:

1. Short and Quick: Rather than put a large amount into a single account which may raise questions, small amounts are placed in many accounts and then moved between accounts to re-assemble them into larger amounts.
2. Buy and Change: Saw this a lot at Brooke and Walters – shell companies that do very little other than act as a vessel for funds to pass through. They may contract for services – say consulting – or buy property, but the profits soon move from one shell to another until they end up in someone's pocket. Often the shells are in jurisdictions with low policing of firms

and few control over money flows. Valin's bank, in part at least, could be a shell?

3.  Property: Real estate deals – buy – wait – sell at a profit. Or speculate on land based on insider information – sell at a profit.
4.  Gemstones and Art: Invest in mobile assets – gems, precious metals, rare items (art, antiques).
5.  Now You See It, Now You Don't: Move money between currencies using the best exchange rates. New money (say US dollars) from old (say UK pounds).
6.  Flow: Establish businesses which require a great deal of cashflow-through to function. Sources of cash not fully traceable – e.g. casinos, parking lots, restaurants and bars, movie theatres.
7.  Bank Capture: Buy a bank and use it as a front.

She would see if Tommaso could add to her list.

At ten thirty, she called the telephone number Sir John had provided and arranged to meet him in thirty minutes. They would "do business" and then go to lunch.

Tommaso was a stunningly attractive, tall, and elegant man in his late thirties. A large map of jet-black hair, bushy eyebrows and blue as a mountain stream eyes. His smile suggested that he spent a lot of time at dentists – his teeth were the whitest she had ever seen in any man or woman. He wore a light blue suit, no tie, and a crisp white shirt. His shoes were stylish and Italian. He wore all as if they were custom-made to fit, which she doubted they were. His designer glasses – they looked to be Gucci – suggested he had a designer or artist taste.

"Ah, Miss Hutchins!" he exclaimed. "Sir John spoke highly of you to my father and I when we met a few days ago. I gather you are an "ace" accountant. For me, I am simply doing this work to fund my real passion – art. I paint and draw. I prefer to paint than to pursue accounts, but this work pays well and is not (if you pardon the feeble joke) taxing, and it funds my passion. Please sit and let us do the business, then we can have lunch. You will need these copies, which you may keep". He handed her a large binder of documents, each section marked with a tab showing where it began.

"Mr. Valin has been on our telescope for some time – about five years. He is an interesting character. Well educated at the University of Bologna Business School, where he secured a first degree in finance and then an MBA. He "apprenticed" at UBI Banca and then at Credit Agricole Italia before joining his current bank – Banca Sella di Bari. He rose to the top there quickly – just five years. He is among the youngest head of any bank in Italy at just forty-six. Handsome chap, married as you may know to the daughter of a Mafia boss with ties to the Mafia families of both Calabria and Sicily. No children.

His bank is not very large. We estimate its assets, at the moment, to be around €12 billion – not the smallest bank in Italy – that would be Cassa di Risparmio di Asti – but nowhere near the largest, which is the Intesa Sanpaolo which has assets over €1 trillion.

Most of the bank's transactions appear to be legitimate – normal banking transactions from companies, pensioners, families, small shops, and street vendors. We are concerned about one-third of the bank's transactions. Some of these are for the Legion of Christ – a legitimate organization which sometimes sails close to the wind concerning financial regulations. But some are suspicious – lots of small new accounts, which a few months later get consolidated – all funded initially with cash. Valin is also out and about on the property-flip market – buying a property with the bank's money and then, after a few months or a year, selling it again at a profit. He takes a commission on sales. You will see in the binder that we have documented fourteen such deals just in the last twelve months."

"Tell me about the bank and the Vatican," she asked.

"Good question. We are not regulators for the Vatican Bank, thank goodness. Indeed, I don't think anyone has their eyes on just what is going on over there. Also, you should realize that the Vatican has no central control over its finances – each dicastery – that is what they call their operating units or ministries – has control over some funds, and the Secretary of State operates his own financial systems and operations, independent of all others. A real financial mess. I suspect Valin and others are exploiting this mess for their own ends. Two ways: one is persuading them to engage in property deals. The other is to offer them investments – shares or equities – which they claim will produce good returns, but which then do not, but someone has pocketed the cash.

I think Valin is doing this, and I would not be surprised if others are too. Also, the Vatican is currently a cesspit of narcissistic homosexuals and sycophants – sorry, it is one of my favourite subjects to talk about with my father, who is a journalist. He has been tracing the rise of the homosexual elite inside the Vatican for years and has even written about it. It is a major problem. Those who speak out loud against homosexuals in public are, in my father's view, likely to be the most entangled in homosexual activity in private."

"Just how is Valin exploiting the situation?" she asked.

"Well, he is always in and out of the Sodano empire – the Secretary of State for John Paul II or the "real" Holy Father as some refer to him. He's also pally with the Pope's personal secretary, Stanislaw Dziwisz, who is, let's accept, a shady character. My father went to see him and asked if the Pope would say mass one morning – he offers a mass every morning in his private chapel – for a writer he knows the Holy Father admired and my father knew well who had just died – the Polish writer Zbigniew Herbert. Dziwisz wanted €5,000. My father said no and arranged for a mass to be said elsewhere."

They explored more of what was in the binder and what the regulatory authority might do. Soon it was time for them to stroll out for lunch. She found him good company – knowledgeable, energetic, and sometimes self-deprecating. She also realized he was focused on his work as a technical challenge – he did not see it as a political or a social campaign but more as a matter of building a concrete case for the "prosecution." She realized that he and she were more alike than her first impression.

Lunch was nothing spectacular – a simple ragu with linguine, a wonderfully rich selection of cheeses and bread and a nice glass of red wine. They parted just after one o'clock, and she was now free.

The concierge told her about a concert at the Oratory of San Francesco Saverio del Caravita. An all-Vivaldi concert, including an organ piece played on the Priori Organ that Mozart once played. The concert was at three. She had time for a short rest before she went.

A simple program of Vivaldi music – Violin Concert in G, Concerto for Strings and Continuo, Concerto in A played with strings and the organ and the seemingly obligatory Four Seasons. All very splendid and in such a wonderful setting of a church built in the first half of the sixteen hundreds. She was glad she had followed the concierge's advice and taken a cushion – the seats without one would be painful, especially after two hours.

She took a meal in her room and had an early night. No dreams of battles in the Vatican or of talking babies. Indeed, no memorable dreams at all.

## February 14th

Before breakfast, after a shower and a careful selection of warm clothes for the day – it looked like rain was in the forecast – she reviewed the binder Tommaso had given her again to make sure she understood just what Valin was up to. She had missed something. During the last year, Valin had created over sixty-five shell companies, some of which had as a director another of their targets – Michael Major, the Member of the European Parliament for Lancashire. There was a connection, and it was direct.

From her notes, she remembered that Michael Major was a Catholic – could he be a member of Regnum Christi? Might that be the connection? She also remembered that he had inherited some £30 million, but this had grown in just six years to over £65 million – might this be connected to Valin? She was anxious to share this information with Sir John and Riya over breakfast.

Riya was there alone. She smiled warmly as Miss. Hutchins arrived – sharing a sense that they were engaged in a productive conspiracy. Sir John joined them a few minutes later.

Breakfast ordered – salmon frittata for Riya, eggs benedict for Sir John and a simple selection of pastries for Miss. Hutchins together with lashings of coffee.

Sir John, once the food had been consumed and pleasantries dispensed with, began the proceedings:

> "A most productive day yesterday for me. I have established, through two distinct conversations within the Ministry of Economics and Finance and through a conversation with Cardinal Ratzinger who is the Prefect of the Doctrine of the Faith – the Vatican's "controller" of the message and chief enforcer. I'll come back to him, though it is most interesting.
>
> First, my conversations in the Ministry. I met Luigi Di Conte, the most senior bureaucrat, and his number two, Francesco Mariano. They suggest that there are three factors at work here. The first is a rigorous, systematic attempt to take over the Vatican Bank by the "new" Mafia – the smart sons and daughters of the old gangsters and thugs with names like Rocky "The Face" Silosso or Jack "The Butcher" Adorno. They see white-collar crime as their new bread and butter, and money laundering is the key. They are aided and abetted by Valin and others, including both Sir John Rabkin and Michael Major, though Rabkin's role is more on turning already laundered money into assets. They think Calvi – the murdered banker under Blackfriars bridge – had got greedy and stole a lot of cash for himself. He was also a poor banker, losing too much money for the new Mafia. They see Valin as more compliant and less likely to bolt – in part because of who his wife is.

Second, they are seeking to leverage not just the Vatican Bank but its purchasing power around the world. The Vatican Bank has an asset value of around €7 billion, and the Church has big investments in banking, insurance, chemicals, steel, construction, real estate and, since 1995, information technologies – all great vehicles for the various interests of the cadre behind these schemes.

Finally, they can also shift funds quickly to jurisdictions where financial policing is less intrusive and skilled – Mexico, Panama, the Grand Cayman Islands, and Cyprus. Using the Vatican Bank and Valin's bank, they can move funds around in a kind of merry-go-round that would be difficult to trace. With this new thing – internet banking happening now at scale – it will be easier, faster, and less traceable. Something like ten banks in Europe are now doing significant transactions on this internet thing, which I must admit I have difficulty getting my head around. Now let me turn to my other meeting.

Cardinal Ratzinger asked Pope John Paul II if he could leave his role and move to the Vatican Library as an archivist in 1997 – he felt he was getting too old for the rigorous challenges of his role. The Pope refused. Ratzinger is, I must say, a most intelligent and cautious man. In 1998, he received several complaints about our Legionnaire – Maciel. He also noted that American press had published articles about Maciel that accused him of serious sexual misconduct with both men, young boys, girls, and women and of having several children. He personally cannot abide the man, even though he knows he is a favourite of John Paul II, who has no tolerance for bad words about Maciel.

Ratzinger is deeply concerned about the current sexual politics within the Vatican. He suggested that over half of the curia – the men who run the church – are homosexual, and these gay priests essentially control the Church, funded in part by money from Maciel and other "dubious" sources. The late Pope Paul VI would do nothing about it, and John Paul II will not hear of intervention either. Ratzinger is distressed; hence he wishes to lead a life of contemplation and scholarship – he used to be a Professor at Tubingen and later at Regensburg in Bavaria and has written several books and academic papers. He wants "out," but no one will let him leave.

He knows Valin and said, "you should not trust him". While he has the ear of many with influence, it is only because he plies them with cash and offers them a few luxuries. It is like the medieval days – priests selling pardons. But Ratzinger's key insight was that Valin is the front for a larger conspiracy to control the levers of the Vatican through its financial system, especially the bank. There is a cabal whose aim is to secure implicit control of the Vatican Bank as a front for several dubious and nefarious activities, he called them. Not just Maciel and the Legion but a wider group are seeking control – he suspects the modern Mafia. He called them "the business-educated sons of gangsters" are in play. We're talking about the 'Ndrangheta here.

"What does he plan to do about Maciel?" asked Riya.

"His hands are tied. Ratzinger wanted to suspend him and require him to hand over control of the Legion and Regnum Christi to the Vatican. At the same time, a team would investigate him, the organizations he controls, and their operations. The Cardinal Secretary of State, who we know is partly funded for his lavish lifestyle by the Legion, says no, and so does the Pope. Apparently, the Pope sees Maciel as a saint-like figure who has saved and supported millions. Pope John Paul's personal secretary, Stanislaw Dziwisz and his henchman George Wisz threatened Ratzinger if he proceeded with any sanctions, investigations, or other actions. Ratzinger said, "I will be condemned if I do nothing and if I do something, I will be punished".

"This all kind of confirms what I found out," Riya began. "But first my news. I happen to know that Valin, Major and Rabkin are in Rome right now. They are here for a major performance at the Opera. The Rossini Opera Armida is rarely performed, but there are two performances here in Rome this week, and our three musketeers will be there tonight. Renee Fleming, and Gregory Kundle are both singing lead parts, and an Italian conductor called Daniele Gatti is leading the orchestra at the Rome Opera House. I got us all tickets. It will be my first opera. I am more of a Rod Stewart, Rolling Stones, or Elton John person. We're in different parts of the opera house to observe what goes on."

"The reason it is not performed often," said Miss Hutchins, "is that it runs for around four hours, involves a single soprano and six tenors and is a nightmare to stage. But it will be fun, assuming we can last the evening". Sir John looked unsure but nodded his agreement. Riya continued.

"I spent some time at the Polizia di Stato – the headquarters of the national police service and then over at the Giardia di Finanza, which deals with financial crimes of all kinds. Fascinating! They are interested in Valin, but they are also interested in his wife, whom we have almost entirely ignored. She is, you will recall, the daughter of Victor Amuso, boss of the Lucchese crime family of New York – one of the five families that ran rackets in New York and across the US. Her father is serving life in prison for various murders, though he seems to be still pulling the strings from his prison cell."

"His daughter, apparently a very beautiful woman, is called Ginevra - Ginevra Amuso-Valin. She is highly educated – a law degree from Harvard and a master's in finance from Stanford – and is very well connected. She is a director of several companies both here in Italy and in the US. She gives the appearance of being a legitimate businesswoman, but she is a Lucchese. She is part of a crime family. According to both of our Italian colleagues, we should see her as such. Our Italian friends see her as the "brains" of the firm."

"The Giardia di Finanza team is working on the idea that the Valin bank is a front for the activities of the 'Ndrangheta and that it is focused on moving money from crime to real estate or other instruments that make it legitimate. Drug money, prostitution, sex trafficking, and extortion monies all become legitimate – real estate, artworks, shell companies, and land. They also think that the Lucchese family, now run daily in the Bronx by Patrick "Red" Dellorusso, using some of the shell companies Valin has created in the US, the UK and Italy as a way to move money. The Valin's are the bridge between the "old" Sicilian mafia and the new Calabria mafia.

"As far as the Vatican Bank is concerned, both of the people I met with today think that Valin is trying to secure access to the Vatican Bank and other parts of the Vatican's financial operations as a way to "clean money" – after all, they are buying and selling properties all over the world and are making what they see as "investments" and what Valin sees as "opportunities."

"What it looks like is a real linking of New York, Italian interests, the Vatican, and the various shell companies," Riya concluded.

"And when we look at the shell companies," added Miss Hutchins, "we see three things. First, both Michael Major and Sir Andrew Rabkin are directors of some of them. Second, Ginevra Amuso-Valin is named as CEO of nine of them – all outside Italy. Third, some have significant connections to the Vatican, with Dziwisz as a director of the two."

They ordered more coffee and began to chat about these observations. The consensus they reached was that this was becoming such a complex web of deception and lies that it must be difficult for all the participants to keep their stories straight. Sir John reminded them of the story of Laurens van der Post – the close mentor and counsellor to the Prince of Wales and "discoverer" of the "lost" bushmen of Kalahari – who died in 1996. After his death, it became clear that almost everything he had ever said about himself was untrue. He could not separate truth from fiction. When asked what he had died of, his long-time doctor had replied, "he had become weary of sustaining so many lies!". They laughed.

But they saw the point. With so many threads and so much complexity, what could the three of them do to be of use to their government or other governments and regulators?

Riya had collected some files on loan from the Giardia di Finanza and from the Polizia di Stato. She gave one thick folder to Miss Hutchins and two thinner ones to Sir John, keeping a small pile for herself.

> "I suggest we study these and meet again for lunch, say at that nice place I spotted on my way back from my meetings yesterday. It's called Terra di Siena on the Piazza di Pasquino – I'll call and

arrange a quiet table at the back. Shall we say one o'clock?"

Miss Hutchins briefly returned to her room, put the files in a small briefcase together with her daybook and her New York pen and took this along with her hat and a pair of gloves and went for a walk, intending to find a suitable place to sit and read and make notes on the documents Riya had shared.

She reflected on what Sir John had said about Laurens van der post. She had read one of his travel books about Japan. She had also heard him on the radio talking about conservation and the threat to land posed by population growth. She remembered that his funeral was attended by Margaret Thatcher and Prince Charles and some Zulu Chief – there was a picture in the Daily Telegraph.

As she walked, enjoying the sights of Rome, she began to think of what they might focus their energies on. Surely, she thought, they should only look at anything which connected all this activity they heard about to Great Britain, its banks and its financial rules and regulations. They couldn't untangle the challenges of the Vatican, which sounded horrendous. Nor could they trace the flow of dirty money between Italy, the United States, and those places where the Legion and Regnum Christi operated. They had to focus on the British angle.

She found a nice place to sit. A large Roman wall prevented a chill wind, and she had a good river view. It was quiet, and the light was good. She began to read the documents Riya had shared, which were largely company reports for some shell companies, including three from the UK companies. She was in familiar territory.

## At Lunch

The restaurant was quiet – they were early by Roman standards – but the food was outstanding. She had a Caprese Salad with some of the tastiest tomatoes she had ever eaten, and luscious mozzarella with a few torn basil leaves and wonderfully rich olive oil followed by linguine with clams. All helped with a glass of Vermentino.

The food finished, and they each had another glass of wine and began to discuss the materials Riya had shared.

> "I am finding the situation overly complex and beyond the capabilities of the three of us if we continue to look at the big picture," Miss Hutchins began. "But if we focus on what this network is doing in the United Kingdom – how it touches us – then we can stay focused and keep our eyes on the issues that affect us. We should advise the Finance Action Task Force, established by the G7 leaders in 1989 and based in Paris at the OECD, of any other issues not directly connected to the UK.
>
> I have looked into the companies in which either of the Valins – husband or wife – has an interest in the UK and have explored what we can see from their filed tax submissions – all in the folder Riya shared this morning. I have five observations:
>
> First, we are talking about very sizeable sums coming into these accounts. One company received

a transfer of £76 million from an Italian company, only for half of this to move out to a US company two days later for "consulting services." In all, of the nine companies I reviewed, a total of £700 million moved in and out of them, sometimes between them, in a single year, yet the companies do not seem to produce goods, sell services, or employ a great many staff.

Second, four companies have provided loans to Sir Andrew to support his publishing empire. One of the suggestions is that we encourage our tax people to undertake a full audit of his various companies and their pension funds. I suspect he is so far in debt that he uses all sorts of money-moving tricks to keep his companies afloat.

Third, the companies in the folder of which Ginevra Amuso-Valin is CEO and which are based in the UK only do business with companies she is CEO of that are based in New York. Funds flow mainly from New York into the UK and then out of the UK into Italy. If we were to trace, say, six of these transactions, I suspect they would each end up in Panama or Cyprus or a place where we would lose sight of the money. I suspect but have no proof that the daughter is a chip off her father's block and is the money laundress of the Lucchese family.

Fourth, the Vatican is involved in property deals in London and other parts of the UK and Europe, using some of the Valin companies as the middleman to buy property, lease and maintain it and then sell it later for a profit. At least, that is what the Vatican presumably wants to happen. As we saw with Monsignor's account of the proposed Vatican London property, there is some double-dealing. The Vatican buys from a company that owns it through Valin, but Valin owns the property in the first place. We should advise our friendly Monsignor of all of this.

Finally, Michael Major is involved in two ways. He is a director of some of these companies and is paid as a Director. Second, he is advising the Legion and Regnum Christi about their investment strategy and encouraging them to flow their funds from around the world – especially from their stronghold in Mexico – into the Valin companies and banks. In nineteen transactions I looked at – all from Medellin, which we know is one significant centre for drug trafficking – funds ended up in London, New York and Rome. I think we should put a trace on Michael's financial activity.

I also want to say that, while I do appreciate being asked to be here and spend time in this lovely city and I am looking forward to spending what will feel like a lifetime with Rossini this evening, I am not sure we can do much by traipsing around Europe. We would be better off focusing on digging into accounts and transactions at home. I am sorry, Sir John, if this disturbs your thinking, but you did ask me to be straight and direct – I am afraid I know no other way."

Sir John smiled, as did Riya.

"Riya and I said the same thing before you joined us at breakfast this morning, Miss Hutchins – not as eloquently, I might add," Sir John responded. "I think that this trip has been immensely valuable in untangling the mess Riya and I have been looking at for the last year.

Let me suggest that what we now know but didn't before we came here is that there is a highly organized and systematic approach to taking dirty money and making it clean that involves companies operating within UK law and involving several UK citizens, including our Michael Major and Sir Andrew Rabkin.

Second, they use a variety of mechanisms to turn dirty money into clean money, but they are also using our financial institutions and systems to make this possible.

For cover, they are involving religious organizations – Catholic institutions like the Vatican, the Vatican Bank, the Legion of Christ, and Regnum Christi – both as a way of moving money and as a way of covering that moving of money. Who is going to question the Vatican buying a multi-million-pound building in Chelsea? While some individuals in the Vatican and the Church may be "in the know" – Maciel and Dziwisz, for example, and perhaps Cardinal Sodano – others in the Vatican are caught in this web.

We also see links to the New York crime family – the Lucchese – and we suspect to one or more drug cartels in Mexico. The drug business in Mexico is big business. I attended a session with our US colleagues late last year who suggested that the Mexican drug business was a $19 billion to $25 billion business growing fast.

Our focus has to be on looking at the UK angle – that is what this team has been asked to do – and suggesting actions we can take to reduce, preferably prevent, money laundering.

I do like your specific suggestions, Miss Hutchins. I want to think more about each of them and meet with you when we return to London to plan a course of action. Riya, do you have anything from your review of your files or to add to these observations from Miss Hutchins and myself?"

Riya looked intently at each of them before she spoke.

"Just two things. When you look at each of the UK companies, they are not using a large array of banks. They are using three. Lloyds, the Royal Bank of Scotland and the Bradford and Bingley Building Society. Whether these banks know what they are dealing with or more importantly whom they are dealing with, we need to find out.

Second, one of the files the Italian financial police shared with me that I reviewed relates to Sir Andrew Rabkin. Miss Hutchins is right. He is playing a shell game within his own companies, some of which are based here in Italy – a newspaper and an academic publisher. He looks to me to be robbing

Peter to pay Paul – using cash from one enterprise he owns to pay the debts of another he owns and then lending money from that corporation back to the first one...snakes and ladders. He can't go on – unless he goes criminal. We should take a close look and keep a close eye.

I suggest we end our visit to Rome early and decamp to London. We should also look carefully at interactions this evening at the Opera. Still, I think trying to unpack what these men and women are up to through observation rather than through analysis of accounts will be difficult, don't you agree, Miss Hutchins?"

She did, as did Sir John. They returned to the hotel, where Miss Hutchins took a bath and her traditional napette. They agreed to dine early in the hotel and go by taxi to the Opera.

## A Night at the Opera

All of the glitterati of Rome were present in the foyer and in the grounds of the Opera House, including the President of Italy, Oscar Luigi Scalfaro. Cardinals Ratzinger, Sodano, Furno, Tonini and Scholte were all there too, dressed in their finest robes. Some of the leading figures in Italy – Silvio Berlusconi, Vittorio Gassman, Sophia Loren, Bettino Craxi, Romano Prodi, Ennio Morricone and the famous conductor Ricardo Chailly – were also mingling with the crowd. All dressed to the nines. All looked elegant and at each other, paying no attention to the onlookers and commoners.

Miss Hutchins found herself sitting next to Franco Modigliani and his wife Serena. He was an economist working at MIT in the United States but was visiting Rome and decided he should take the opportunity to "sit through four more hours of Rossini," he said. He loved opera and played recordings while he worked. His wife was also an enthusiastic opera goer, "whenever we can." She looked around and spotted Michael Major, just two rows in front of her, sitting next to a very young and attractive man with flowing hair. Across the aisle, she could see Cardinal Ratzinger take his seat and begin to study what looked like the opera score – he was, after all, a competent pianist and enthusiastic operagoer.

The opera is set at the time of the Crusades near Jerusalem. Key characters are introduced – Rinaldo, Gernando, Ubaldo, Carlo and so on – and, eventually, Rossini introduces Armida, a Princess of Damascus and a sorceress who immediately engages in intrigue and sets the men against each other. The plot is, to say the least, a stretch and involves demons and spirits and a Prince of Hell, but the music is rich and lyrical, as one might expect from Rossini. Soon, the unreality of the plot was overtaken by the beauty of the singing of Renee Fleming, which was exceptional.

There was an interval at the end of the first act, and Miss Hutchins saw Michael Major leave his seat and quickly go to the bar, where he picked up pre-ordered drinks for himself and his young male partner. Valin and his wife soon joined him and then Cardinal Sodano. They had an intense discussion. Miss Hutchins thought she saw an envelope pass between Valin and the Cardinal but could not swear to it. She certainly did see that the Cardinal was very taken by the young man accompanying Michael Major, and he reciprocated the attention.

Act two involved quite a technical spectacle. A forest gradually turns into a truly amazing pleasure palace and Armida sings the most famous Aria from this opera D'Amore al Dolce Impero, and Renee Fleming sang it so beautifully that the audience rose to its feet and gave her a standing ovation. She sang it again, and the plot continued. Miss Hutchins marveled at the set design and the way it could transform itself from forest to pleasure palace and then back again.

During the second interval, shorter than the first, Valin was nowhere to be seen, but Sir Andrew Rabkin appeared at Michael Major's side, and they spoke intently. It looked, at least from her vantage point, that Sir Andrew was unhappy, but about what she did not know.

The final act, shorter than the other two, shows Armida ranging in emotion from love to pity to anger and then ends with her seeking revenge and flying off in a rage. It was all very odd, but by then, the audience was simply exhausted. Four hours and nine minutes, not including time for applause and standing ovations.

As they returned to the hotel, they compared notes. The Valins, during the second act, had spent their time in an intense conversation with Cardinal Sodano, and Cardinal Ratzinger had a deep conversation with Ricardo Chailly. He doubted that Chailly and Ratzinger discussed a business deal. More likely the tempo and tonality of the performance.

It occurred to Mss. Hutchins that the opera was a version of what they were observing. A woman with very high needs to control the situation and its consequence - Ginevra Amuso-Valin – is using several men (her husband, Michael Major, Sir Andrew Rabkin, Fr. Maciel, Stanislaw Dziwisz and others) for her nefarious ends linked to the bigger picture of the ambitions of the Lucchese crime family. As she explained this to Sir John and Riya, they each smiled. It seemed too cute and pat to be true, but it did make some sense at a superficial level.

## February 15th

At breakfast, Sir John announced that he and Riya would be returning to London and would initiate some tax audits and fraud investigations of the shell companies. He would also start drafting some suggestions for the Prime Minister. He would appreciate any input Miss Hutchins wished to have but clarified that she was free to stay in Rome for the period they had agreed – until February 20th, all expenses paid. She could visit some of the sights, attend concerts or galleries and perhaps write a short document for them to consider on her return to London. He wanted to finish his report by the end of the month.

She said she would stay but that she wouldn't take any action which might alert their targets to any activity or alert the Italian authorities. She would, since he had asked, have lunch with Tommaso Bellucci to explore some ideas if Sir John did not object. He did not.

After they departed the dining room with a sense that they were not finished but, in many ways, were beginning what might turn out to be a long journey, she shook hands with both of them and returned to her room.

She called Tommaso and arranged to have lunch the next day. She also called the Concierge and asked him to arrange for tickets to a performance she had seen advertised on the Verdi Requiem for tomorrow evening.

Today, however, she was determined to undertake a personal Caravaggio tour – exploring his paintings across Rome. Some were in the Villa Borghese, as she had seen on her first day but wanted to see again. Some were in the Church of San Luigi dei Francesi. Some were in the Church of Santa Maria del Popolo, two are in the Capitoline Museums and others in the Vatican Museum. She would be exhausted, but she was in no rush. She could take her time.

On her return at close to six that evening, she was truly worn out. Being a tourist on the hunt for Caravaggio's is hard work. She ran a bath, filled it with bath salts and a "bath bomb" which produced masses of bubbles, undressed, and luxuriated in its warmth. She washed her hair – tourism is also a dusty business – and tried to remember the twenty paintings she had seen. The most memorable, for her at least, was The Entombment of Christ in the Vatican and the Road to Damascus – St. Paul in the Santa Maria church.

She sat and opened her journal. She began writing suggestions for new rules and regulations to deal with the kind of concerns and challenges they had explored. She had four big ideas. She wrote:

1. Who is the ultimate beneficiary? Who benefits from a transaction, and who receives the transaction? It's not just about where the money comes from but where it ends up.
2. Not all players are equal – some are riskier than others. The Valins are a greater risk than, say, Cardinal Ratzinger. Don't treat them all the same. Use risk-based decisions.
3. Strength reporting – banks and financial institutions should not hesitate to report suspicious transactions, even if they have no "proof" of it being money laundering. Better safe than sorry.
4. Train, Train, Test and Train – many staff in banks and financial institutions have no clue about all this. They need to keep better records and be subject to audit and oversight.

Though tired, she lay on the bed, pen still in hand and journal open. She began reflecting on what all this meant for her. She made a list:

- I can be sociable with the right people - Riya and Sir John.
- I enjoy thinking, analyzing, and understanding. I like to find "simplicity on the other side of complexity" (who said that?). It's a bit like advanced academic work.
- Unusually, I seem to be able to get on well with "new" people – people I have not met before (Tommaso).
- I enjoy learning a lot. This is kind of new to me – money laundering.

- Not working fulltime but having some work to do is nice. Maybe I should talk to an agency about freelancing?
- Somehow, I feel more relaxed working on a project than working day to day in an office.
- I seem to have a lot of energy. More than when I worked fulltime.

She felt herself drifting off to sleep. She closed her journal, placed the top on the pen and placed both on the bedside table. Turned off her light and went to sleep.

She dreamt of sailing on an ocean in a sailboat, eating canapes and drinking champagne with people she did not know. She enjoyed it but got concerned when a young man threatened another young man with a gun. No one was hurt, but the incident left everyone nervous and upset. She went from happy to anxious in seconds, and the dominant feeling was of persistent anxiety.

## February 17th

Tommaso Bellucci was on time for lunch. She had chosen the restaurant on the advice of the Concierge at her hotel. Set atop of the Hotel at the Spanish Steps, the Imàgo is a highly regarded rooftop restaurant opened in the 1950s. She secured a wonderful table with a view across Rome. Tommaso was impressed with her choice of venue and her choice of table.

> "This is wonderful. I have never eaten here before," he said.

"Me neither, but I understand it is amongst the best places to eat in the city," she said.

They perused the menu, ordered some drinks – he just sparkling water and she a negroni – and then chose their food. She opted for an octopus salad followed by a lemon risotto, and he chose a Caprese salad followed by gnocchi Sorrentino – gnocchi in a tomato and mozzarella sauce.

They chatted about her time in Rome, the Caravaggio's, the opera and as they finished their second course and her second negroni, they began to talk business.

"My Minister, Giuliano Amato, has been talking with your Chancellor, Gordon Brown, over the last few days about money-laundering, especially focused on Russian dirty money but also dirty money from Italy, the United States and Asia. It looks like they want the EU Finance Ministers and the G20 Ministers to take some sort of concerted action on this. What do you know about it?", he asked.

"Nothing, but I suspect Sir John is close to these conversations. He has been tasked with recommending some plan based on the work he and his small team, with whom I am associated, have been doing. I think they are struggling to get a handle on just how big the issue is, and the various forms money laundering can take."

"And, I suggest, how our financial institutions are willingly or unknowingly involved", he added.

"Your financial police unit must have some suggestions – some understanding of how all of this works, surely?" she asked.

"Ah, yes, the Guardia di Finanza – a fine institution!", he said with a smile. "They are more focused on the drug trade. They don't understand all of the financial nuances. They want to stop the import and manufacture and sale of drugs. They are a military operation focused on enforcing drug laws. This money laundering issue is way above them. It is more of a policy issue – one that we in the Ministry need to focus on with the Central Bank. My Minister is meeting later this week with Antonio Fazio – our Central Bank Governor. I understand that this issue you and I are discussing is high on their agenda – what can be done to regulate the banks?"

"It is a good question," said Miss Hutchins. "In 1990, there was an EU directive focused on suspicious activity – deposits above an agreed amount or movement of funds to suspicious accounts must be reported. It was improved on in 1995 when non-banking institutions were included. Maybe we expand this and lower the amount we agree is suspicious. We may also need to further strengthen policing of non-banking financial institutions – lending providers, foreign exchange offices and so on. The current EU directive is too narrow. Each country needs a national financial money laundering policing unit. What do you think?"

"You are aligned with some of the thinking within our Ministry and others across the EU. We certainly need to update the directive. What we need to focus on as well is what we refer to as cyber-laundering – using the internet to move money around the world quickly".

"I don't understand how all that works. Do tell."

"It took off big-time in the United States in 1995 and has been growing steadily worldwide ever since. A person sitting at home with a computer connected to the internet can log into their banking account, move money from one account to another, pay bills or make financial investments in a limited number of funds – usually bonds and mutual funds. Banks call it their "brick and click system" – you go to the bank to deposit money, but once it is in your account you can move it and use it. Paychecks are deposited electronically; taxes are paid electronically. It will just grow and grow. In Canada, there is a bank called ING which allows its clients to do all their banking online – they get cash by visiting a branch or the branch staff will visit you."

"So, our bad people can use these systems to move money between their accounts and to pay bills from shell companies?" said Miss Hutchins.

"Exactly. We are also seeing major money moves between accounts in different countries – money moving from Italy to Panama and then from Panama to Cyprus, for example. Difficult to trace".

"Sir John is working on recommendations for Chancellor Gordon Brown and our Prime Minister, Tony Blair, I understand. Our foray here was to better understand some of the nuances of money laundering."

"Do remember," responded Tommaso, "that the reason Valin and his friends are so interested in the Vatican Bank and the Vatican's financial empire is that it is not part of the EU and not subject to the same regulatory controls. You might, as we are thinking here, need to negotiate separate arrangements with the Vatican. Your Ambassador to the Holy Sea, Sir Mark Pellow, spent some time at Hambros Bank for a few years so has some knowledge of financial systems. He was also in Washington for awhile. You might want to connect with him."

"Good idea. Are you working on a detailed plan to counter money laundering to present to your Minister?"

"I am working on a part of this — the part that deals with the internet — but not the whole plan. There is a small team. I will keep you posted, but no doubt Sir John is being kept abreast of developments by your Ministry people."

"I am wondering," she began hesitantly, "just how aggressive any government policy or banking policy can be? We do not want to inhibit legitimate business activity which often involves the sudden movement of large amounts of money around the world. We just need to finesse our regulations to stop the bad guys. It is difficult".

"Exactly! If it were easy, we would have acted by now. Also, the "bad guys" you mention seem always to be one step ahead. This is especially the case with the movement of money using the internet. They have smart people working on this and we have smart people. It's a race."

They chatted for a few more minutes before Tommaso had to return to his office. She stayed and enjoyed the view before she left.

On her return to her hotel, she called the office of the United Kingdom Ambassador to the Holy Sea and was connected with Sir Mark Pellow's secretary, Janet Albright. She arranged to meet with him for a drink at her hotel at five that evening – dropping Sir John's name helped.

She took her napette, changed, and went to the lobby around four thirty to await his arrival. He was not difficult to spot. A tall – over six feet – very English-looking gentleman in a white suit, white shirt, and an Oxford tie, carrying a black wooden cane with a silver horse's head handle, arrived. She raised her hand in greeting, and he approached.

"Miss Audrey Hutchins, I assume?" he asked.

"And Ambassador Sir Mark Pellow, I assume?" she said in response, smiling at her visitor. "Or should I say, Your Excellency?" she added with a smile.

"Mark will do fine," he said with a smile, never overly keen on the formality of titles.

She guided him to the lounge bar, and they ordered drinks – her a white wine spritzer and he a large dirty gin and tonic.

"So, you are part of the team who has been looking at the Vatican bank with Sir John, I gather?" he asked, looking somewhat puzzled.

"Not quite. While that was part of our expedition, it was not the main focus. We were much more interested in the operations of a certain Italian bank and its Chief Executive and his wife, the daughter of a New York mafia boss", she said. "Ah yes, Mr. Valin and his very beautiful wife Ginevra. Met them several times at various functions. As a former banker, I would be very suspicious. He seems more than keen to buy friends and influences than to earn their trust."

"Quite! I am pretty sure he is a front man for some dubious characters both in the Church and in the underworld of money movers. I think he sees the Vatican Bank as a vehicle for his nefarious schemes".

"Ah yes, the Vatican Bank. It has never really recovered from the Calvi and Marcinkus scandals and its dealings with shady characters worldwide. Just one of several issues I keep trying to raise with the Secretary of State, Cardinal Sodano. They need to get their finances in order, especially given what

I see coming as crises for the Church. But I am sure that Mr. and Mrs. Valin are seeking to use the bank somehow."

"And what crises do you see for the Church, Mark? Remember I have signed the official secrets act, so I understand the need for discretion."

"Yes, I am aware of your status. I had my staff check you out before I came for a drink. Where to start? There are real tensions within the curia. A group of Cardinals, unhappy with where things are going, meet annually and sometimes more often in Switzerland – at a secluded monastery. These cardinals, which include our own Cardinal Basil Hume who often brings along his likely successor, Cormac Murphy-O'Connor, are concerned that not enough change is happening quickly enough and that many of the recommendations of Vatican II are being quietly put aside. In particular, the idea of decentralization of the church's governance is opposed by John Paul II. They are also concerned about the emerging legal and financial challenges associated with pedophile priests – there appears to be a great many of these and this could bankrupt some dioceses, especially in the United States. There are also issues about married priests, communion for divorced and remarried Catholics and other issues. I suspect that many of these will soon come to a head and the Church will find itself deeply challenged."

"What makes all this more difficult," he continued, "is that John Paul II is not a well man. It appears, according to some sources, that he has Parkinson's disease – early stage – but also is showing some signs of early onset dementia. He has also had some cancer scares. His staff are covering for him, but I have met him several times recently, and I can attest that he is not the Pope that secured election in 1978 – twenty-one years ago".

"That is sad to hear – he brought so much energy to the papacy when he began and was an inspiration", she said.

They both sat in silence for a few minutes, taking a sip of their drinks.

"The other issue, which I am sure you have been made aware of," began the ambassador, "is that the Vatican is literally a hotbed of homosexual liaisons. There are more gay men per square mile in the Vatican than, I suspect, anywhere else on earth. Yet these same people – some of them very senior – actively and aggressively campaign against gay rights and homosexuality. Indeed, a colleague has suggested to me that the more aggressively a priest campaigns against homosexuality the more likely it is that they are homosexual".

"Yes, we had a briefing from an insider that suggested that not only was this a moral and ethical challenge for the church, but that the homosexual clique was also seeking to gain power so as to protect themselves. Very difficult," she added.

"What, if anything, can I help with Miss. Hutchins?", asked the ambassador, checking his watch.

"I am not sure, other than I think we need to know – that is, Sir John needs to know – if you see any emerging and new issues with Vatican bank or the financial dealings of the Vatican that raise your hackles as a former banker. Our focus is on improving the 1995 EU directive on money laundering but also on developing tougher laws and regulations for both the UK and the EU."

"I will do just that, Miss Hutchins – first checking with my superiors that such sharing of information with Sir John is appropriate, which I am more than sure it will be".

They chatted a while longer, but soon the ambassador left, and Miss Hutchins sat with her thoughts and another white wine spritzer.

After dinner – seafood risotto with broccolini – she sat in her room listening to some Corelli on the radio. Her thoughts drifted between concern about the state of the Vatican and its several pending challenges and concern about the extent of money laundering in her own country. She thought back to the numerous accounts she had reviewed during her working days and tried to remember if she had ever seen anything suspicious in the transactions she had been required to review. She could not remember any and was sure that she would have noticed.

She made some notes in her daybook using the New York Wahl pen, trying to capture some of the insights that she understood were emerging. Then she readied herself for bed.

One thought kept occurring to her: where did this new confidence in talking to strangers suddenly come from? An amiable chat with an Ambassador and an Italian government official. Several long, interesting conversations with Sir John and Riya, who she really knew only slightly. No hesitancy in talking to others, despite years of avoiding new encounters. Was this a new Audrey Hutchins emerging from her shell?

## February 18th – March 1st

Audrey Hutchins stopped being detective, scholar and inquisitor and returned to her role as tourist – which she found to be much harder work. After several forays into galleries, churches in hidden corners which contained simply magnificent artworks, shopping, long lunches, and afternoon napette, she was more than ready to return home.

At the airport, she wondered if she would ever return to Rome. She doubted it. It was a truly incredible city, but difficult to navigate and a place which had its rhythm, rules, and routines which no tourist could ever penetrate.

Her flight left just after two in the afternoon, and she was back in her apartment in London at five-thirty. As on previous occasions, the concierge had arranged for a cleaning team to come in the day before and the apartment was spotless. She felt glad to be home.

She walked around her neighbourhood, bought a few groceries, and returned to make a simple meal – a simple salad with various meats and cheeses. A glass of Pinot Gris and she was happy as she listened to some baroque music on Radio Three.

Over the next few days, she dealt with her mail, stocking up on pantry items and wine and visiting the local library. She needed a break from worrying about money laundering, the challenges faced by the Vatican and the state of the banking industry. She was, after all, not working – at least not working full time.

She checked in with Riya. Riya explained that they had done a lot since they were together in Rome. Tax audits had begun for Sir Andrew Rabkin and Michael Major. A review of the issues associated with bank security and compliance had been commissioned by the Governor of the Bank of England, Eddie George. Sir John had a meeting with Cardinal Basil Hume essentially sharing our concerns about the Valin's and the Vatican Bank. Cardinal Hume, whom Sir John said did not appear at all well, added to these concerns some challenges faced across the Church over how monies collected for the Vatican – Peter's Pence – were being used.

Riya suggested she come to the office again on 3rd March when Sir John would be back in the office – he is dealing with some personal issues at the moment, nothing to worry about – he is moving house and off to live in the country. He has also bought an apartment in London, having sold the house he inherited.

Miss Hutchins attended a concert at the Wigmore Hall –
Beethoven string quartets Opus 74 known as the "Harp"
and Opus 95 known as "Serioso" – and one at the Festival
Hall – Elgar, Delius, and Holst. She also was engrossed in a
novel about a quartet by Vikram Seth – An Equal Music. A
beautifully written and poignant account of the players'
life in a string quartet. She decided she must read other
novels by Seth – the librarian would place on hold his
novel A Suitable Boy when the current reader returned it.
This novel had won several prizes.

## March 1st St. David's Day

Miss Hutchins decided to spend a few days in Paris. She
wanted to catch a rare performance of Pierre Boulez's Le
Marteau sans maître, which Boulez himself would conduct.
She had read that the piece, written for a small chamber
orchestra and a solo alto, had a huge impact on the
classical music chamber scene, and she wanted to
understand why. No better way than listening, especially
since Boulez was to talk about the work after the
performance. He was seventy-five years old, so who knew
what chance there would be to experience this again?

There was also a remarkable exhibition of the French
romantic painting with forty works from Eugène Delacroix,
Théodore Géricault, Jean-Auguste-Dominique Ingres which
The Guardian said was one the best staged exhibitions in
Europe. She had to see it.

She caught the 1026 Eurostar from St. Pancras and arrived
in Paris just before 2pm. She took a taxi to her usual hotel,
Hotel George V, and was shown to her suite. A quick
shower and a change of clothes later, she left the hotel to

find something to eat. She headed for Le Petit Pontoise, which the concierge had recommended, and she was not disappointed. A very rich but elegant cassoulet with a glass of Chateau Neuf and she felt "at home."

The concert was held at Studio des Champs-Élysées, the same venue the work was first performed in. Around eight hundred people were present, and there was a lively atmosphere.

The music is very layered, complex, and sometimes demands a lot of both players and the audience. It was, however, clearly a piece full of imagination, energy, and passion. The solo alto - Nathalie Stutzmann – was outstanding. Even though the entire piece lasts just thirty-five minutes, it has a profound impact, and Miss Hutchins was moved by it. She sometimes reacted negatively to abstract pieces, which this was, but on this occasion, it captured something about being alive that spoke to her.

In his talk, Boulez explained that he saw this piece as a manifesto or statement about a new kind of music for a new age of composition. For him, it marked the end of a period of experimentation and the real beginning of his compositional statements – more controlled, more organized, and more structured. He had written it in 1955, and the initial reaction was mixed. By 1970, the piece was seen as a benchmark for twentieth-century composition. He said his choice of instruments - flute, xylorimba, vibraphone, guitar, viola, and percussion – forced him to think carefully about sound, interaction, energy, vibrancy, and tone.

Walking back to the hotel – it was a surprisingly warm evening – she wondered why this music spoke to her in such a direct way.

## March 2<sup>nd</sup>

The exhibition of romantic paintings was at the Musée de la Vie Romantique on Rue Chaptal in the ninth district. She took a taxi and was there just after two in the afternoon. She was almost immediately drawn to a portrait of Princess Alberta de Broglie by Jean-Auguste-Dominique Ingres. It was as if the image on the canvas was sharing an intimate idea with her. Two others of his paintings had a similar effect, especially a portrait of Madame Louis Leblanc. She spent three hours at the exhibition and looked at each painting which resonated with many. Some were powerful statements to her about confidence and integrity.

Later, after a supper of mussels in white wine, she reflected on her two experiences in Paris. The music spoke to her of dissonance and cohesion – how what began as a collection of sounds, seemingly disjointed, soon became coherent when you stopped trying to impose pre-conceived notions on the music but let it speak for itself. She thought of her own life – trying to impose order on the structure and preconceived notions of what a woman should be or what a career should be rather than simply being in the moment and letting structure emerge over time.

The paintings showed her what confident women, sure of who they were, looked like, and she felt more like them now than she ever had felt before. The directness of their gaze from the canvas felt like they were looking into her and saying, "you be you, don't try be someone you are not."

She slept well, dreaming of floating on a gondola in Venice and listening to music by Scarlatti. No sign of crawling and speaking babies.

She returned to London and home the next day.

## March 3rd

Miss Hutchins arrived at the office as agreed at ten and was warmly welcomed by Sir John and Riya. After some social conversation and the sharing of a photograph of Sir John's new home in the Cotswold's, they started to focus on the challenges of using all that they had learned to suggest some new actions to stem the flow of "dirty money" through corporations and banks in the UK and Europe. Gordon Brown, the Chancellor, was hoping to lead a group of finance ministers to revise the first EU money laundering directives issued in 1990 and 1995 to take account of current developments, especially the emergence of Internet banking. Eddie George, Governor of the Bank of England, was also considering tightening oversight of British banks, given the concerns.

They explored six or seven key recommendations they might make, given what they knew from their explorations. Key amongst them was the establishment in each EU member state of a team of professional investigators with substantial search and seizure powers to investigate suspected money laundering or the sudden acquisition of wealth. Also critical, in their view, was to broaden the focus from a focus on drug money to sex trafficking, terrorism and the proceeds of crime to wider definition of laundering, such as the rapid movement of funds between accounts and then offshore.

Miss Hutchins suggested that there were also issues around bank transactions – say, from a bank in Britain to one in Cyprus or Panama where the receiving bank was non-compliant with the strict banking regulations in the G10 nations.

The banks were already required to document, track, and report any suspicious sums of money deposited by a customer – with the starting point being £15,000. Miss Hutchins suggested that this should be lowered to £10,000 – based on her review of various Valin-related companies.

By noon they had a catalogue of ideas to recommend. Sir John invited Miss Hutchins to lunch, but she declined, saying that she had decided that it was time to cut down her excessive eating and drinking behaviour and consider her health. All three smiled. Sir John said, "very wise."

> "One last thing then, Miss Hutchins, "said Sir John, "I suspect your work with us is done. Riya will also move on to the Bank of England as a policy analyst in three months' time. I will finish up here, and then I will be retiring from full-time work. I want to thank you, most sincerely, for your insight and support of our inquiry. I thought this work would last longer, but the Prime Minister's office and the Treasury are anxious to get the policy ball moving across Europe. It will be the bright young things leading the charge."

"I have appreciated the opportunity to explore this issue," said Miss Hutchins, "and the opportunity to work with such interesting colleagues. You know where to find me if you need to follow up. Riya, as you can appreciate Miss Hutchins, will do remarkably well in her new work – she is ideally suited".

And with that she left the office and decided to have lunch at the Tate – fish and chips with minted fresh peas. After lunch, she took in the exhibition of Gustav Klimt's symbolist paintings. She looked very closely at his use of gold leaf, especially in his famous painting The Kiss. She found it exquisite.

At home that evening, after a simple supper of risotto with prawns and a small yogurt, she chose to listen to a selection of orchestral music by Gustav Holst. She especially enjoyed the Hammersmith Prelude and Scherzo. Originally written for brass bands, this orchestral version is luscious and lyrical. She truly enjoyed it.

After a bath, she read for a while – finishing the Equal Music book. She drifted off to sleep.

In her dream, she was the lone woman in a meeting of Cardinals at the Vatican. Each one of them went up the altar and came back to their pew with an envelope full of cash. When she went to the alter, there were no envelopes left, but there to greet her was Ginevra Amuso-Valin dressed as a cardinal. She smiled at Miss Hutchins and said simply, "not this time."

## March 4th

Her adventures as a money laundering detective over, she pondered her life again. It seemed to her that she had experienced more endings in the last year than she had in her lifetime, except for the deaths of her parents and her aunt. She wondered what her life had in store for her, not that she had any concerns.

Taking a walk around Knightsbridge, her eye caught a newspaper headline. Sir Andrew Rabkin was missing and presumed dead. She bought a copy of The Daily Telegraph. The newspaper report she read at a nearby coffee shop clarified that this was a developing story. The key facts were that he was on his boat, Destiny, and the crew last saw him just after midnight, sipping champagne at a table on the upper deck. He was, they said, deeply unhappy. The captain said that he had taken several ship-to-shore calls that evening, none of which had made him happy.

The financial reporter for the Telegraph wrote that it was understood that the various banks he had borrowed money from to fund his publishing empire had called in their loans – a total of £850 million. It was also thought, the reporter wrote, that an audit of the three pension funds he controlled would show that he had illegally used some of these funds to support his business. Analysts suggested that these pension funds now had unfunded liabilities of over £300 million.

She was shocked. She had seen him looking well and very happy at the Opera just a few weeks ago in Rome. The coincidence of all of this struck her immediately. Robert Maxwell, a larger-than-life newspaper owner and textbook publisher, had died in almost precisely these circumstances in 1991. He, too, had massive debts, had raided pension funds, and was playing the banks off against each other. He, too, had gone missing from his boat, Lady Ghislaine. No one at the time understood just what happened. His body, when found, was subject to an autopsy which found that he had a massive heart attack and had drowned. His companies went bankrupt, and the government topped up the pension funds.

There have been several documentaries about Maxwell's life and death. Some suggested he was killed by the Mossad or the KGB, both secret services he was thought to be working for. It was also revealed that some of the funds he was using to prop up his failing businesses were from Russian government sources, and it was also suspected that he was able to access "dirty money" from the Mafia.

She sat for a while. Too stunned to move. When she eventually stood up to walk back to her apartment, she took her time and was lost in thought. Could the Mafia be behind his death? Was Valin involved, she wondered?

She decided to have an early meal at a Chinese restaurant not far from her apartment. It was a small, family-run restaurant which specialized in Cantonese food. She chose the steamed fish in a spicy sauce with chow mien noodles. She had a Chinese beer with the meal – a glass of Tsing Tao. She took her time – the restaurant was not too busy. And made some notes in her daybook. She jotted down reflections on her feelings on hearing of the death of Sir Andrew. One of the notes she made was focused on the mafia connection and the way in which this may be shaped by the Valin's.

She also reflected on how quickly life can spiral out of control and how something you thought you were "on top of" suddenly becomes a dragon that breathes fire. She was glad there were no dragons in her life. At least none she knew about.

At home that evening, she decided that Vaughn Williams would reflect her mood. She chose Fantasia on a Theme by Thomas Tallis – a piece she had always loved. It was her "go-to" CD when she felt unhappy or disturbed. She followed it with the Five Variants of Dives and Lazarus – rarely performed but wonderfully rich and evocative.

She slept fitfully, her thoughts full of dreams and images of the Valin's, various cardinals in league with them and the sense of danger that all of this suggested. In part of her dream, Rabkin was on stage singing in a Rossini opera when Valin and his wife suddenly attacked him, knocking him to the ground repeatedly.

On waking, she called Sir John Aston only to discover that he was in Europe on business and would be away for several days. She was not sure who answered the call – it wasn't Riya – but she realized she had forgotten to ask, but they said that he would connect with her on her return.

## April 11 – 12$^{th}$

She had not heard from Sir John, which made her anxious. She had busied herself sorting out some of our her own financial and tax matters, adding to her music collection and exploring Bristol, Bath, and Edinburgh – all for the first time. She loved Bath. Such elegant buildings, a wonderful

Abbey church and the fashion museum, which had an intriguing display of clothing worn in Britain since 1600. She also managed to spend a few hours at the Jane Austen Centre.

While she was dining – she was spending two full nights in Bath – she was reading an account of the Jesuits and their history. She had a wonderful meal at The Dark Horse – sat in a quiet corner, drinking a glass of lightly oaked Chardonnay, and eating duck in an orange sauce.

As she sat, she kept thinking about the work she had done with and for Sir John Aston and wondered why he had not been in touch. She began to wonder if he had, as he had planned to do, written his report and retired to his new home in the Cotswold's and said goodbye to his past. She hoped that was the case. Her fear, small as it may be, was that he had decided to take some sort of action which put him in harm's way.

She wondered why she was so concerned. After all, he was a work acquaintance – a man who had both appeared in her life suddenly and then, seemingly, disappeared equally suddenly.

She took the four o'clock train back to London and was back in her apartment by seven. A letter from Sir John awaited her, suggesting they meet at noon the next day for lunch at Wilton's in Jermyn Street. She loved eating there – it was first opened in 1742 and for over two hundred and fifty years has been one of the best places to eat in London. She was, much to her surprise, delighted with the invitation and began to think about what to wear.

# April 13<sup>th</sup> – Lunch

Wilton's specializes in seafood – it does offer a small number of meat and vegetarian dishes – but it would be a shame to eat here and not have at least half a dozen oysters or some crab with avocado or a shrimp and lobster cocktail. She was exploring the menu when Sir John arrived.

He was dressed in a dark suit with a waistcoat complete with a gold watch and chain and a bright yellow kerchief in his top jacket pocket. He looked tanned and vibrant – she was truly happy to see him.

> "Miss Hutchins! So wonderful to see you and see you looking so well, I must say. What a wonderful pattern that dress has!"

> "Why thank you, it's Laura Ashley's Blue Gingko and Hawthorne – I loved it as soon as I saw it."

> "Well, you look very attractive in it," he said. "Sorry about the formal wear, been with the Prime Minister and Gordon Brown for a few hours – very focused on the banks and what they can do to stop some of the money movement, but more about this later. Let's focus on food and wine."

They each examined the menu in silence, almost as if they were studying the book of common prayer. Their items chosen, they agreed on a crisp white wine – a bottle of Pouilly-Fume and some sparkling water.

Their first courses arrived. She had chosen the lobster and shrimp cocktail, and he had the marinated salmon with dill and mustard sauce. Both plates of food looked elegant, and if the noises they made when taking their first taste were anything to go by, both were splendid. While they ate, they talked about small things - travel, living in the Cotswold's versus London, being in Bath, and their time together in Rome.

The second course showed their different tastes. She had chosen the grilled monkfish with green peppercorn butter, and he had chosen the lamb cutlets. These both came with an assortment of vegetables.

A selection of five kinds of cheese and biscuits followed with a glass of vintage port (a 1956 Taylor Fladgate) and coffee.

"You may want to know what has been going on, Miss Hutchins," Sir John began.

"I think we've known each other long enough for you to call me Audrey, Sir John," she responded.

"Yes, thank you Audrey – and in my case, we can forget the Sir, unless it's helpful – you know in case we meet a policeman or have to use status to get a table at a smart place like this! But back to business. I submitted a rather long set of forty recommendations to Gordon Brown a few weeks ago and we've been testing around twenty of them across the finance ministers in Europe. Going quite well, except for the Germans. Hans Eichel, their Minister, wants to get the credit for a new money laundering agreement rather than Gordon Brown, so he is being awkward. This means that the French are asking questions – the Germans and French seem to think the EU is their plaything rather than a collective. But progress is being made. Ironically, the death of Rabkin kind of helped shine a light on just what a risk we have across the world."

"How so?" asked Miss Hutchins.

"Well, he was using Valin to move money around so fast that by the time any of the banks decided to look into a transaction, it was no longer on their books – a kind of rapid money-spinner – "dry cleaning" the bankers call it. Money comes in at 10 am and is gone by noon, moved to another bank until it lands where it can be used to show that a payment has been made on a debt."

"One big development is that the lumbering giant we know of as Interpol has started to work on this file and has a team of sixty full-time people across Europe working on money laundering, especially as it relates to drugs and terrorism. A different group is looking at sex trafficking and the flow of money. In addition, the heads of the largest tax authorities have agreed to coordinate some of their audit activities – all of Valin's companies in eleven countries are being audited by their respective tax authorities simultaneously. It's got Valin scared. Mrs. Valin – the very beautiful Ginevra – is in Palermo meeting with the families and some of their smart people".

"One other piece of news. Cardinal Ratzinger has decided to act on Maciel and is initiating an investigation, despite the opposition of both Sodano and John Paul II. I got this from our friendly Monsignor, who has been asked to gather all of the relevant information. There are a growing number of newspaper and television reports of his misdeeds appearing in both the US and Mexico. The Church has to be seen to be at least trying."

"Well, progress then?", she asked, her head tilted so that it was more of a question with an exclamation than a simple statement.

"Some, yes. I am afraid the wheels on this bus go round and round very slowly. But enough of this. I am retiring from all this to-and-fro and am settling into a quiet life in the Cotswold's. My former wife has accepted, finally, all the arrangements our lawyers have been working on for the last eighteen months and I can focus on my real interests."

"Which are?", she asked, genuinely interested.

"Well, don't laugh, but I own a small publishing company which published limited edition poetry books and a quarterly poetry journal – quite successfully, in fact – and I also sponsor a small chamber ensemble – they perform baroque music and occasionally, just occasionally mind you, let me conduct which I enjoy. We're working on a scaled-down Messiah with a small orchestra and choir to perform at St. John's in Chipping Campden – just two performances, but a lot of fun. I have wanted to conduct the Messiah since I was fifteen and heard it performed in that same church. I must have been to seventy performances, carrying a score with me which is annotated in the hand of Sir Malcolm Sargent no less."

"Ah yes, I have several recordings of the Messiah, including one by the English Chamber Orchestra, which I find the most satisfying. I am sure it will be wonderful," she said.

"Will you come – I know it's months away. But I would like you to be there."

"I would love to. I will make the needed arrangements," she said.

"You could stay with me – I have six very quiet bedrooms. You would have a lot of privacy, I assure you."

"Let me think about this, John," she added.

"The orchestra – they call themselves a "band," would you believe, despite having a perfectly good name, The Baroque Consortium – are doing a few other concerts between now and then, but we start rehearsals for Messiah in November. The choir has sung it many times, but we have soloists about to graduate from the Royal College of Music. They need rehearsal with each other, which we're doing initially in London and then with the band in Chipping Camden in December."

"Given your interests, John, I am surprised we haven't run into each other at the Wigmore Hall or the Festival Hall or Saint Martin in the Fields – you know at concerts and performances? I am at these a lot."

"Yes, I have avoided these for some time since my former wife is at all of them, and I am doing everything I can to avoid her. It is silly. We're finished and the divorce is final. It's all over. But whenever I see her it kind of ruins the experience of the music. She is a big fan of ballet, which I never was. She doesn't like opera, which I love, and she hates baroque music, which is my passion. I don't know why we ever thought our marriage would work." He paused and looked at Miss Hutchins. "I am so sorry – you don't need to know all of this. I do apologize."

"No need to apologize, John. I do understand. Whenever I hear this kind of story – and I heard them a lot in my last position, believe me – I just feel glad that I never got involved in "relationships." I am very much a loner and am happy being what some used to call a "spinster" – a word which, I understand – is now out of fashion. I am a "happy, single woman of means" who has not any intention or desire to marry."

"Very wise," said Sir John. "My former wife already has a man in her sights – a Duke. He lost his first wife to cancer and is very lonely. We have known him for many years. The Duke of Cumberland. He and I are the same age – we went to school together. Janet will become his second wife and Lady Cumberland. I hope he makes her happy. I certainly failed."

"Shall we order some more port?" asked Miss Hutchins, anxious to change the subject.

"Sorry. No, no more for me – I have a meeting in an hour, and then I need to get back to the house. I hope I did not bore you with all my domestic troubles, Audrey."

"Not at all. I am pleased you felt comfortable enough with me to share, though therapist I am not – I assure you!"

The conversation came to a natural end. Sir John paid and was on his way. Miss Hutchins took the opportunity to visit Hatchards bookstore in Piccadilly. Several floors of some of the most interesting books available. She had an account there since she was in school – a gift from her aunt. She had a book on order which should have arrived by now, but also took the opportunity to browse. She found a comfy chair and a book of poems by Seamus Heaney – The Spirit Level. The poems were very moving. She especially loved A Dog Was Crying To-Night in Wicklow Also. It was no wonder he won the Nobel Prize for Literature, she thought.

The book she had ordered was waiting for her at reception when she went downstairs again – the second and final volume of David Cairns biography of Berlioz – a composer the author had championed for many years., especially in his years as music critic of The Times. The first volume –

which explored the first thirty years of his life – she had found fascinating and compelling. She was looking forward to reading this volume, listening to the four Berlioz symphonies, sipping a glass of rich red Merlot, and nibbling on some cheese and biscuits. That would be her evening.

She took a cab home, sorted some things out and sat herself down and thought about Sir John. Was he making a pass? Was he trying to suggest a relationship? She didn't think so. He was lonely yet had his passions – music, poetry, policy, food, and wine. He seemed wealthy, even after the separation settlement.

From her reading about him in the library, his father made a fortune investing in the mining of rare metals. As an only child, he inherited. He married Janet Newcombe when he began his work in government twenty-seven years ago. They did not have children, and she worked, initially at least, as a designer for a large furniture company before moving on to work as chief designer for John Lewis fabrics. She left quickly and became "a lady who lunches." Lady Janet was on the board of the Royal Ballet Company and several other arts-based organizations in London. She had seen pictures of her – a tall, long-legged thin as a rake woman with flowing, straight brunette hair. Very attractive, yet austere. In the two photographs she had seen, Lady Janet had looked as if she had just sucked a lemon.

She put on the recording of Berlioz Symphonie Fantastique, poured a glass of Merlot and sat in her favourite chair, a small plate of cheese and biscuits with grapes by her side. She began reading the Cairns book –

Berlioz: Servitude and Greatness. She was quickly absorbed in the words, music, flavours, and taste. Time flew by. She was happy.

## April 15<sup>th</sup>

Reflecting on her luncheon with Sir John, Audrey decided to contact Riya. They arranged to meet for lunch at Camino's on Bankside – a Spanish Tapas Restaurant – tastes which would be new to her.

Riya was already seated when Miss Hutchins arrived. She wore a simple yet elegant green and gold silk saree. She looked truly magnificent.

> "Before you say anything. Audrey, I am wearing the Saree since I am to attend a reception later this afternoon at 11 Downing Street for visiting EU Finance Ministers that Gordon Brown is hosting. I thought I'd dress for the occasion. Yesterday was the Bangladesh new year – April 14<sup>th</sup> – and my parents were down from Bradford, and we celebrated with friends and family here in London in Spitalfields, where there is a large Bangladeshi community. We always celebrate at the Monsoon restaurant. My mum bought me this new saree and I think it really suits me, what do you think Audrey?"

> "Well, I must say, you do look wonderful," said Miss Hutchins, "you will no doubt attract the attention of many. Will Sir John be there?

"No, he is in Amsterdam now and then on to Brussels. We're getting close to an agreement across the EU finance teams. Gordon Brown is working the phones, and his team is all over this as a strategic priority. The Prime Minister has raised this at heads of government meetings and is encouraged by the response,

For myself, becoming more focused on the next step in my career – the move to the Bank of England and working with the analytics team on the policy implications of the data we are exploring. It's what I worked on in Rome for the EU before I met Sir John and worked on the money laundering file.

Look, Audrey, if this all works well, we will have done good work, but we both know that it will only have a modest impact. What the authorities are up against is seriously organized crime. Not just the Mafia, but the Russians, North Korea, and Iran – they all have their fingers in the money laundering business. The internet is changing the rules of the game and the speed at which the game is played. It is no longer like cricket; it is more like Formula 1."

"Yes, Riya. I have been thinking the same. Two steps forward, one step back while the Valin's and their like take four steps forward. We are in a race, but we carry the handicap."

They looked over the menu. Miss Hutchins asked Riya to order, since she was unfamiliar with many items on the menu, though understood something about them from the English translation provided. Five tapas were ordered: Albóndigas, Patatas Bravas, Gambas al ajillo, Calamares a la Romana and Tortilla Española. Audrey had no idea what each of these would taste like. Riya also ordered two small glasses of a Spanish red wine – Garnacha.

As they sipped their wine, Riya asked.

"Any how, Audrey. What have you been doing? "

"Nothing much. A few concerts, sorting out my very quickly growing collection of CDs, books, and fountain pens. Thinking about travel. I feel I used up a lot of my emotional energy on the work we did, though I did learn from that."

"What did you learn, Audrey?" asked Riya, sounding deeply and genuinely interested.

"That I can, with the right challenge and the right people, be a team player and that I am good at identifying patterns and shapes, especially when looking at financial data," she said, somewhat cautiously.

"I would add, said Riya, that you are also passionate about places, art, music, and ideas but cautious about people. I saw something of me in you. At Oxford, my nickname was "Hermit the Odd" – a play on "Hermit the Frog." I was always shying away from social events, studying, and learning how to use statistical tools. I loved problem-solving more than people meeting. I was the first in my group to master and use multi-

183

dimensional scaling and to explore its use in a model of economic wellbeing – work that propelled my career after I graduated. Using some ideas developed by a Canadian economist who writes about a quality-of-life index, I developed an alternative analytic model to the gross domestic product that looked at the economy as being about people, not just a basket of goods and services."

"How interesting, Riya. Is this what you will be working on at the Bank of England?" Audrey asked.

"In part. The Governor wants the policy committees to have a broader understanding of the real state of the British economy when they are making decisions about interest rates, monetary policy, money supply, foreign exchange rates and banking controls."

"One other thing I came to learn, Riya", said Miss Hutchins, "was that I don't need to work to have meaning in life. I already have everything I need, I need to focus on what I can do with the energy I have. And what I choose to do need not be about accounting, auditing, or anything to do with my past life. I am a free woman, independent-minded and independent in terms of what I choose to do with my time."

Riya looked her straight in the eye "Good! That's the spirit!" she said.

The food arrived, and they began to eat. Both made the noises satisfied diners make when the food is both excellent and beyond expectations. Miss Hutchins fell in love with patatas bravas and the Albóndigas. The wine was so tasty, taking the edge off the spicier food.

They continued to chat casually, as if they had been classmates in school and shared a long history, when they had really known each other for just a few months.

As she was leaving, Riya asked Miss Hutchins to stay in touch since, she said, "I think we are kindred spirits".

## April 9ᵗʰ

She had also bought a notebook computer – a Dell Inspiron. She had taken some classes on how to use it and was getting used to the very idea that from Netscape, one could search for information online with something called Yahoo – typically, an American company created it. She used it to write letters which she could print on the printer she had also bought. She used it to manage her financial matters, using something that was called a spreadsheet that did all sorts of things automatically, which she had spent years having to do manually. She used it to catalogue her very large collection of compact disks, which now totaled over 5,000. She was constantly surprised at just what the Dell notebook could do.

## April 16ᵗʰ

Concorde was not as full on this occasion as on the last, and it was not as fast – a good ten minutes later than her previous flight. Still, she was in New York from London in less than four hours.

She had chosen to stay at The Hotel Carlyle on the Upper East Side in Manhattan. An art deco hotel, it was often home to stars of stage and screen, Presidents, Prime Ministers, and other celebrities. She checked in and was escorted to her room by a very handsome and elegant young man, who showed her around the small suite. She tipped him generously.

She wanted to visit the Frick Collection – something she had not done before. It was supposed to house an exceptional collection of European paintings, sculptures, decorative arts, and furniture from the Renaissance through the early 19th Century. These included paintings by Rembrandt, Gainsborough, Bellini, van Dyck, Holbein, Renoir and, perhaps most famous of all, Vermeer's Girl with a Pearl Earring. She was keen to look at the works by Goya, especially his portrait of Lady Maria Martinez de Puga.

When she eventually found it, she was surprised. Goya had painted this in his late 70s and had worked very quickly, as can be seen from the bold brush strokes. In contrast to his royal portraits, this looks and feels very modern. The sitter looks controlled and straight ahead as if thinking about her future. Miss Hutchins looked at the painting for a good thirty minutes. She found herself wanting to know more about this woman. She would use her new computer to find out more.

## April 17th

String quartet at the Lincoln Centre. The Guarneri, renowned for their performances on Bartok and Beethoven quartets, were performing Schubert's String

Quartet No. 13, generally known as Rosamunde, and his single movement quartet Quartettsatz. She had seen the quartet at the Wigmore Hall performing all the Bartok quartets over three concerts on consecutive nights and thought them outstanding. A clear, focused sound, terrific, shared understanding of the music and an ability to respond to the conditions – each venue has its own way of sharing sound, and any ensemble must understand how to play the venue and their instruments.

They were, as she expected they would be, incredible. Such contained passion, lyricism and energy. She had read an account of Schubert's life and tragic death at just thirty-one. Despite his age, he made a major contribution to music and was a big influence on many other composers, especially Brahms and Schumann.

## April 20th

She had a few days wandering around New York. Visits to the Met, the Guggenheim and a lunchtime concert at the Lincoln Centre with the Kronos Quartet from Seattle. They played ten short pieces from their newly just released CD called Caravan. None was longer than 9 minutes, and the shortest was just four. Such a different experience from the Guarneri, but magical. She especially enjoyed a short piece called The Gallop of a Thousand Horses by Kayan Kalhor. The music sounded like a cross between Klezmer, modern jazz and classical. She was intrigued and loved it.

Later that day, after a light supper taken in her room at the hotel, she was at Carnegie Hall. It was a most memorable concert. Lorin Maazel conducted the Vienna Philharmonic in a stunning and moving performance of

Mahler's Fifth Symphony. She noticed Pierre Boulez was in the audience – he had just been appointed composer in residence. Also, there was Daniel Barenboim, who was to perform several times during the coming season.

She had never really taken to Mahler until this performance. It is a very long symphony – the performance was over an hour long – and it is complex, but Maazel seemed to find the right tempo and textures, and the orchestra was on top form. The program notes reported that Herbert von Karajan once said of this symphony that "You forget that time has passed. A great performance of the Fifth is a transforming experience. The fantastic finale almost forces you to hold your breath." For this performance, he was right.

She dreamt of being in Marrakesh in the Souk – she had never been – and getting lost in a maze of alleyways, stalls, street traders, silk winders and snake charmers. All the time, she could hear music from the various concerts playing as fragments.

## April 21st

She took a flight from New York to Toronto – a city she had never visited before. She took a room at the Royal York Hotel and asked the concierge how far it would be to walk to Roy Thompson Hall where she would hear the Toronto Symphony. It was not that far and there were some good restaurants en route, including a good French one which the concierge strongly recommended.

He was right to do so. Le Sélect Bistro had a wonderful classical Parisian ambience to it. She had a perfectly cooked lamb steak with ratatouille, pistachios and pommes Anna. This was served with a red wine and port reduction. Very tasty. She finished with a tarte au citron and an espresso. A most enjoyable and refined meal.

The concert turned out to be a powerful evening of Shostakovich's Leningrad Symphony – his seventh - and Prokofiev's second piano concerto. Yukka-Pekka Saraste conducted, and the pianist was Janina Fialkowska. Roy Thompson Hall has wonderful acoustics, even though it seats around 2,600 people. The concert was very powerful. Miss Hutchins was moved to tears as she listened to the Leningrad, knowing the impact it had on German troops who listened to it at its premier as it was broadcast to all on the Russian-German front line in 1942. One German general said of it, "as we listened, we knew we could not win this war."

The Prokofiev aways surprises. It begins with a lyrical theme on the solo piano, which the orchestra picks up, and the interplay between the piano and orchestra begins in earnest. The soloist was superb, and the orchestra found the right tone and volume to let the piano shine.

She spent the rest of her time in Toronto sightseeing – eating at the rotating restaurant on top of the CN Tower, exploring the Royal Ontario Museum and the Art Gallery of Ontario. She even took a bus down to Niagara Falls, reminded of a work colleague once saying she had been and was very disappointed: "just a lot of water falling off the edge of a cliff." She was from Norway.

## April 24th

Toronto to Vancouver. Miss Hutchins was surprised at how long this flight took – five hours. Then she remembered that Canada was the second-largest country in the world, Russia being larger. Canada is so big that it would be possible to "fit" forty-one Great Britain's onto its land.

She had bought a biography of Emily Carr, the Canadian painter and writer whose works she wanted to see in Vancouver. She was an expressionist painter who used bright colours and sought to "translate" her experiences with Indigenous people into vibrant, powerful images. She had seen some of her paintings in London and the Met in New York, but a major exhibition was being held at the Vancouver Art Gallery, which she now wanted to see.

She stayed at the Hotel Sylvia on English Bay in a small suite and bathed after the flight and taxi ride downtown. A little run-down but quaint. Her room had a kitchenette so she could make simple meals and tea. Not that she needed to. Within a ten-minute walk, there were Indian, Greek, French, Italian, Malaysian, and British restaurants, not to mention fantastic coffee shops and a bakery.

She took a small boat taxi across to Granville Island market and explored the eye-catching displays of fruit, vegetables, fresh fish, meats, cakes and bread. Nearby were stores selling hats, books, jewelry, clothing, art supplies and even a chandelier.

She strolled amongst the art galleries, restaurants, print shops and artist studios, feeling happier than she had done in some time. She stumbled across a shack selling fish and

190

chips, ordered and sat at a table and enjoyed them more than any fish and chips she had ever eaten – fresh haddock, thick-cut chips served with a tangy coleslaw. As she ate, she looked at the sailboats in the harbour, watching them exit the safety of their moorings with grace and dignity. A calmness came over her and she felt at peace.

Later that evening, after a walk around Stanley Park and a meal at a Bistro near the hotel, she sat in her room overlooking the ocean and made some notes in her journal.

> I like who I am becoming. Through travel, art, music, and food, I feel anchored in my life. They each connect to me and help me understand who I am.
>
> I no longer feel I have to "fit in", or that work shapes who I am. I am me.
>
> If I can pursue an interest, for example, in art or music or a place, why not? I have the means. Why hang onto all the money when I could use it to make sense of who I am?
>
> My last therapist told me once that, "when you do discover that you can be yourself and not someone you are supposed to be, then it will be liberating!" I am beginning to feel that she was right.

She read over her writing a few times, turned off the light and slept well. No dreams.

## April 25th

There were thirty-five Emily Carr paintings in the exhibition at the Vancouver Art Gallery as well as several of her sketchbooks, letters, and ink drawings. Also displayed were paintings by Matisse, Derain and de Vlaminck – all modernist painters pursuing similar ideas and techniques to Carr's. These artists were known, at the time, as part of the "fauvist" movement because of their use of bright colours and vivid imagery.

She spent three hours in the galleries. She was especially taken by three of Carr's paintings called, "Scorned as Timber, Beloved of the Sky", "Big Raven," and "Totem Poles, Kitwancool." There was a simplicity about the composition of each of these, yet they were vivid and powerful. Truly engaging paintings. Bold, brash, and yet inviting.

The Matisse painting in the same style included in the exhibition was Luxe, calme et volupté (Luxury, Calm and Pleasure), which was painted in 1904 – very early in his career as an artist. It is frequently seen as the first painting in the fauvist genre. She noted it was on loan from the Musée d'Orsay in Paris. She was surprised she had not seen it. After all, she was more than familiar with many of the works at the Musée.

She left the gallery and went for a stroll down Robson Street. Full of elegant shops selling leatherwear, handbags, and jewelry. She found a small restaurant and sat down for an early evening meal. Shrimp cocktail, steak frites with a peppercorn sauce, followed by a sublime Panna Cotta.

She took out her notebook and Dubai pen and wrote:

> "The distortion of shape seen by the eye and vivid
> colours characterizes the Carr paintings. It is as if
> she wanted us to feel and experience what she was
> seeing rather than picture it like a photograph. She
> wants us to engage with the experience she had of
> "being there." Matisse and the others are inviting
> us in the same way. When you stop trying to
> impose form and structure on these images, you
> encounter not just the idea of a totem pole or a
> raven, but the emotions associated with these
> encounters.
>
> I felt the same way about the Kronos Quartet's
> short pieces for Caravan. They were too short to let
> one explore the structure and impose form but
> long enough to connect emotionally. Powerful,
> lyrical, and sometimes jarring pieces that
> heightened alertness and sensitivity. Just in the
> same way that Carr and Matisse's images did."

Pleased with her writing, she walked back to her hotel
down Denman Street and enjoyed the sense that she was
in a community.

## April 27th

At the suggestion of the Concierge, she took a taxi to
Steveston – about fifty-five minutes from the hotel. A
fishing village built where the Fraser River meets the
Pacific Ocean and where the salmon were once caught in
abundance, it retains a village feel and has interesting
shops, walks and eateries.

She bought a matching bracelet and earrings set as well as a new book, Alias Grace by the Canadian writer Margaret Atwood. The book is based on the true story of Grave Marks who came from Ireland to Canada but found herself accused of murdering two people in 1843. Atwood uses the real events, as the back cover of the book says, to tell the story behind the events leading up to the murders and reveal the real story of Grace. Miss Hutchins had read one previous novel by Atwood – The Handmaid's Tale – and, though dark and disturbing, she had found it compelling and very well crafted.

She sat on a bench overlooking the estuary and marveled at how enchanting the place was. Fishing boats were pulled up on the dock and were selling fresh seafood. Lots of shrimp, crab, lobster, salmon, and other enticing temptations. What is more, none of this was expensive, especially given the prices she had seen at the Granville Island market.

What was she doing? she asked herself. Sitting on a bench looking out at the Pacific Ocean on a lovely day. This time three years ago she was auditing a company's books in Harrogate and thinking that this was what she would be doing for the rest of her working life. But, having given up working, she now found herself a woman of leisure and means, travelling the world in search of great music, good food and memorable art. She was spending down some of her money, but she had plenty, and her investments were showing strong returns – nothing to worry about.

But what should she do? What was her purpose? She took out her journal and the Dubai pen and began to write:

I don't need to earn a living to have a purpose.
I don't need to be part of a team or a workplace to
have a purpose.
I don't need to earn an income to have a purpose.
I don't need to find religion to have a purpose.
I don't need a partner or companion to have a
purpose.
I don't need to engage in politics to have a
purpose.
I have a purpose as an art, music, and food
explorer.
I have a purpose in travel and encounters.
I have a purpose in just being me!

She sat back and read through her list a few times. She thought about how she could use her travel and love of arts and food to be creative. She wondered if writing about her experiences would provide an additional layer of meaning and purpose. She seemed capable. The question is would anyone be interested? An idea began to percolate. She had a sudden thought – perhaps all those hours of therapy were beginning to pay off.

She found a nice restaurant and had the most delicious seafood risotto she had ever eaten.

## May 1st

The Vancouver Symphony, with its conductor Kazuyoshi Akiyama, played the Brahms Second Symphony and a work by John Adams called, A Short Ride in a Fast Machine, both of which she enjoyed. In the second half of the concert, a very young Canadian called James Ehnes played the Sibelius Violin Concerto and was sublime.

In her notebook that evening, she wrote: "I want to listen to more Sibelius. I think he struggled with questions of identity and purpose. It comes through his music."

## May 3rd

She had had a few wonderful days exploring Vancouver and was highly delighted with her "discoveries". Excellent meals, lovely and very helpful people, and great sights. She had especially enjoyed her day trip to Whistler, a ski resort northwest of Vancouver. Though the idea of flying down a mountainside strapped to two long pieces of laminated wood held no interest to her, the shops, the views, and the food were remarkable.

Flying back to London on an Air Canada flight that would take over nine and a half hours, she was pleased to be on a single seat on the upper deck of the Boeing 747-400 with no one sitting beside her. She would finish the Margaret Atwood novel and make notes in her journal. She had some ideas for an article she might write, though she was unsure what she would do with it if she ever finished it.

The meal was a nice baked salmon in a cream sauce with roti potato and carrots, followed by a lovely lemon tart and various cheeses. The coffee was a little bitter, but she tempered it with a snifter of brandy. Between naps, she finished the novel and had five pages of notes and ideas in her journal.

## May 4th

The flight landed shortly after one-thirty in the afternoon."
Her driver was waiting for her, holding a sign, "Miss
Hutchins", in his gloved hands as she exited with her
luggage. A friendly man, he had her back at her apartment
in just forty-five minutes. He asked where she had been.
She told him about New York, Toronto, and Vancouver. He
smiled and said that his son was in Vancouver, learning to
be a doctor at the university. He had been over twice and
thought the place magical. So did she.

The apartment, as always, was spotless and comforting. It
embraced and comforted her. She was pleased to be
home.

She had waded through her mail, dealing with bills, a tax
issue, and concerns about the possibility of some
construction affecting the apartment. For the first time,
she experienced jet lag – tired, fuzzy thinking and a level of
lethargy she had only experienced when she had the flu or
a nasty sinus cold.

She had started to write about the Emily Carr paintings
and the art genre she was a part of, so far, around
fourteen hundred words. She would need to tighten it and
add more about how the notebooks shed light on Carr's
thinking as an artist, but she was pleased with the writing
she had done so far. All those years of reading the London
Review of Books, The New Statesman and The Spectator
were paying off.

She went for a walk and found herself outside Harrod's.
She didn't like Harrod's or the man who owned it,

Mohammed Al Fayed. It wasn't that he was Egyptian; something about him made him unattractive, even odd. He had become prominent after Princess Diana and Fayed's son, Dodi, died in a horrible car crash in Paris and had promoted the idea that they were killed by British special forces on the orders of Prince Phillip. Despite several investigations and an independent second autopsy, no evidence had been produced to support his conspiracy theory. The lack of evidence did not appear to stop him from repeating his theory at every opportunity. The Home Secretary, Jack Straw, had said, "no", to his applications for British citizenship on more than one occasion.

Nonetheless, she decided to walk through the store and found its stationery department on the lower ground floor. She loved exploring stationery stores. Always had done so, ever since she was a young girl. All the tools of writing – paper clips, staples, bulldog clips, inks, ink cartridges, index cards, folders, pens, pencils, rulers, and erasers. She didn't buy anything but began to think if she was to see writing as part of her future, she might need to equip herself appropriately. Harrod's was not the place to do this. Much better prices at W.H. Smith's, Waterstones, or Ryman's. She smiled, thinking of herself as a potential writer.

Back at home, she finished the article on Emily Carr and the fauvists, printed it on the printer attached to her Dell computer and sat back to look at it. It ran to just a few words over one thousand and read well. But what to do with it? Given the connection to French painters like Matisse, Valtat, Puy, Derain and Vlaminck, she wondered if the Paris Review might be interested. She found an email address for the editor and used her email to send the article with a cover note, suggesting places in the text where it would be helpful to show an image. Despite its name, the magazine is published in New York and explores art, literature, film, music and poetry. Founded in the 1950s, she had found a copy in her room at The Carlyle and took to it.

Satisfied with her day, she made a frittata with eggs, some bacon, cheese and broccoli, poured herself a glass of oaked Chardonnay, and chose to listen to Scarlatti.

## May 12<sup>th</sup>

She had telephoned Dr. Michelle May and invited her to join her for lunch. Her former therapist had initially hesitated, concerned that Miss Hutchins was looking for therapy with salad. Miss Hutchins had assured her that she wanted to connect to share where she was on her journey in her new life. Dr. May had agreed.

Miss Hutchins arrived first. Lunch was at Rules in Covent Garden, the oldest restaurant in London. It had been there since 1798. The joke was that some of the wait staff were from the original team. That is not true, of course, most seemed to be from Australia or New Zealand. She ordered some sparkling water and waited for Dr. May to arrive.

She did not have long to wait. Michelle May wore a stunning powder blue pantsuit, a white silk blouse, matching gold earrings, a necklace, and a bracelet. Her hair was shorter and in a different style from when she had last seen her, but the new style not only suited her but made her look much younger. She also looked to have lost some weight.

"Well, this is nice," Dr. May began.

"I hope so," said Miss Hutchins, "I haven't been here in ages – we had a client who loved this place and ate here at least once a week and insisted on our team meeting him here before we got down to serious accounting business in his offices, which are nearby."

"You are looking well, Audrey, very well. But I am starving. Let's get to the menu."

They studied the menu and were quick to make decisions. Dr. May ordered the smoked duck breast, broad bean salad, and a glass of sparkling water. Miss Hutchins ordered the smoked haddock, leek, and onion tart with a simple green salad. Their waiter, a young lady called Amelia from Melbourne, tried to encourage them to order some wine, but they both declined.

"So, what have you been up to since you left the accounting company – Brooke and Walters, if I remember correctly? Travelling, I expect?" asked Dr. May.

"Well, yes, amongst other things. I had a brief spell working for the cabinet office, then explored Rome, Paris, Dubai, New York, Toronto, and Vancouver, taking in wonderful art galleries, concerts, great food, and the sights. Been quite the journey," responded Miss Hutchins.

She spent the next twenty minutes recounting, in general terms, what she had been doing since she ended therapy towards the end of October last year.

"So, you have decided not to be what others want you to be and to be who you are – a wealthy, smart woman who loves music, art, food, and travel? Is this what you are saying to me Audrey?", asked Dr. May.

"Yes, plus I hope to turn my interests into something tangible through writing. I have made a start – a short piece on the paintings of Emily Carr and others who were part of a "movement." I have submitted it and will see what happens. I think, even if I say so myself, I write well. My training in accounting taught me to be focused, concise and insightful. I hope that comes across in my writing," Audrey said.

"For what it's worth, Audrey, I am delighted. It seemed to me that part of your struggle, when we spent those hours together, was trying to understand how you might break out of the patterns you had used to cope with the sudden loss of your parents and, not long afterwards, your aunt, to whom you were very close. You are in your thirties, realizing you can be what you want if you work at it. Excellent."

"I still feel I am on a journey, not sure where the station stops, or what the destination is, but I am more willing now than I ever have been to take and enjoy the journey."

"That's the spirit!" said Dr. May. "I did enjoy our lunch, but I have a 1:30 client, so I must go, but I must say, Audrey, this has been a delight. Stay in touch. Be well."

With that, Dr. May left, leaving Audrey to reflect on their conversation and what it represented. While she had formally ended her therapy last October after a decade or so, she saw this lunch as the real end of that period and a signal of a new beginning.

## May 19<sup>th</sup>

The Paris Review accepted the article with some minor edits. She would get a proof copy in a few days, and it would appear in September. Her first published article. She was thrilled. She could now call herself an author.

She had just read Bruce Chatwin's book, Songlines. It captures a great story – how Aboriginals in Australia, as young men, take journeys along ancient routes known as "song lines" in the outback to develop their resilience and test their determination and become "men" as a result of this rite of passage. Beautifully written, it is really a celebration of man's desire to wander, travel, experience and connect with the earth. She found it very moving. She also saw the book as a masterclass in writing. If she was to write about her travels, Chatwin's work was the gold standard.

She had heard Chatwin interviewed on the BBC several times. He was an eloquent, intelligent speaker. Always creative in his use of words and able to engage his audience in encounters in such a way that you could almost feel you had been with him on his journeys. She remembered an interview he did with Clive James about his book In Patagonia – he made the place sound so alluring, almost magical. If she remembered correctly, he had written one or possibly two novels. She would look them up at the public library the next time she dropped in.

He died young – at just forty-eight. He had been involved in several homosexual relationships and, from one, contracted AIDS, probably from an Australian man he grew very close to. This occurred long before he met and married Elizabeth Chanier, an American photographer and artist, in 1965.

She wondered what she might write next and whom she might write for.

## May 23<sup>rd</sup>

She went to Hatchards bookstore and explored a shelf of books written by writers about writing. If this was her new craft, she should treat it as a professional task, not a hobby. She sat in a comfortable armchair and started reading.

One book she looked at quoted J.B. Priestley, the Bradford-born novelist, playwright, and broadcaster who believed in working hard to keep the writing simple so that it would be easier for the reader to understand. He said, "if any man thinks the kind of simplicity I attempt is easy, he should try it for himself." She knew what he meant.

The book also noted that Oscar Wilde once said, "I write when I'm inspired, and I see to it that I'm inspired at nine o'clock every morning." He emphasized the discipline and rigour of the work. It was a job that required timelines, focus and determination. This reminded Miss Hutchins of an interview she had heard on the BBC with Ian McEwan after he won the Booker Prize for his novel Amsterdam. He said that he sat at his desk six days a week and wrote for about four to five hours, went for a walk, had lunch and a nap. Then looked over what he had written and edit out between a quarter and a third of the manuscript. She distinctly remembered him saying, "You don't sit there and wait for the blue flame of inspiration. You write!" It had stuck with her at the time.

Writing requires discipline, focus, routine, and determination. Just like auditing. Just like all hard work, she thought.

She did not buy a book about writing but instead paid for a guide to which journals, magazines and newspapers accepted work from "freelancers" and how to submit the work. It was a hefty volume but full of suggestions as to where she might place whatever she wanted to write.

Later that afternoon, after a light tuna salad with a simple dressing, she took a cab home and opened her journal. She listed four things she might write about:

1. Finding Mahler – about how she had disliked and resisted his work for many years, but having heard a wonderful performance of the Fifth Symphony, she was hooked. She would include recommended recordings.
2. The Middle East, Desert and Art – using her notes from the visit to Dubai, she would write a short travel piece about what to do for art in the desert.
3. Caravan and Music – she would review the Kronos Quartet CD when it appeared next year, having

heard them play most of the music live in New York.

She wondered what Sir John would think if she wrote about money laundering or the Vatican. She had signed the Official Secrets Act, but many issues and concerns they had dealt with were now in the public domain. She would ask him. She was especially interested in what was happening with the Legion of Christ and its disreputable founder, Maciel Degollado.

## May 27<sup>th</sup>

She had seen them before – the list of writing workshops, courses and private writing coaches that appeared at the back of the London Review of Books. She had not considered them, but now she was interested. One, set in the Yorkshire Dales, appealed to her. It was in a property once owned by the writer Ted Hughes at Lumb Bank, near Hebden Bridge, and was close to some lovely countryside. Run by an organization dedicated to supporting writers founded in 1968, it had in the past some wonderful instructors including Beryl Bainbridge, Ian Banks, Hilary Mantel, and Salmon Rushdie. The idea was to write, share, learn and improve.

She was not a big poetry reader but had read Ted Hughes' collection, Birthday Letters. The poems in the collection span a period of several decades, from the time Hughes first met and married Sylvia Plath, through their marriage and separation until her death in 1963. The poems have been referred to by some as "confessional poetry". She had found the writing taut, full of emotional anguish and pain but also self-effacing. She knew she could never write poetry, nor did she want to.

What she wanted to write was non-fiction. Interesting observations and insights. She registered for a course in June at Lumb Bank and started work on her piece about finding Mahler.

## May 31ˢᵗ

She had a working draft of her Mahler article, exploring why she had resisted Mahler for so long and what had happened to change her thinking. Though the New York concert was a turning point, she had been listening to more music from the grand tradition Mahler came from as well as several recordings of Mahler's symphonic works – all ten symphonies, loving the Bernstein recordings. She was at the right stage of her own development and self-understanding to better appreciate his work and its emotional tones.

Her insight was that Mahler's music is deeply introspective and emotionally intense. His compositions explore themes of love, death, spirituality, and other existential questions. The profound depth and emotional weight of his music can be challenging for some listeners who may prefer more accessible musical experiences, such as Mozart or Haydn. Mahler's works often demand a certain level of emotional investment and patience from the audience (some of the symphonies are very long with some lasting over an hour and half), which may not resonate with everyone. She had listened to several recordings of each symphony, listing her preferences at the end of the eighteen-hundred-word article.

In the mail today she had received confirmation for her writing retreat in Yorkshire and was delighted to learn that the guest tutor for the four days was Bill Bryson. She had devoured his funny, insightful book, Notes, from a Small Island and found his writing creative, imaginative yet grounded in observation. She wondered what he might think of her writing and what kind of person he might turn out to be.

## June 14<sup>th</sup>

She arrived at Lumb Bank, thanks to a driver who picked her up at home and took her all the way there – a drive of over two hundred and twenty-five miles. For some of the ride she read Bryson's book about his travels in Europe – Neither Here nor There. He has humorous things to say about most of Western Europe, especially France, Italy, Monaco, and Luxembourg. When she wasn't reading, she was looking at the view, which was mainly dull until the car left the M6 and joined the M62 towards Leeds. After the cityscapes, she luxuriated in the look and feel of the Yorkshire moors and dales and marveled at how untouched it all looked.

Ted Hughes' old house once belonged to the owner of a wool mill – John Armitage and his family – and was built in the middle of the eighteenth century. The family-owned mills in Huddersfield and Leeds and used the house and grounds as a place of retreat and rest. A large house in some twenty acres of woodlands with a stunning view of the Calder valley near Heptonstall. Busy farms, small cottages and sheep dotted the landscape. Ted Hughes sold it to the Avron team who ran the writing retreats but lived there as writer in residence until 1997. Now it was one of three bases for writing retreats and creative writing classes run by Avron. Eighteen bedrooms, including five double rooms, a well-stocked library and lots of quiet places to read, write and think. She was looking forward to it.

Dinner was to be made by the guests, following recipes and instructions left by the kitchen staff, using pre-prepared ingredients. A Caprese salad, pork chops with apples and pears, green beans and small jersey potatoes, and an apple pie (already made) with cream. Simple, but looked very tasty. The pork, the recipe said, was from a farm just six miles away and the apples from a local orchard. Audrey prepared the Caprese salad – sliced tomato, intermingled with mozzarella di bufala cheese, sprinkled with fine shreds of basil and, when served, some very lovely olive oil, salt and pepper.

Two other guests – an elderly woman called Joyce and a young man called Andy – prepared the main course, though there was little to do – and Linda, a lively lady from Warrington, said she'd make sure the dessert was "up to snuff." A fifth participant would arrive just in time for dinner. She was called Janet and was coming from Canada, though she had been in Scotland for the last several days visiting an aunt.

They sat together at dinner and, while enjoying the simple but very tasty meal, introduced themselves.

Andy, in his "other life" he said, was a painter and decorator. "Puts money in my pocket and is not demanding work mentally. A lot of time setting up ladders, cloths, paints, brushes, and rollers and then hours of dull work. I started using the time thinking up stories. When I got home, I wrote them down. Then on my days off, I polish the writing and send them off to various magazines. Had eleven short stories published so far. Doesn't pay. Not in it for the money. Very satisfying. I also am a decent cook, experimenting with different recipes and ingredients is very satisfying. Last week I made Nasi Goreng – Indonesian fried rice - for the first time. Spicy and very tasty. It all beats painting a ceiling!"

Joyce, who said she was seventy, had been writing since she was ten. "I started with a diary, which I have written in every day since my mother gave me my first diary for my tenth birthday. Two complete volumes a year for sixty years. When I look back at them, they are full of ideas, stories, tall-tales, rumours, inuendo, bits of scripts from plays or TV shows and, well, anecdotes. A treasure trove. When my husband died six years ago, he left quite a bit of money, so I don't need to worry about the basics. The kids all left Britain years ago – one lot lives on the Greek island of Crete and the other in Spain – on the coast at Almeria. I have no need to worry about them. I even get to visit from time to time, though it gets very hot in both places in the summer, so I tend to go when its winter here." She had written two novels. Both had sold reasonably well. She was working on a third but was a little stuck with the plot. She was hoping for a breakthrough over the next few days.

Linda, who acknowledged that she was "the baby of the group" since she was just twenty-seven, wrote for women's magazines about health, wellness, and mental health. She had trained as a psychiatric nurse but gave it up to focus on writing. She was married to a man who worked in Warrington Council in the planning department

– Tony – and they had bought a house in Padgate, which they had done up. She said something she had written appeared almost every week in one or other of the magazines aimed at women – New Woman, Bella, Red, She and Prima were her "go to" places for her articles. Her most recent looked at how to manage stress. "It doesn't pay as much as nursing," she said, "but it is much more satisfying. I write an article each day during the week and three of the five get published somewhere, which is not bad. Keeps us in wine and beer!"

Janet arrived just as they finished the Caprese salad. "Sorry I'm late, train delays just outside Berwick-on-Tweed. But here I am – starving!" They had saved her a portion of the salad and delayed serving the pork chops until she had finished. As she ate, they each introduced themselves again to her. "Well, so nice to meet each of you and no doubt we'll get to know each other better over the next few days. I'm Janet from Vancouver in British Columbia and my day job is in sports administration. I am part of the Canadian Olympic administration staff, looking after our athletes, coaches and support personnel both in between and during the Olympic games. That's what pays the rent and keeps me in Chardonnay. My passion, however, is writing about the people I work with. Profiles of athletes and what drives them so hard. I mean, think what it takes to be a kid growing up on a farm in Manitoba and becoming one of the best athletes in the world and winning a gold medal. Someone has to write these stories, and I decided that one of the people who would do that is me. Some of my stories have become the basis for television profiles of the athletes. The one I am working on now is a full-length book about one of the great Olympians we have right now, an amazing man called Arturo Miranda who competes in the decathlon. I am ghost-writing this, which mean his name is before mine on the book jacket, but I do all the work!"

They chatted about the upcoming Olympic games in Sydney Australia and what it was like at the last games in Atlanta. The only Canadian anyone could remember was Donovan Bailey, who won gold in the men's one hundred meters running in a world record time.

They retired from the dining room into the lounge. Joyce had brought a bottle of brandy. They found some glasses, and each had a measure of the golden fluid. Just as they began drinking, Bill Bryson walked in carrying half a dozen books.

A small man with a beard with a glowing, smiling face, he greeted everyone with a handshake and gave each a copy of the book he was carrying – The Penguin Guide to Troublesome Words which he had written. He joked that it was a list of words "not to use improperly over the next few days!"

He apologized for not joining them for dinner. "My wife, Cynthia, and I visited our old house in Kirby Malham and the current owners cooked us a wonderful shepherd's pie, wonderfully rich gravy, and fresh peas. My favourite. We moved back to the US a couple of years ago, but I simply loved the house here and had to see it. It's just thirty-five miles away. But I am here with you now and here I am staying. Delighted to see that one of you brought brandy – I'll have a small snifter!"

He settled in a comfy leather chair, and they all introduced themselves. They had each sent some writing along with their application and Bryson had read them all. When Audrey introduced herself, Bryson said, "ah, the Emily Carr lady! Loved your piece – lots of insights and ideas but somehow alluring. Made me want to go see the paintings. Lovely!" Audrey smiled, relieved and grateful. A real endorsement.

Bryson explained what he wanted them to do. "Start a piece of writing you really want to write – don't try to fix up something you are part way through. Start anew. I want to help you think about the process of writing beginning to end," he said.

They chatted for around forty minutes and then, gradually, they each drifted off to bed and sleep. Audrey was asleep within minutes of her head hitting the pillow.

## June 15th

Over a classic English breakfast buffet meal, Bill Bryson explained a few things he did when crafting a new piece. First, he worked out what he called, "the through-line" – the core narrative he wanted the reader to take away. For example, the idea that the French are dependent upon tourism but hate being dependent on tourism, and this shows in their behaviour towards tourists is a through-line in his writing about journeys in France. He observed that, "though some French citizens are wonderful, the majority have never forgiven the British for the Battle of Agincourt – and that was in 1415!"

The second idea he wanted to share from his own work as a writer was "storyboarding" – identifying the building blocks of the story, article or piece and then working out the best sequence for these blocks to appear. He showed them a picture of a wall of medium-sized Post-It Notes, each of which had 3-4 bullets conveying the idea of that "block" and how they were sequenced. It was the storyboard of a book he was working on about his travels in Australia. The book's chapters and sub sections were all laid out. "All I have to do is write the damned thing!", he quipped.

The final technique he wanted to share was called "blocking" and comes from work on the stage and the way playwrights and theatre directors work. It refers to the positioning and movement of characters within a scene. In the context of storytelling and writing, blocking involves the physical actions, gestures, and spatial relationships between characters as they interact with each other and the environment. Blocking plays a crucial role in visualizing a scene and conveying the story effectively. It helps establish the dynamics between characters, their physical proximity, and their relative positions in relation to objects, things or the location. By manipulating blocking, writers can create various effects and enhance the reader's understanding of the scene. He shared a few examples from his book, A Walk in the Woods, about his travels in the United States and some of the people he met, especially on the Appalachian Trail.

They chatted for about forty-five minutes and then they each went off to write. Bill said he'd be in the tutor room if anyone needed him. "Knock first, please" he said, "so I can make sure I am awake!"

Audrey found a quiet space and began work on her Mahler piece. She liked the storyboarding idea and began using some paper she'd torn into squares to lay out what the article might look like.

She would begin with some of the unkind things people have said about Mahler's music. For example, the great Conductor, Sir Thomas Beecham, said that "Mahler's music is the only time I ever hear someone knitting audibly". The American composer, conductor and educator, Leonard Bernstein said, cuttingly, "a Mahler symphony is like a universe. It is never finished; it just stops in interesting places." Her all-time favourite quip came from the New Yorker. Their music critic had written that, "Mahler is the musical equivalent of an eyelash curler: He wants to lift you up to ecstatic heights, and he'll torture you a little in the process." She would use this and similar anecdotes to make the point that Mahler's work is like statistics, many people avoid it or think they will dislike it or that it will be too difficult. They, therefore, don't "do the work" needed to make the most of the opportunity the music affords. This would not be easy to write. Somehow, she had to start here but hook the reader into the idea that appreciating Mahler was both possible and desirable.

She also wanted to write something about "being in the right place" emotionally to hear Mahler. Listeners who have never felt anguish, pain, hurt, rejection, or numbness will miss some of the layers of meaning Mahler offers, especially in the symphonies. That would be a difficult idea to convey.

By lunchtime she had five hundred and forty-two words, each painfully written, rewritten and re-sequenced. She felt she was getting there, but it needed more time. She also needed a break. She had been concentrating and writing for four hours.

Lunch was a quiche with salad and a fruit cup with a nice cup of Yorkshire Tea, which she truly appreciated. Joyce said it was too weak for her – she usually had "builders tea", which meant two tea bags rather than one. "You need to be able to stand a spoon up in the mug," she said. Audrey thought this sounded dreadful.

Janet was pleased with her morning writing, Linda not so. Linda said that she found it difficult to "write on demand". Bill Bryson pointed out that writing is a job, just like any other. "You wouldn't expect Andy here to paint and decorate only when he felt inspired!".

After lunch, Bill had them read four short stories from different writers each seemingly about very different things. One was from Alice Munro (Dear Life), another from William Trevor (Widows), J.B. Priestley (One Thing Leads to Another) and the last from Anton Chekov (A Doctors Visit). They discussed not the stories as such – they were all so different – but how they were written. Bill had them focus on the tightness and directness of the writing, how the through-lines were maintained from beginning to end and what phrases or sentences captured the spirit of the story. Audrey found this very interesting. Inspiring even.

They returned to their own writing spaces and Audrey managed another seven hundred words, bringing her total to just over one thousand two hundred. A lot for her. She was pleased, until she remembered the read it and throw away between a quarter and third "rule: suggested by Ian McEwan.

Before dinner, they each read what they had written and Bill Bryson took notes, listening intently, but saying nothing. They each tried to find nice things to say about the work others had done, but they all knew that Janet's writing was a mess. Disconnected, poor structures, incomplete ideas. Audrey did not know where to start trying to help her improve. Janet, however, seemed oblivious to the fact that it did not go well. Blissful ignorance (or willful ignorance?), Audrey thought.

They worked together to make dinner – a mushroom risotto with shrimp followed by an apple tart and custard, both of which were pre-prepared. This was accompanied by a very fine Chardonnay from Canada, which Janet had brought.

After dinner, Bill gave feedback on the writing each of them had done. He was full of praise for Joyce, who had written about attending funerals. It was well written and funny, which Bill clearly appreciated. About Andy's writing, which was about walking into other people's houses as a painter and decorator and being amazed at how some people lived, Bill made five suggestions for how it could be improved. Linda's writing about preparing an Indian meal for the first time, which was both amusing and creative, received fine praise and just a few suggestions for improvement. Audrey's piece about finding Mahler was, Bill said, "clearly a work in progress, but a very strong throughline and needed a better, clear storyline – "early stages, but very promising," he said. When it came to

Janet, he tried to be kind but also direct. "I think you and I should talk one on one, but I want to say that there are gems in here, but we are going to have to help you find them!". Diplomatic.

After dinner, they took a walk along one of the footpaths on the grounds to the top of a hill and looked out over the valley and dale. It looked simply enticing.

Alone in her room after, what for Audrey, was a demanding day of writing, thinking, listening, and working with others, she was surprised to find herself not only happy, but content. No restlessness., self-doubt, anxiety, or concerns. Just a keen desire to continue to write. Not trying to avoid people but wanting to better understand them.

## June 17th

The last full day of their writing retreat. They were now writing their final versions of the pieces they had started writing on their first full day. Despite tears, Janet had pulled through and won praise from all, including Bill, for "finding not just her voice, but a writing process that was delivering a strong, thought-through text." Joyce was seen as the star. Her piece about funerals was now just wonderful – poignant, moving and yet very funny. Bill loved it. Andy's piece was now a short story – five and half thousand words. It read well, "but still needed an edit and some more texture for one or two characters," according to Bill. Linda's cooking story was now sharper, funnier and worth reading. "Will find a home in one of the eight hundred thousand cooking magazines that seem to be available," said Bill.

When it came to Audrey's Mahler piece, Bill was full of praise. "I think what I see here is two parallel stories. The first is how you moved from avoiding Mahler to embracing his music, even loving it. The second is how this process mirrors something that happened inside you – how you shifted from avoiding who you really are to embracing your true-self. Would that be right, Audrey?" Bill asked. She felt embarrassed. Maybe she blushed. She was not sure. It felt right.

They spent the rest of their time finishing their pieces. Then they each read a short story called The Beggar about a very wealthy man who must confront his values, beliefs and prejudices when he meets a beggar on the street. Another example of tight, engaging writing with a strong through-line and excellent character portrayal. Bill asked what they would change. Only Janet suggested adding another character – a female – to provide a "different angle".

Over dinner – steak and potato pie with green beans and mashed potatoes followed by poached pears with ice-cream – Bill asked what they had each learned.

Audrey said that she had realized that whatever she wrote – whether it was about Mahler, Emily Carr or even the Vatican – was also about her. Who she was, what she valued, how she thought, what triggered anger, anxiety, concern, humour. She had not seen this in her Emily Carr piece until Bill had pointed it out. She felt this was a big revelation.

"As an accountant, we did the work and signed it off. If anyone looked back at it two or three years later all they would see is that some anonymous but thorough and competent accountant signed off on the accounts. But when I write, people see both the story and the writer. That is very different."

"Right," said Bill, "which is why it is called the "writer's voice". As soon as you start to read James Joyce or Salman Rushdie or Ian McEwan or (hopefully), Bill Bryson you know that voice and that person - the writer. Indeed, we often look forward to new pieces from authors we like so as to ""hear" that voice.

## June 23rd

The Mahler piece was finished. She sent it to The Gramophone. A long shot – they had a strong stable of contributors and rarely took unsolicited constitutions. She started work on a new article, this time about Sand, Art and Music describing her trip to Dubai.

## August 8th

One of the delights of London in the summer is the Royal Academy Summer Exhibition. A display of art, sculpture, and installations from amateur and professional artists from around Britain and some from other parts of the world. She had attended over twenty of these exhibitions, each with a unique feel since each was curated by a different group of artists with different tastes and views from their predecessors. The two-hundred and thirty-first 1999 exhibition seemed so different from many others since it specifically featured two artists with "exhibitions within an exhibition" – works by the painter David Hockney and three sculptures from Tony Cragg. The sixty-six Hockney paintings and Polaroid images included six of the Grand Canyon, which to her eyes, were simply magnificent. Large, compelling canvases with very vibrant images of the vast space, especially Hockney's A Bigger Grand Canyon – lots of vibrant reds and an oasis garden of green and subtle yellows. Some said these were "garish," but Audrey found them enticing and alluring.

There was also a wonderful exhibition of how artists use optics and the camera Lucinda to create images on canvas using a small prism lens. She was fascinated. To make the point more powerful, there were several mirrors in the galleries, which provided a different perspective for some of the works.

Hundreds of paintings in several galleries – close to a thousand. She liked the images of Chalk Farm by Peter Howson, a collection of etchings in the Large Weston Room and a wonderful image of a Waterfall in Cumbria by Jason Hicklin, which she bought a framed print of for £235. A bargain.

Exhausted, she retreated to the Royal Overseas League and sat in their garden dining area in Park Place adjacent to Green Park for a glass of chardonnay and a crab and shrimp sandwich, which was delicious.

## August 11<sup>th</sup>

A note of acceptance of her article from The Gramophone, which came as a nice surprise. The editor asked if she would like to write an article about composers who were deeply influenced by Mahler, such as Schoenberg, Berg, Shostakovich, and Benjamin Britten. She would have to think about it. She knew little of Alan Berg and only knew some early Schoenberg - Five Orchestral Pieces. She would have lots of listening to do. But it was an interesting challenge. She would think about it but took note of the implied compliment: she was seen as a writer.

She went out to lunch at Noor Jahan on the Old Brompton Road. This Indian restaurant had opened here in the late 1960s and served very interesting food. She had the duck masala with a side of chana masala, some pulao rice and a paratha and a mango lassis. She ate the meal, which was delicious, chatted to the staff and ordered another lassis.

She took out her notebook and the New York pen and made some notes relating to her Dubai article. Then she added:

> So, who am I now? I no longer feel like an accountant, pouring over ledgers, spreadsheets, numbers, tax laws. My thoughts now seem to revolve around phrases, paragraphs, storylines, and through-lines. I think of characters, people, places as potential material. I think I am a writer, even though it's very new to me. Two pieces in respectable places – The Paris Review and The Gramophone – with a potential for more.

She finished her second Lassi and took a taxi to HMV on Oxford Street and bought several recordings of Berg and Schoenberg and then took a taxi home. A napette, followed by a simple salad for supper and then an evening of listening and note-taking.

## September 9<sup>th</sup>

There was a lot of fuss about the coming millennium. The government had spent a lot of money on various projects to celebrate the turn of the century. These included some spectacular domes in Cornwall for a garden called the Eden Project, funding for the National Botanic Garden of Wales and an art gallery in Salford to celebrate the work of L.S. Lowry. Then there was the big dome in London, which everyone complained about.

What was of more pressing concern was the growing fear that computers all over the world would crash, since they were not designed to cope with a date change from the 1900s to the 2000s. Something to do with date adjustments not been programmed in appropriately. Some suggested that aircraft could fall out of the sky or that many systems, like banking and health systems, could simply stop working. Others were convinced that thousands of satellites might drop back to earth like some majestic meteor shower. As she read these stories and saw the amount being spent by companies to "avoid catastrophe" – literally millions of pounds – she suspected that the hype and the potential for big revenues were connected. She was not a betting woman – she had never placed a bet on anything, not even the Grand National – she would bet that all would be fine on January 1<sup>st</sup>, 2000, and that those who had spent millions would be a little red faced.

She read in The Daily Telegraph that Gordon Brown had given a major speech on money laundering at a meeting of EU finance Ministers, who had agreed in principle to revise the money laundering directive and shift from a responsive model to an anticipatory one, based on risk assessment: exactly what she pushed for, and which Sir John had subsequently championed. She felt some satisfaction. A sense of closure.

Since August she had not only finished her article on her Dubai visit, she had shared it with Bill Bryson who liked it, but suggested three specific changes. She made them and sent it to the Paris Review.

She had also finished two more. The article on Mahler's Men looking at the way several composers owed something to Gustav Mahler. To the list provided by The Gramophone, she added Bernstein and Jean Sibelius. Her key observation was that Mahler provided each of them with a model of expressive power, instrumental color, vocal writing, structural complexity, and the blending of Romantic and modern elements. It was long, over two thousand three hundred words, so she suspected that the magazine would want a severe edit.

The other article, which was intended for the Catholic Herald, looked at The Coming Challenges for the Catholic Church. She outlined the sex abuse scandals growing across the US, Canada, and Europe; the challenges with the priesthood and homosexuality; concerns about some organizations like the Legion and the Knights of Malta; and the ongoing problems with the Vatican bank. She did not reveal some of her sources but was very blunt. Her conclusion was that the successor to John Paul II, whoever it was and whenever their papacy began, would be climbing a mountain of challenges. John Paul seemed unable to deal with the issues yet soldiered on as Vicar of Christ and Bishop of Rome.

She had worked very hard on this article but found doing so liberating. It was as if writing this was cleansing for her – lifting some kind of burden she had been carrying, though quite why she had the burden or where it had come from, she was unsure.

She had sent it to Sir John to make sure he signed it off in terms of the Official Secrets Act.

## September 16<sup>th</sup>

Sir John confirmed both that the article about the Catholic church was fine and that he thought they should have lunch at Wilton's soon. She telephoned him in the Cotswold's, and they had made their arrangements. Today was the day.

Wilton's at 11:30 was unusually quiet. She arrived early, was seated, sipping some sparkling water, and looking over the menu. She wore a Liberty print dress, matching green heels and some gold earrings, necklace, and bracelets. She was feeling buoyant, even a little excited at seeing John again. It had been months and so much had happened.

As she looked over the menu, she decided to have the Dover Sole Meuniere with a crisp white wine followed by a Pear Tart Titin and a glass of port. She sat back, relaxed and looked around the room.

She was surprised to see Terry Wogan and Michael Parkinson, two legendary broadcasters, lunching together. They were clearly enjoying each other's company, laughing and smiling. They had, she understood, both hosted TV talk shows and must have some good green room stories to share.

Across from her was another well-known literary figure, Doris Lessing. Audrey had read The Golden Notebook, The Diary of a Good Neighbour and The Good Terrorist – all of which she had borrowed from the public library. She thought her simply a wonderful writer - incisive, introspective, and thought-provoking, exploring complex themes with depth, insight, and a keen eye for social observation. Her work was powerful and resonated with her. Lessing was alone, reading The New Statesman and picking at her food.

Sir John arrived, looking dapper in a white jacket and matching trousers, blue shirt with gold cufflinks, red tie, and red pocket handkerchief. He also looked tanned, as if he'd been working on it to look younger. He had also changed his spectacles. No longer tortoise shell and oval, these were gold rimmed and round. He looked spritely and several years younger.

> "Audrey, so good to see you – looking well and alluring, I see," he said.

> "Why thank you. You're looking well yourself. New glasses?"

> "Yes, thought that now I am a free man I should indulge in some new clothes, glasses, and a new watch. My grandfather loved watches. When he died my father found forty-five watches neatly packaged in a drawer, all of them valuable. We kept half a dozen and sold the rest. As a young boy

I became very fascinated by watches. This one is a Breitling Chrono Avenger. A watch I have always loved and admired, but my ex always suggested it was an extravagance and a symbol of vanity. Now she is gone from my life – she did marry the Duke – I bought it as a symbol of my independence. Take a look."

He took off the watch and passed it to her to look at. It was surprisingly heavy. The watch face was yellow, and the hands were largely white with black at the centre. Three small dials and a date. It was, she had to admit, gorgeous. It also looked expensive.

"Picked it up in Portobello Road market. Second hand, but it is in very good condition. I think of it as a symbol of my new life as a man of leisure, well almost."

"You have finally left the Cabinet Office then?" asked Audrey.

"Almost. Doing some part-time consulting on the draft money laundering regulations the EU are considering. By the way, you will be interested to know that our Italian friends have arrested the Giuseppe Valin. Apparently Valin tried to move around four million Euros through several subsidiary companies to a company in Panama, but the Panama company was a shell created by the Italian authorities to mimic one of Valin's. I don't know all the fine and gory details, but it looks like a strong case. He has been forced to step down from his position at the bank, at least for now. His wife is

226

indicating that she knew nothing about it, she was in Paris shopping at the time."

"How are the Cotswold's?" asked Audrey, keen to change the subject. She felt that the money laundering and accounting were the "old" Audrey Hutchins. The one she was trying to move beyond. "I don't know why I didn't move there years ago. I love the peace and quiet, the walks, the local pub where I am now thought of as a regular – they do a wonderful fish pie with minted peas – and I can focus on my poetry journal, which is doing very well, now that I can devote time to it. I am getting thirty to forty submissions a month. Its quarterly, so I can select some quality material. The books – five a year if I can find the right poets – are also ticking over nicely. We sponsor an annual poetry competition – the South Downes Poetry Competition it is called. They get close to three hundred and fifty entries a year. Some are simply dreadful - doggerel and dustbin material - but there are always real gems and really good writing. I don't judge, just sponsor some prizes. This year the judge is Wendy Cope, a wonderful and very successful poet. I should send you one of her collections. Serious Concerns is my favourite."

"That would be very kind, John. I will look forward to reading it. I have become a bit of a writer myself, as you saw in the piece about the Vatican and the Church, which the Catholic Herald has now agreed to publish. I even went on a writing retreat with Bill Bryson in Yorkshire, she said with a smile."

She chatted about writing as the new focus for her life – a way of connecting her interests, passion, and skills. She told him that she found writing as a way of connecting her inner self to the outside world, which she had found liberating.

John reminded her of his invitation to come to both a rehearsal and performances of the Messiah he was organizing and conducting and to stay with him, if she felt that was appropriate. She agreed to come down in December for a rehearsal and a full performance the next day. She would also stay at his house.

After another half hour of conversation, focused mainly on the challenges of living a single life – shopping and cooking for one when all the cookbooks assumed meals for four, food waste, current political tensions and some issue about travel becoming much more complicated – they parted. He gave her a peck on her left cheek, saying it was so good to see her and to see her looking "so well and refreshed," which she took as a compliment.

## September 20th

Leipzig is home to the Mahler Festival each May but hosts concerts throughout the year at the Gewandhaus, home of the Leipzig Gewandhaus Orchestra. Its principal conductor is the American born Swede Herbert Blomstedt - apparently a demanding but wonderful conductor Audrey had seen him several times at the Festival Hall. She had heard musicians talk about his preciseness, sensitivity, and eloquence. He lets the music speak for itself but encourages the musicians to follow the score and the tempo marked in the score. "We're not here to improvise and play jazz, ladies and gentlemen, we're here to make the composers music come to life", he had once told the London Philharmonic in rehearsal who seemed to have "gone astray" while playing Bruckner's Fourth Symphony. He did have a sense of humour. She remembered a piece about conducting she had read in The Guardian. Blomstedt had told the violas in the San Francisco Symphony, "look, I'll pretend to conduct and you can pretend to follow," which caused much laughter but led to better playing.

Audrey had flown into Berlin and then down to Leipzig for a performance of Mahler's Second Symphony arranged by Bruno Walter for two pianos. She was intrigued. She also had tickets for a second concert with the full orchestra playing Sibelius 5th Symphony and a new work for her – a Clarinet Concerto by the Finnish composer Magnus Lindberg. She had heard Lindberg's second Piano Concerto at the Festival Hall played by the gifted Australian Piers Lane with the London Philharmonic and liked it. Very modern, all sorts of different rhythms, tones, and textures, but a rich piece of music. She had purchased a recording of the piano concerto and listened to it occasionally, especially when she was tired of the standard piano concerto repertoire. She was looking forward to both concerts.

She was staying at Hotel Fürstenhof, an elegant old hotel adjacent to the old town. Her room had a small balcony overlooking the square and was furnished with wonderful art deco furniture. The bathroom was very large and had both a huge bath and a shower. The dining room was one of the most elegant and inviting she had ever seen.

After a light lunch – a salad with a selection of charcuterie – she walked to the Bach Museum. Housed in the former home of the wealthy merchant Bose family, who were close friends with the Bach family who had lived across the street at St. Thomas Church, it contains all sorts of artifacts, musical instruments, manuscripts, and memorabilia connected to Bach. Bach was cantor at St. Thomas's Church in Leipzig for twenty-seven years, and he composed many of his great works in this city. Audrey saw a cabinet in which Bach stored manuscripts, fragments of his St. Matthew Passion original manuscripts, a violin and viola used in the orchestra Bach directed and many other items of interest. She found it all fascinating.

Following a napette, she took a light evening meal and walked to the concert. Settled into her seat in the centre stalls, she was ready to be intrigued. How could a demanding orchestral symphony be performed on two pianos? She soon had her answer. It was a remarkable piece of work. Bruno Walter had done a magnificent job transcribing the music and the two pianists, Maasa Nakazawa and Suhrud Athawale, did the music justice. It was very powerful and moving. She would love to listen to this again, but apparently there were no current recordings. The performers secured a six- minute standing ovation which the young man next to her told her was very unusual.

Back at the hotel she needed a drink to calm her down after the energy the concert created. She ordered a negroni and sat alone at a table by a window. From her handbag, she took her notebook and Dubai pen and made some short notes.

1.  What other transcriptions of symphonies exist? Liszt Beethoven and Wagner. Busoni does Bach. Stokowski and his transcription of Mussorgsky's Pictures at an Exhibition. What others?
2.  What are the challenges of transcribing something as complex as a Mahler symphony? Who to ask?
3.  When transcribing something as "big" as a symphony, what does the transcriber do to ensure the core messages of the music are intact? Do they have to be critic, interpreter, spiritual medium? How is authenticity enabled?
4.  What do performers have to <u>unlearn</u> when performing such a major work?
5.  Given the intimacy of the performance of Mahler #2, what are the secrets of securing the audience's approval? After all, they are used to hearing #2 in a very different way and with a very different sound!

She had a feeling that another article was emerging. If it did, she could write off this trip as a "research cost" – she was sure a great deal had been written about this challenge, so a trip to the British Library would be helpful.

## September 22nd

She read the program notes very carefully. She wanted to know more about Magnus Lindberg and his music before the orchestra began playing his Concerto for Clarinet. The Sibelius was, as always, glorious – a rich, endearing tapestry of sounds that invoke a sense of majesty and pride. Soaring melodies, subtle tonal language and rich evocations leave a lasting impression. The orchestra was in top form.

The program notes said that, while Lindberg had sanctioned this performance, but still felt that the concerto needed more work and intended to offer a revised score at some point in the future. Lindberg had been writing and performing since he was a teenager – his first long piece was performed when he was just sixteen. His most recent composition before this concerto was called Fresco. Commissioned by the Los Angeles Philharmonic, the twenty-two-minute piece "involves immensely powerful structures which are sustained like a massive bridge, with occasional moments of crisis, allowing the tension (but never the interest) to dip before once more building to a climax" according to her program notes.

He seemed very prolific and enterprising, having formed his own musical organization called Toimii (apparently meaning "it works" in Finnish). For this group of musicians, Lindberg had written a major work called Kraft, which also required a full orchestra. It had received strong endorsements from many, though some critics remained skeptical (including Arnold Whittall of the Gramophone) she recalled.

As it turned out, the Clarinet Concerto even in this "draft" performance, was magical. The clarinet soared, sang, engaged and was a breath of fresh air, leading the orchestra on a magical journey. The soloist – Sharon Kam – was outstanding. Very expressive and played a complex score with ease, grace, and imagination. She was highly engaged with the orchestra.

Audrey was engrossed in this music. It seemed to capture so much in such a short time, just twenty-four minutes.

She heard so many themes and rhythms that touched her, as if the music was speaking to her in some way. It was as if Lindberg had written a concerto that captured much of her life journey. Intense, with lots of tension between the clarinet and the brass section, some discordant notes, but transcendental. Shaken a little by these thoughts, she returned to the hotel just a short walk away.

## September 24th

On her return from Germany, she had received an invitation to meet with the editor of the BBC Music Magazine, Oliver Condy. He wanted to talk to her about writing a few columns for the coming edition of the magazine. Founded in 1992, it focused on classical music and was, in many ways, a competitor to The Gramophone. She had agreed to meet him at the magazine's offices for coffee and a chat at ten-thirty at their offices in Bristol.

The 8:13 London Paddington to Bristol train would get her to Bristol in good time to get from the station to the magazine's offices. She arrived early, bought her ticket and a coffee from the Costa coffee shop located beside the platform, and boarded the train and sat in her assigned first-class seat facing the direction of travel. The train was a new one – comfy seats with lots of leg room and a small table. She had a single seat and a small window. Her journey would take about an hour and twenty-five minutes. She settled down, took out her notebook and Dubai pen and began to make notes.

What would I like to write about?
- Reviews of new releases? Concerts?
- Profiles of composers and their music?

- Transcription idea?
- The work of conducting – maybe profiles?
- Music and humour? The quips and quotes from musicians about each other and the music they have to play?

What don't I want to write about?
- Opera, ballet, jazz.
- Concert halls
- Hi-Fi systems, speakers, equipment and devices.

She decided to be open minded about the conversation. After all, it was not a job interview, just a discussion between an editor and a freelancer. That is what she was now: a freelance writer.

Condy was welcoming, as they sat with some of the nicest coffee she had tasted in a while. He told her it was made from a blend of roasted coffee beans which were mixed following a precise recipe from the writer Honoré Balzac. He had arranged for a local coffee roaster to supply them. Very deep, rich with a hint of a caramel flavour. She loved it.

He chatted about what he wanted to bring to the magazine – new writers, new perspectives, and some different material. He had read her piece about Mahler in The Gramophone and really liked it. "A kind of cross between music appreciation, psychology and sociology" – just the kind of thing I am looking for.

He asked what commitments she had to The Gramophone. She told him that she was just beginning her writing career, having spent the last several years as a senior accountant. Having left that profession behind, she had been writing about her experiences of travel, art, food, and music. The Gramophone had kindly taken two of her pieces – Finding Mahler and Mahler's Men – but she had no contract, no commitments, no sense of loyalty. She wanted to write and find homes for what she had written.

She told him about the two pieces she had written for The Paris Review, the new one about her Dubai experience would appear in December and she had another piece she had written about fountain pens for Stylus Magazine, shyly admitting to a slight but growing addiction to collecting them.

They talked about some potential contributions. He liked the idea of an article looking at the strange things conductors say and do and the idea of an article about symphonic transcriptions, like the Bruno Walter's Mahler transcription. He suggested she write something about the way music is used to comfort, console and calm or to excite, enliven and engage.

They talked payment. He said that, on average, they paid freelances sixty-five pence per word or around one thousand pounds for a fifteen-hundred-word article. They shook hands, with her agreeing to treat the BBC Music Magazine as having right of first refusal on material she wrote which focused on music. He asked her to write the fun piece about the conductors as start. "Let's call it a 'look-see' so we can find out how to work together," he said.

She was on the noon train home and back in her apartment just after two fifteen.

She was excited. After all, she had just begun to see writing as her new "career" and here she was chatting with an editor who had asked her to write because he had read an article she had written in a rival magazine. She poured a small glass of sherry and started listening to a recording of Vaughan Williams Sea Symphony.

## October 3rd

She had found researching the article on conductors a great deal of fun. When you think about it, it is an odd job. The hard work occurs in rehearsals. Conductors work with orchestras to ensure that they perform the works on the program in particular ways – tempo, volume, subtle shifts of sound between different sections of the orchestra can all make a difference to a performance. Some, like Bernhard Haitink, say almost nothing, but convey messages non-verbally, especially with their eyes. Others can't stop talking about Leif Segerstam, the extra-large Finish conductor, has said remarkable things. One orchestra created a collection of things he had said during his years of conducting them. They included an instruction to "keep an irony rhythm," or "more grease in the pianissimo, "or "you won't get lost because at the end. I will turn and look at you stoppingly!" His rehearsals had much confusion, yet performances always seemed to go well.

Sir Thomas Beecham was legendary for his quips and quick wit. Once, a young opera singer said, during a rehearsal, "I can't perform well while lying down in bed." Without missing a beat, Beecham said, "Some of my very best performances have been from that position!" When asked if he had ever heard any Stockhausen, he said, "No, but I believe I have stepped in some!" Perhaps his best advice to an orchestra was his two golden rules: "Start together and finish together – the public doesn't give a damn about what goes on in between."

After spending several days in the British Library and on a search engine with her Dell computer, she had more material than she ever expected to find. Eugene Ormandy's time with the Philadelphia Orchestra alone was worth nine pages of notes. Her favourite quote of his was, "Why do you all insist on playing when I am trying to conduct?" But she had the material she needed, and the article was almost writing itself.

## October 14th

Oliver Condy called to say he loved her conductors' comments piece, and it would run in their January 2000 edition. She was delighted. He asked her to start work on the article about transcriptions. He had arranged for her to talk to Sir Roger Norrington, the conductor and advocate for baroque music to be played on authentic instruments, about transcriptions and the challenges it poses for the transcriber. He gave her contact information and suggested they meet for lunch.

She did not hesitate to contact him and found him very happy to meet with her. They arranged to meet for lunch, and he said he would bring a list of recordings she should listen to before she wrote the piece. He sounded friendly and interested in the idea of the article.

## October 23<sup>rd</sup>

He was, as she expected, on time for lunch. A small man, bald with bushy hair on each side of his head and a slight stoop, he had an elfish smile and looked to be a fun person. He suggested they dine at Launceston Place in Kensington, near her home. She had not eaten here for years, so she was pleased to do so. Lunch was a simple menu. He chose ceviche of sea bass and calamari with lovage, and she had the chicken liver parfait with grapes on a waffle, a new dish for her. He wasn't drinking "performance tonight and quick rehearsal at two-thirty," he explained.

He began to share some of his thoughts about transcription. He thought Stokowski's Bach transcriptions were simply dreadful – "a travesty in an attempt to sell popular music!" he exclaimed. He suggested some key challenges with the task of transcribing large symphonic works – conveying meaning with fewer or different instruments, losing some of the textural richness and nuances, missing the interplay between different sections of the orchestra and losing the dynamic appeal of thirty to fifty players when you reduce it to four hands, as with the Mahler second symphony transcription by Bruno Walter. He was not against such transcriptions, but suggested it was an art and a skill that few possessed.

He pointed out that some composers had transcribed their own work – for example, Dvorak and Stravinsky, and that well known composers had transcribed work they truly admired. Liszt transcribed four Beethoven symphonies, Mahler a symphony by Mozart and one by Schubert. Others, like Bruno Walter and Erwin Stein had transcribed

Mahler symphonies – the second and the fourth, both for four hands on the piano. Tchaikovsky's Fourth Symphony had been transcribed by Sergei Taneyev, composer and professor of music and a close friend and colleague of Tchaikovsky who had edited and overseen the publication of all of his works. All are reasonable, if we accept the very idea that a symphonic work can be played on two pianos.

There have been some failures. Not just Stokowski, but a very sad example exists of attempts to transcribe Mahler symphonies scored for large orchestras so that they can be played by smaller chamber ensembles. He had attended just such a performance in Dresden and had to leave. "So much pain!" he said.

After dessert and a chamomile tea, he took his leave, suggesting that she chat with Julian Anderson, who teaches composition at the Royal College of Music and a prolific composer of orchestral music, choral music, chamber music and opera. "He'll suggest some more items to add to the list."

She had truly enjoyed this encounter, though she had said little. He had treated her as a serious writer who was looking at an idea and needed his help. He had given it freely in exchange for a very tasty, if simple, lunch.

She had told him about her conductor's quips story, which he liked a lot. He shared one she wished she had used. Bramwell Tovey, the principal conductor of the Vancouver Symphony, was conducting the City of Birmingham Symphony which completely lost the plot playing a rehearsal of Bartok's Concerto for Orchestra. Tovey told them, "That sound you just made is only required in

certain pieces – none of which have been written yet!"
The resultant laughter permanently endeared him to the
orchestra. Norrington loved this story. He could relate to
it.

He was between performances. His main work was now in
Stuttgart with the Southwest German Radio Symphony
Orchestra, but this week he was conducting performances
of Haydn and Rebel with the English Chamber Orchestra
and spending some quiet time in "the money pit" – his
manor house in Berkshire.

Back in her apartment, she made detailed notes and
started to develop her storyboard using some Post-it notes
she had bought at Ryman's on the walk home. She would
start drafting tomorrow. As she did so, she would begin to
list questions she had for Professor Julian Anderson.

## November 3rd

On a whim, she had packed a bag and taken the train to
Paris, arriving at the Gare du Nord at two o'clock – just
two and a quarter hours after leaving St. Pancras. She took
a taxi to Hotel George V, her go-to Art Deco hotel on
Avenue George V in the eighth arrondissement. She was
pleasantly surprised to find that she had been upgraded to
the one-bedroom Suite Anglaise which came with a
stunning lounge, full kitchen, dining room and a private
butler. "In recognition that this is your thirtieth stay with
us madam," said the very charming man at reception.

Her butler, Hénri, made her green tea and a toasted ham
and cheese sandwich with a few greens, tomato and a
light dressing as a lunch and left her. Luxury.

She needed to have a break. Her writing was, as had been suggested, now a full-time job. Since she began writing, she had seven articles accepted, two rejected, and a direct approach to write on a regular basis for the BBC Music Magazine. The Paris Review in New York seemed to like her writing and the Catholic Herald would soon publish her explosive piece about the challenges within the Catholic Church.

She wanted to see some paintings, experience some new food, and smell the air by walking alongside the Seine. She took a bath, changed into some comfortable clothes and what her mother used to call "sensible shoes" and went for a walk.

Strolling past some shops, she found herself inside Hermès leather goods store, lured in by the fresh smell of leather and the wonderful artful display. She was drawn to a collection of items called Lizard, made from the hides of African water monitors. Working with Monique, the very elegant young assistant, she bought a leather notebook cover, a pen case for two pens, and a shoulder bag in which these items would all fit. All were in the stunning green-gold lizard leather. Monique explained that this required care, a gentle application of a leather conditioner every seven or eight months. "If you take it to any Hermès store, they will do this work for you at no charge."

This was the second Hermès bag she had bought. When she first came to Paris some twenty years ago, she had bought a small clutch bag from this same store.

Pleased with her purchase, she walked down the street to Le Bistro Marbeuf, one of the oldest restaurants to continually serve food since the 1920s. She ordered an Auvergne salad and andouillette's in mustard sauce with fries. It had been some time since she had eaten this salad - potatoes, ham, cantal cheese, mixed greens, shallots, chives, and a zippy vinaigrette dressing – it is what she fell in love with the first time her parents had brought her to Paris. She had asked for the small plate, but even so there was a lot. She ate most and asked for the remainder to be packed so she could take it back to her hotel.

Andouillette's are an acquired taste. They smell, largely because some of the meat inside the casing is from the tripe of the pig as well as other offal. They are similar in many ways to Welsh faggots. She had always loved their richness with the unctuous mustard sauce they were usually served with. She chose a robust Burgundy, in this case the Marchand Tawse Pinot Noir 1994. Rich, yet silky on the tongue and full-bodied. Just the right pairing with the rich, tasty sausage and chips.

On her way back to the hotel, she stopped in the Palais du Stylo, one of five shops in Paris that specializes in stationery and fine fountain pens. She bought three new notebooks made from paper made in Étival-Clairefontaine in Nancy in the Meurthe Valley bound in light brown tanned leather. She also bought a Visconti Rembrandt fountain pen in emerald green and silver – just the right weight in the hand and a wonderfully free writing flow.

Exhausted from her rich lunch, two glasses of wine and expensive purchases – her day had already cost her £2,500 – she returned to her hotel, changed into her nightwear, sat in a comfy chair, and began reading the novel she had brought with her. She had chosen to bring Tracy

Chevalier's novel, The Girl with the Pearl Earring, inspired by the painting she had seen in the Frick collection. Such artful writing, tense emotions shared in economical prose.

After an hour of reading, she went to bed which the butler had kindly turned down, placing a pitcher of iced water and a tall glass beside her bed.

In her dream she imagined herself on a small boat drifting on a very blue lagoon, her left hand trailing in the water. Music was playing – it sounded like Mozart – and she was happy. On the boat bench was a book, a gin and tonic and a pen and paper. It was lovely and warm with a cool breeze.

## November 4th

A concert later today – the Mozart Concertante featuring a solo violin and solo viola. One of her favourites.

She spent the morning in her room making notes on an idea she had woken with. A piece about food that some thought wonderful, but others could not stomach. The andouillette was a good example, but there were others – tripe, calf's liver, hákarl, marmite, natto, haggis, century eggs and escargot, for example. She had eaten all of these except the fermented fish hákarl, seen as a delicacy by some in Iceland. She had no objection to any of them and would be willing to try hákarl if she could find some. She was a willing food adventurer, though she did like to eat excellently prepared food, whatever it was.

Some people did not like cilantro – they found it so bitter and distasteful. Others could not stand black licorice. She wondered about different levels of taste sensitivities and the different taste thresholds people have. She had read that some people were "super-tasters," very sensitive to subtle tastes and flavours, especially bitterness, that most people did not taste at all. She also remembered from this same article – in the Daily Telegraph a few years ago – that there were "hyper-tasters" who were also sensitive to flavours and tastes but in different ways from supertasters. She would have to investigate.

She also had the sense that food allergies were on the rise. Growing up, she did not know anyone who had a food allergy. Now it seemed half the population had one. She wondered why? She had read that it was about the spread of mass-manufactured food and the use of chemical additives. Others think that the growth in people reporting food allergies is connected to environmental changes impacting immune systems. Another line of investigation.

She remembered the fuss over former President François Mitterrand's final meal. Dying of cancer, he insisted on dining with a few close friends and eating a small, rare bird. – an Ortolan. This songbird was historically captured, force fed, and drowned in Armagnac before being roasted. It is traditionally eaten whole, with the diner covering their head with a napkin to capture the aromas and to hide the act from view. Eating this was illegal when Mitterrand did it, but he died the next day, so he could not be prosecuted. He had been President of France, after all. She added social conventions to her reasons people disliked certain foods. She noted that it was now fashionable to dislike foie gras and fur coats.
She made a list of questions to explore and people she needed to talk to. When she looked at her watch, it was

eleven fifteen. Time for a bath, lunch, and the afternoon concert.

The concert was to be at Salle Gaveau on the Rue La Boétie, not far from the hotel. The soloists were two young players, both French – Renaud Capuçon and the viola player Antoine Tamestit. Both were young – very early twenties – but both had been performing solo since they were teenagers. The Age of Enlightenment chamber orchestra was playing both the Mozart Concertante and the rarely performed Les Nations by Francis Couperin. The conductor was Philippe Herrewegh, who founded the orchestra in Paris almost a decade ago.

She had read about Les Nations. Couperin wrote to convey the music of different nations and styles – France, Spain, the Holy Roman Empire and what was then known as Savoy – parts of France and Italy, including Turin, Annecy, Aosta, Geneva and Chambery. A rich, evocative piece intended to showcase his mastery of different styles – a kind of portfolio from which he hoped to secure commissions. She had two recordings of this, her favourite being Jordi Savall's with the English Consort.

She arrived about twenty minutes before the performance was due to start and sat in the middle of the audience, well able to see the entire orchestra. The program notes in French were very detailed, and her French was just good enough to make sense of most of them. She was especially keen to know more about the soloists, who would perform after a short interval.

Renaud Capuçon had won the Menuhin Prize when he was just sixteen – he was now just twenty-three. He had played with orchestras all over the world. His performances of the Ravel, Saint-Seáns, Bartok and Tchaikovsky concertos had won special praise, though his repertoire was much broader. Antoine Tamestit was just twenty but already a highly regarded viola player. He had already played with the Vienna, New York and London philharmonic orchestras, and his next performance was Berlioz's Harold in Italy with the Frankfurt Radio Symphony Orchestra. The two young men promised an exciting afternoon.

The Couperin was excellent. Lots of shifts in the musical dynamics, textures, and tones. The orchestra did not play the full score – it would take close to two hours – they played just the French and Savoy sections. After a fifteen-minute interval, the orchestra began the Mozart. From the moment of the first solo note played on the violin, Audrey knew she was listening to a truly outstanding performance. In the second movement there is a succession of descending intervals, then the viola goes up to a minor second, then there's a development so full of hope and tenderness that is truly heart-wrenching. She was almost moved to tears.

Such a wonderful, moving, and memorable performance. It made her trip to Paris so worthwhile.

Her butler had, as she had requested, laid out a salad niçoise for her evening meal and a bottle of Chablis was chilling in an ice bucket. She kicked off her shoes, sat and devoured the food. The music had made her hungry.

The butler had left the radio on, tuned to Radio Classique. An early Beethoven string quartet was playing. Wonderful sounds. She took out her notebook, now enclosed in her Hermès cover, and wrote some reflections on her day. Her key message to herself was simple: "live the life you enjoy and that brings you satisfaction, not the life others want you to lead!"

## November 10th

Back in London, she had finished her food article and it was to appear in The Sunday Times Magazine, with photographs showing each dish. She was thrilled. A real milestone on her journey as a writer.

She had started on a new idea exploring "what had happened to classical music's child prodigy performers?" She had made a list of some of those she wanted to profile – Yo-Yo Ma, Itzhak Perlman, Martha Argerich, Joshua Bell, Gabriel Montero and a dozen others. She was also tracking down information about those who began as musical prodigies but walked away, like the French pianist Hélène Grimau, who took a break from performing "to grow up!"

She loved the story of the violinist Hilary Hahn, whose debut at eleven with the Baltimore Symphony did not go well. She had difficulties remembering some passages and sequences, but the orchestra and young soloist made it through the demanding Tchaikovsky concerto. Within months she was playing with other orchestras across America and studying at the Curtis Institute for Music in Philadelphia. Now she was in high demand – one of the leading violinists in the world.

One story she wanted to dig into was that of the British violinist Nigel Kennedy. A student of Yehudi Menuhin and

247

later at the Julliard in New York, he was a prodigy who stunned the world with a very fresh and vibrant performance of Vivaldi's Four Seasons and by his unconventional appearance on stage – jeans, leather jackets, spiked hair and Dr. Martin boots and a nose ring. She had seen him play the Korngold concerto with the London Symphony Orchestra and found his appearance distracted from the music. More recently, he had started playing "fusion" – classical with jazz, classical with rock. She wondered if she could get to talk to him. There was no doubt that he was an outstanding player.

Maybe there was a book to be written with this material?

Her work was interrupted by a call from Michael Mearns, the "new" man at her old place of work. He wanted to meet for a drink after work today if that were possible. Intrigued, she had said yes.

They met in the bar of the Hotel Russell on Russell Square. A very Victorian, luxurious room with comfy seats arranged in small clusters for two or four people. When she arrived, Michael Mearns was already there. He smiled, rose and held out his hand to greet her.

> "Miss Hutchins, so nice to see you, and you do look very well I am pleased to see," he said.

> "Good to see you too, Mr. Mearns," she responded.

> "Can I get you a drink?" he asked.

The waiter arrived, and she ordered a negroni and he asked for a refill of his white wine spritzer – a Chablis mixed with sparkling water, a drink she associated with hot days and Paris, not cold and damp days in London in November.

"Thank you for coming, Miss Hutchins. We have missed you at the office which, by the way, is doing very well. We have won a significant number of new clients and have expanded the practice with a branch in Holland."

"I am pleased to hear it, Mr. Mearns. You have done well."

"Well, yes – we are growing. I hired nine new staff. But it has been a lot of work. A lot. I have decided to move on, rather like you. I am leaving the company in a month's time and moving to the United States. My sister has a thriving new company in California which is using the internet to manage supply chains. She started it two years ago and it has attracted a great deal of venture capital and investment. She wants me to be her head of finance and I have agreed. I see the internet as a game changer for all sorts of things. It will be an adventure."

"Yes, so I understand. I can see some significant possibilities and also some challenges. Game-changer it certainly is."

"I wondered if you would be interested in return to Brooke & Walters as the Managing Director. You were such a strong, focused accountant – integrity at the heart of your work, thorough, and insightful. Just what we need in the MD. You wouldn't have to worry about all the people stuff. Ian Pringle, the new human resource person, is excellent and well respected in the firm. What we need is technical and professional leadership. The company would benefit from your expertise, Miss. Hutchins."

He sat back and looked intently at her, almost as if he was pleading. She looked at him carefully. There was something about him she disliked. The arrogance with charm, sharpness with cunning, scheming with calculated precision. She couldn't put her finger on it. But she disliked him.

"Well, what an interesting proposition, Mr. Mearns. I am sure you have plenty of colleagues inside KPMG who could take on this role, yet you come to me. I am going to have to disappoint you, I am afraid. You see, since I left the company, I have done very little accounting work and focused my energies on a change of career. I am now a freelance writer and, though I say so myself, doing quite well. Of course, writing doesn't pay well, but it gives me far more satisfaction that an audit or advice on best practices in bookkeeping ever could. I can't go backwards, Mr. Mearns. I am doing what I should have been doing all along."

He looked deflated but chose not to argue or try to persuade her. He raised his glass and offered a toast "to the writer!".

They talked for a further forty minutes, he about the move to California and she about her writing. She left the Hotel Russell at five forty and took a taxi home.

One thing he had said caused her to think. He suggested that, while she had been lucky to place several pieces as an "unknown" writer so quickly, she would do well to have an agent – someone who would negotiate opportunities and promote her work. She would investigate.

## November 17th

She had found a routine that worked for her. Waking at around six thirty, showered, did her hair and teeth, and then had breakfast, usually coffee, toast, and granola with yogurt. Then to her desk no later than seven thirty. Write solidly until around one, with music playing in the background. Her word target was now two thousand words each morning.

Out for lunch, a walk, and some fresh air. Deal with mail, phone calls and other matters. Back at her desk at four. Review all she had written with a view to culling or identifying sections that needed rewriting. Finish by six.

Make supper with ingredients bought fresh that day, often fish or pasta, then read while listening to music or the radio. She had read somewhere that all good writers spend a good few hours each day reading.

Today she was scheduled to see Michelle Robinson at Peters Fraser & Dunlop, literary agents, at three o'clock. She had a portfolio of all of her accepted work and an outline of the book on musical prodigies, which she thought might also be a documentary suitable for television.

She wore a curve-skimming light brown dress with a light leather jacket from Dior that matched her Hermes bag and accessories and light brown two-inch heels. In the full-length mirror in the hallway, she felt and looked stunning.

Michelle Robinson was no spring chicken. In her late fifties, she had been an agent with PFD for two decades. The company was the agent for many well-known names – Brian Blessed, Melvyn Bragg, Lloyd Grossman, Henry Kamen, Tim Rice, Simon Schama, among them. Michelle now handled the "newcomers."

Miss. Hutchins introduced herself, explained her journey to writing and shared her portfolio of accepted pieces, including the pieces from The Sunday Times and the Catholic Herald. Michelle was impressed, especially when she discovered that these had been placed without an agent. She was also pleased by the account Miss. Hutchins provided of her meeting with the editor of the BBC Music Magazine and with the material she saw which had appeared.

> "What is it you think we can do for you? You seem to be doing very well without us," observed Michelle.

> "Yes, I have been very surprised myself. I have a book idea which could also be a documentary for television looking at the perilous journeys young prodigy musicians take and the remarkable lives they then lead as well as those who begin the

journey and then drop out to pursue some other dream," she explained and shared her outline with Michelle.

Michelle liked it a lot and could see all sorts of possibilities. A book, profile articles, and a television documentary. They talked for over an hour, ending with contracts being signed and timelines tentatively agreed. As she was leaving, Michelle said, "when did you realize you were a writer?"

She carefully thought about her answer, and then said "when I was fourteen, but I didn't begin to write until recently. I was sidetracked into a career at which I excelled but which did not satisfy me. I only came to my writing when I left that career behind me and started to do only what I wanted to do."

"Good for you, Audrey. You and I will get along just fine," said Michelle as she gave her a hug and said goodbye.

On her way home, she stopped off for a drink and light meal at Margaux, near her apartment. Mainly French with some Italian dishes, she chose the black ink tortellini with crab served with a lobster emulsion and a glass of chilled Vermentino. Settling down with her notebook and her Visconti Rembrandt pen, she made some notes:

- An author with an agent and seven published pieces all in one year.
- A soon to be book author if PFD can secure a deal.
- A former accountant – turned down the opportunity to return to the profession.

- A woman of means who travels, dines, and goes to concerts without feeling any guilt or anxiety that she is "missing work".
- A woman who is disciplined as a writer.
- An avid reader – a book a week, sometimes two.
- A single woman who is busy and proud.

She looked over her list and smiled. The food arrived. She devoured it. It was simply exquisite.

## November 22$^{nd}$

The telephone woke her. It was just after five o'clock in the morning. No one had ever called her at this hour. It was going to be a wrong number. She got up, walked to the living room, and picked up the phone. It was Tommaso Bellucci, the handsome young man she had seen several times in Rome. He sounded anxious.

> "I am sorry to ring you so early, Miss. Hutchins, but I am at the airport in Rome, and my flight to London leaves in just a few minutes. It is urgent that I meet with you. I land in Stanstead just before eight and will be in London at Liverpool Steet by nine. Can we meet? I need to see you before my meetings at the Treasury and with other officials at eleven? It's important."

> "Of course," she responded. "I'll meet you from the Stanstead train at platform eight. If we miss each other, wait under the station clock. See you soon!"

She quickly showered, dressed, made coffee and a slice of toast, packed her notebook, Dubai pen and purse in her handbag, and left her apartment just after eight. A taxi dropped her off at Liverpool Street station well in time to meet Tommaso.

He couldn't be missed. A tall, distinctive, smartly dressed and a stylish man with a distinctive head of curly hair, a very slim briefcase and a raincoat over his shoulders striding down the platform with confidence and panache. He waved as he saw her at the ticket gate and hugged her when they met.

> "I am starving, Miss Hutchins. Take me to breakfast, and I will explain the reasons for my call. I do apologize for calling so early."

> "Do call me Audrey and no need to apologize. I could tell from your voice that you felt it important. There is a very good traditional British breakfast place just a few minutes across the street – the Breakfast Club Spitalfields. A former client always insisted on meeting there and it is very good."

They walked for a few minutes, turned down a small alley, and there it was. A classic breakfast café. A few booths, several tables, a bar with seats and some very friendly staff. They sat in the booth at the back of the café, and ordered coffee and traditional eggs benedict, orange juice and wholewheat toast. She warned him that the coffee would not be what he was used to with his espresso in Rome.

> "So tell me what you need to tell me, Tomasso."

"I could not reach Sir John or Riya, so I connected with you. I trust you know how to find and brief them, Audrey?"

She explained that Riya was now at the Bank of England as an analyst and Sir John had retired to his manor house in the Cotswold's to spend more time on his poetry publishing business and music. He looked puzzled but carried on.

"As you may know, we arrested Valin. At first, he would not speak, even though he was charged with sixty-three counts of fraud, nine of conspiracy to commit fraud, four money-laundering charges and one charge related to banking regulations. All civil charges, nothing criminal. For two weeks, he said nothing. Then, all of a sudden, following a visit from his wife Ginerva, he started singing like a bird.

"He began naming names of people who he bribed or paid "fees unconnected to services rendered" to make his work possible. They include five Ministers in the Italian government, three senior cardinals in the Vatican, senior government officials in seven EU countries and nine executives in banks across the EU, including two in the UK. He claims his wife is the brains behind all of this together with Michael Major. He says his wife is having an affair with him and is going hang him out to dry.
The bank he ran until his arrest does some legitimate business but is really a front for two corrupt organizations – the Legion of Christ and his wife's family business, the Mafia and the 'Ndrangheta.

What got me worried about you, Riya and Sir John was his revelation that one of the enablers of Valin's schemes here in the UK was Sir Dominic Sosta in the cabinet office. A devout and deeply committed member of the Legion, he shares everything the government is planning to do with Major who shares it with Valin. My concern is that Sosta is the man Sir John reports to.

Given that charges, some criminal will soon be laid against both Michael Major and Ginevra Amuso-Valin, I thought I should warn you. I wanted to make sure you were safe."

They were both silent as they ate their perfectly cooked, soft poached eggs, ham and English muffin with fried potatoes in a hollandaise sauce and sipped at their coffee.

"Who are you meeting with today, Tommaso?" she asked.

"The head of the UK fraud squad, senior officers from the serious crime unit and the cabinet secretary. I am part of a larger team; the rest of the Italian team is already here. Valin has evidence related to the murder of Calvi in London and to the murder of seven others, all linked to money laundering or fraud. One of the murders is that of Sir Andrew Rabkin. His evidence and statements point to his wife as the "mastermind," and Michael Major as the director of operations with Dominic Sosta as a point man here in London."

"I don't think Sir, John, Riya, and I are in any danger. Are we?"

"Your names were on a list found in a search of the Valin's villa. He knew you were investigating his money laundering and that you had met with various authorities and someone senior in the office of the Secretary of State Sodano in the Vatican. The annotation against your names says, "policy people with links – Sosta keeping an eye.""

"I see. I will let Riya and Sir John know. What do you think will happen now?"

"Valin has so much information that it could cause an earthquake in several governments and the Vatican if all were arrested and charged. No one wants that to happen. Words will be spoken, and some, like Sosta, will take retirement if he co-operates. In our government, this has already happened. Two cabinet ministers, nine senior public servants and a deputy director at the Guardia di Finanza have quietly departed. I am not sure what will happen at the Vatican. Sodano is paid every month by the Legion. He is not going anywhere, but I suspect a few Cardinals will be moved on."

"We are most concerned about his revelations about the Banca di Roma, which seems to be involved as is both the Bank of New York and Deutsche Bank. We are looking at a lot of money and some significant public figures. It will be very messy. New money laundering laws, regulations and practices will have to be developed – precisely what you, Sir John and Riya were working on," he said.

They sat in silence for a few moments. Then Audrey smiled.

"If I were still working on policy and regulations for money laundering, I might be very worried. After all, we are talking about very large sums of money, murder, serious crimes, and the Mafia or 'Ndrangheta. But I am not. Since we met in Rome, I have changed my career and focus for my life. I am now a writer who travels. I have left that world behind me."

"I wish I could just paint, Miss. Hutchins. It is what I want to do. But I also need to eat, pay rent, and enjoy some good wine. I work so that I can paint and live."

"I understand, Tommaso. I do. I am very fortunate not to have to worry about money – I can focus on what I want to do, which is to write. Though I say so myself, I am very good at it. If you are to make your meetings on time, we need to get you in a taxi and on your way. I sincerely appreciate you reaching out to me and ensuring I am in the loop about the Valin disclosures. I will make sure Sir John and Riya are informed."

She paid for their breakfasts and hailed him a taxi, giving instructions to the driver about his destination. Just before he got into the black cab, he hugged her and whispered, "Take care, Audrey."

Returning home, she made herself an espresso. Then she called Riya, who answered on her mobile phone. Riya listened intently, asking a few questions occasionally, and then thanked Audrey for making sure she was in the loop. Given the disclosures, she felt a need to share information with the head of security at the Bank of England, something Audrey thought was wise.

In talking with Sir John that afternoon, he said he was due to have a briefing for Sir Michael Gower of the Serious Crimes unit at the Metropolitan Police. Apparently, they had a four-hour meeting with Dominic Sosta, whom Sir John referred to as a "toad", who after an initial denial of any involvement, confessed fully to being involved in Valin's schemes, though denied that there were any threats to persons or violence associated with what he did. It was about the money. Apparently, he has a gambling addiction and needed the cash to pay off his debts.

> "The bottom line, Audrey, is that Valin's talking and confirming what we suspected. I don't think we are under any threat. What I do think is that all this will strengthen the resolve of EU Ministers to introduce the new policy and regulations we have been proposing and to strengthen their enforcement of them. If they don't, governments will fall, and heads will roll. They all want to stay in power. If they want to stay in power, they will have to act.

No need to buy a bullet-proof jacket and a Baretta just yet, Audrey!"

She agreed. They chatted about her upcoming visit, how the preparations and rehearsals for Messiah were going and about Riya's new work at the Bank of England.

By the time she had a light late lunch, it was three o'clock. She had yet to open her mail. Six items. Three bills, an invitation to join the Writers Guild, "the trade union for writers," a letter from the Chartered Accountants professional body asking if she would be interested in joining their committee on professional standards, some junk mail and a long letter from Michelle Robinson at PFD.

Michelle had met with a commissioning producer at the BBC, and they were very interested in the Prodigy documentary and book idea and wanted it to be ready to launch to coincide with the Young Musician of the Year competition. The next competition was in 2000, probably too soon. But the one after that in 2002 would fit very well. Attached to the letter was an outline of fees paid to authors of BBC books and documentaries, plus "day fees" for attending meetings. Michelle asked Audrey to get back to her as soon as possible.

Audrey phoned Michelle. They arranged to meet for lunch. The rest of her day was spent making notes for the Prodigy book and a walk around the shops in Kensington. She needed a break. She came back with cheeses, prawns, and some lettuce leaves. A prawn cocktail was on her menu for this evening.

## November 29th

Audrey arrived early for her lunch with Michelle Robinson. Lima was a new Peruvian restaurant that recently opened in Fitzrovia. The menu was full of items new to her, but looked very enticing. She ordered a negroni and studied the menu. Michelle arrived, looking exquisite in a simple linen outfit.

> "I can't stop arranging lunches here, Audrey. The food is to die for. Wonderful simple food but, believe me, a taste of heaven. I am working my way through the a la carte menu. Today I am having the smoked char siu pancetta – a lovely piece of fish with a shroud of pancetta with a delicate sauce."

> "I was tempted by that but have chosen the octopus and crab causa with miso sautéed aubergine," said Audrey.

> "You'll not be disappointed. Now I need a drink. A dreadful morning with that awful bore Lloyd Grossman. Full of himself, yet he has nothing to say. Ah well. Onward and upward!"

Michelle ordered for both of them and asked for a prosecco. When the drink came, she immediately asked for a second one.

> "It's looking very promising, Audrey. Your BBC Music Magazine articles and your piece for the Sunday Times convinced them you could write. They also checked you out with the editor of the

music magazine, who confirmed that you were one of his new and up-and-coming talents. I think we can close this deal. A book by August 2021 accompanied by a script for the documentary – essentially blocks about the five people we feature in the program - no room for anymore. The book can have as many as you like. I think we can get £25,000 for the package, less our fees. A real kick-start for your book writing, Audrey."

"It sounds too good to be true, Michelle. I have just started writing and this is a big opportunity. I don't know what to say…"

"Say "yes", Audrey. Then we can enjoy our meal."

They talked some more about the writing of the book, the contracts with the BBC and the arrangement with PFD. Audrey signed an agency agreement and Michelle said she would take care of the rest. "You write, I negotiate!"

As Michelle had promised, the meal was remarkable. Freshness, rich flavours, and finesse. She would be back.

Later, at her writing desk, listening to the Shostakovich cello concerto, she began elaborating her ideas for the Prodigy book. She may begin with a powerful story of someone who started with great promise but who left classical music behind for a different career. She had enough ideas about whom to include. The challenge would be about who to leave out. Then some kept trying but failed, like Joyce Hatto, who showed remarkable talent in practice sessions but went to pieces during performances. She decided to include two winners of the BBC Young

Musician competition – oboist Nicholas Daniel who now taught obo and conducting in the United States as well as clarinetist Emma Johnson who was a prolific performer, with many recordings to her name.

## December 8<sup>th</sup>

A call from Riya arranging lunch later that day at The River Café. The café had become a go-to place for all sorts of people – Richard E. Grant the actor and his wife were having lunch with the actor, Alan Rickman. The editor of The Daily Telegraph, Charles Moore, was lunching with Boris Johnson, the newly appointed editor of The Spectator. It was a place to be seen.

The Italian menu was intriguing. Audrey decided to have a drink of Bussola Valpolicella Classico and await Riya's arrival.

She did not have long to wait. Riya arrived in a dark pantsuit with a fine silk blouse, pearl earrings mounted in silver, and a matching necklace. She knew how to dress to impress. Almost every diner turned to look, even the women. They ordered – veal risotto for Audrey, and the Dover sole for Riya.

> "Audrey, it is so good to see you. You look younger each time we meet. You must be doing something right!"

> "I think it might be the wine!" said Audrey with an impish grin.

"Thanks for the heads up about the Valin's and all that. I briefed our security team, who were subsequently briefed by Serious Crimes and the fraud squad. We have Deutsche Bank, HSBC, and Lloyds Bank and a few others on a high level of scrutiny. We have sent a team to Coutts to take a long hard look at a few issues relating to compliance with banking regulations. It's all a go I tell you. Did my reputation at the Bank a lot of good, being ahead of the game. So, thanks Audrey." Riya raised a glass, as if offering a toast.

"Felt I had to make sure you were alerted. Make sure you were safe, Riya."

"I appreciate that, Audrey. I do. The assessment from our team and the police is that I, you and Sir John are not in any danger, especially now that Dominic Sosta has been dismissed following his full confession. My boss thinks they should take away his knighthood. Not going to happen. It will all be covered up, you'll see."

The food arrived, and they both topped up their drinks. Audrey shared her news about the book and television documentary, signing with PFD and the new ideas she was working on.

"That is excellent, Audrey. Just wonderful. This is why you look so much younger. You're doing what you should have been doing all along. Writing!" After a pause, Riya continued. "I have news too. I am getting engaged this weekend. You'll love him, Audrey. He is a musician. Plays with the BBC

Symphony Orchestra – principal viola. Trevor Herbert is his name. He's from South Wales - Cambrian. He is so gentle, kind, and caring. We've known each other for ages, but we have become very close over the last six months. He proposed a few weeks ago. I said yes. At least it will stop my mother and aunties from trying to arrange a marriage with some ugly old fat Bangladeshi doctor from Leeds!"

"I am so happy for you, Riya. So happy" – and she was. Genuinely happy. "When is the wedding?"

"Not sure yet," replied Riya. We are in no rush. You will meet him very soon – he has been cajoled by Sir John to play in the Messiah, we're coming down in a few days for the final rehearsal and performances, staying at Sir John's. I gather you will be there for two nights too, is that right?" asked Riya.

"Yes, I am. I arrive on the afternoon of 12th and leave in the morning of the 14th. I am to be driven by my usual driver. We could include you too if it would be helpful?"

"So kind, Audrey. But no. There are three others from the orchestra coming, so we're driving down in a people mover with instruments, luggage and a case of champagne. Sir John persuaded them all to play. It is just Trevor and I staying at the house. One of the other players – the woman who is playing the harpsichord – has a house nearby, and the other two are staying with her. Do you know, don't be shocked now, but I have never been to a performance of Handel's Messiah before. I will be a Messiah virgin – probably an inappropriate thing to say," she said, smiling broadly.

Audrey laughed, "Well, you are in for a treat. This must be my twentieth Messiah. Always different, always inspiring."

Riya asked Audrey about her writing and was very impressed with her BBC book and documentary series and the other writing projects that Audrey had started sketching out. She was especially interested in the idea of profiling women chefs in the UK who were close to a Michelin star but had yet to be recognized. None held one yet, but it was only a matter of time. She was thinking of Clare Smyth at Restaurant Gordon Ramsey, Angela Hartnett, and Sally Clark. She would ask her agent to pitch this to The Sunday Times.

Riya had another surprise. She had been promoted at the Bank of England. She was now leading a project on "true" indicators of economic well-being, based on the work she did for her Master's degree at Oxford and work in New Zealand on the economics of happiness. Rather than just look at the cost of a basket of goods, her team would look at the economics of health, raising children, transport and other factors that make up "living." The idea was to give a snapshot of the health of families, communities, and individuals in economic terms. After Christmas, she was travelling to both Canada and New Zealand to explore just how they are measuring economic well-being and, more importantly, what they are doing with the data. She wondered if Audrey would like to join her.

"You mean as a travelling companion, Riya?"

"More as a consultant or advisor. I value your judgement and you have "presence". I think you'd be an asset. I need someone who understands Britain, someone with experience, to advise and consult with during these visits. I can get carried away and enthusiastic. I think you'd help to keep me focused and grounded. We can pay you, of course. I know you are writing and have projects to complete, but you can do that anywhere. The round trip – Ottawa and then Wellington – would just be ten days in mid-January. Will you think about it? "

"I will think about it, Riya. I will let you know my decision when we are together in the Cotswold's."

They chatted for a further twenty minutes, and then Riya left, having settled the bill for the meal. Audrey ordered a negroni and thought for a moment. She wondered why Riya would want or need her as a colleague. Was it a confidence issue? Was it really about expertise and "presence"? She was baffled. No doubt it would sort itself out.

She paid for her negroni and took a cab home.

## December 12th

The time between her last lunch meeting at Wilton's with Sir John Alton and arriving at his front door in Chipping Camden in the early afternoon of December 12th had, for Audrey Hutchins, gone quickly and had seen significant changes in her life.

Thanks to Michelle, she now had a book contract and a commitment in principle to a one-hour documentary for Channel 4. In the new year, she would meet with a producer called Dominique Leclerc, who had overseen several very successful documentaries. Michelle said he "loved the idea," especially when he saw the list of prodigies she wanted to profile and saw it was not the usual suspects – Mozart, Paganini, Clara Schuman, and the rest. A focus on modern players who young viewers could connect to. Michelle said he was already asking an assistant to research archive footage to see what was available.

She also had some close encounters with difficult people. One was the manageress of a bookstore she sometimes popped into not far from her apartment. She was accused by this very angry woman of stealing a book - as if she would. The book in question was about Marie Antionette by Antonia Fraser – not at all interesting to her. The woman was adamant that Miss Hutchins was the one who stole the book, and "now she is back looking for the next book to steal!" How ridiculous. The police were called. A nice policeman calmed the manageress down and assured her that the matter would be investigated. He asked Miss Hutchins to accompany him to the station. As they left the bookstore and turned a corner, he stopped her and said, "sorry about that – it's not the first time she has done this...I suggest you go on your way and forget about it and not return there again for a while". She took his advice.

Then there was the recent encounter with Riya. She had announced her engagement, promotion and made an offer. Unusual. Audrey had decided to say no, but to find a positive way of doing so. She really had a lot to do with the book and several meetings with the BBC.

And now here she was in the Cotswold's at the door of Sir John Aston's impressive house – a small manor house set in five acres of land with a windy drive between the gate and the front door. They had chatted by telephone and agreed she would come for a rehearsal today and a performance of the Messiah tomorrow. She had been driven by a service she now used all the time to get to and from the airport or to events outside of London. Far more efficient than rail or buses and much more comfortable.

Sir John greeted her at the door, took her suitcase and welcomed her to the house.

> "Just in time for afternoon tea and champagne before we dash to rehearsal. Meet Trevor in the dining room, Riya's other half. Riya is upstairs getting changed. She'll be down in a moment."
> "Nice to see you too, John!" Audrey said with a smile.
>
> "Ah yes, welcome Audrey," said Sir John as he gave her a peck on the cheek. "So much to do, but all is going well. Our four soloists are just excellent. They

have mastered their parts, even though for three of them this is their first Messiah."

She walked in the direction of voices and found a large dining room with a table full of sausage rolls, sandwiches, pate, dips, cheeses, toasted slices of bread, crackers and biscuits and champagne. She helped herself.

A very handsome, tall young man with a full head of straight black hair approached her.

"You must be Audrey. I am Trevor, Riya's fiancé. I have heard a lot about you. Riya really thinks the world of you," he said, smiling.

"I can't imagine why," Audrey said also with a smile. "We worked together briefly on a project with Sir John. We did enjoy working together – Riya is a very smart woman. You're lucky to have found her."

"That's what she tells me all the time," Trevor said. "I think she admires you for taking charge of your life and making such a big career change. From accountant to writer and having such success so quickly. It's the focus and determination she likes. She also tells me you're "as smart as a pin," whatever that means."

Riya joined them, giving Trevor a hug and Audrey a peck on the cheek. They chatted for some time before Sir John ushered them into cars and they went to the rehearsal.

Audrey had been to one rehearsal before. The Philharmonia Orchestra held an open rehearsal for a performance of Scarlatti and Couperin conducted by Christoph von Dohnányi. She had been fascinated at the attention to detail he encouraged the players to "attend to," especially markings in the scores about tempo. That rehearsal did not involve a choir of thirty people or four soloists. This one did. She was interested to see how it would unfold.

Sir John was very much in his element as conductor. Thirty-two musicians had been assembled and, after just three rehearsals, were playing well. The choir was a little ragged on the first chorus he asked them to do – All We Like Sheep – but after a time, they too were singing well and together, managing the complexities Handel had built into the score. It was the soloists who most impressed Audrey. Christina Stiles had a wonderful alto voice, and Thomas Theobalds's bass voice was deep and resonant. His singing of Why Do the Nations Rage So Furiously Together was just magnificent. Sir John, clearly pleased, thanked everyone and encouraged them to be early and sober for tomorrow's performance in the medieval Church of St. James.

Back at the manor house, Sir John tucked into the food left out from earlier and gave everyone another drink. He was very pleased with the rehearsal and the quality of the singing. They were all in bed by ten-fifteen.

## December 13<sup>th</sup>

After a light breakfast of coffee, croissants and toast with a rich marmalade, Riya and Audrey decided to go for a walk around the "town." Trevor and others in the orchestra wanted to rehearse and Sir John had urgent errands to run in preparation for the evening.

Chipping Campden is not exactly a large town, but it has an interesting High Street full of antique shops, crafts and art shops, a high-end jewelry store and a lovely bookstore that also sells compact discs. Riya and Audrey visited each, stopping at The Old Tea House for a pot of tea and some egg sandwiches.

Audrey told Riya that she would not be able to accompany her on her visit to New Zealand and Canada - she had too much to do with the BBC project and other commitments. Riya, clearly disappointed, said she understood. Audrey hoped she did.

Riya asked if Audrey thought Sir John was "interested" in her – "after all," she said, "he is on the market and would be quite a catch!"

> "What do you mean, Riya? Do you mean is he interested in me?"

> "Well yes, Audrey. I mean, you two are about the same age, get along well, both very smart and well educated and seem to me to be a good fit."

> "I can assure you, Riya, that such a thing has never occurred to me and I am pretty sure that it is the farthest thing from his mind. He is still recovering from his divorce, and I doubt if he is interested in a relationship with anyone, least of all me. I certainly am not. I have never been as content and as happy

as I am now and I wouldn't want to give up my life as is for some many, even if I did like and admire them."

"Just thought I'd ask," said Riya with an impish smile.

After their tea and sandwiches, they drove to Hidcote Manor to see the wonderful gardens created by Lawrence Johnston and now run by the Royal Horticultural Society. They were glad they did. Arranged as a connected sequence of outdoor "rooms," they were enchanted by the winter garden, which still had colour and vibrancy. They had to use their imagination for other rooms – it was very late in the year.

As they were leaving, Riya suddenly said to Audrey,

"I hope you were not offended by my request for you to come with me to New Zealand and Canada. I asked you because I respect you and trust your judgement. I am also a little nervous. This is a major project for the Bank and a real test for me. I wanted reassurance and someone to explore ideas with."

"Why not a colleague from the bank?"

"To be honest, I wanted to do this on my own. Remember I told you that my nickname at Oxford was "Hermit the Odd"? Well, now you know why. I am a loner, really, but you I feel I can connect with, and I do not feel you are judging me. Work colleagues would. I feel safe with you. Trevor too, of course. I'll be fine. Really."

"So kind, Riya. I appreciate the gift of trust. You will be fine. Just listen, learn and imagine. That's all you need to do. I have not yet been to New Zealand, but if my experience of visiting Canada is anything to go by, you will be warmly and openly welcomed, and they will be happy to share with you. Nice people."

"So, I gather. I want to try poutine – it is a combination of chips, cheese curds and gravy. Sounds very Indian to me – a bit like khichdi, but it is supposed to be a classic Quebec dish that is catching on across Canada."

"Sounds truly awful!" said Audrey, not attempting to hide her disgust. "Do tell me about it when you get back."

They returned to the house to find everyone having a nap. Audrey went to her bedroom, lay on the bed, and fell asleep.

The performance was not flawless, but it was wonderful. Sir John relished his role on the podium and was masterly in directing the compact orchestra and engaged choir. All of the soloists were on top form and the packed church showed their appreciation with frequent applause. They stood, as is now tradition, for the Hallelujah chorus and she thought she heard some in the audience singing along with the "Amen" chorus. There was a six-minute standing ovation. The highlight for Audrey were the complex choral pieces – especially And with These Stripes we Are Healed. The whole performance spoke to her about her own journey in the last two years and how she too felt healed.

At the after party, when Sir John reminded everyone that they were expected to do the same again tomorrow to another sold out crowd, he congratulated all on a wonderful performance – "moving, engaging and largely on tempo!" he quipped.

After a while, he came over and sat with Audrey.

> "You being here, Audrey, means a lot to me. We worked together well and now you have seen me in my other world – at home doing the things I love. I gather that you are now doing the same – writing. We are kindred spirits, Audrey. I knew it the first time we met. If you need to get away from London, this place is not far and you'd be welcome anytime.
>
> The team we had – you, Riya, and me – did good work, but more importantly, I think we all grew together. I was healing from my divorce and being sidelined at work, Riya was trying to decide whether to say "yes" to Trevor and to move to the bank and you were on a journey to become the person you have always wanted to be. We're each getting there, Audrey. You and I may be getting on, but we're getting there. Be true to yourself – do what it is you want to do, and you will be fine. That's what I think."

He got up, gave her a hug, leaving her surprised and yet feeling a sense of satisfaction. Someone else was on a search for meaning and purpose and was making progress. Always more to do, but she was indeed getting there. Time will tell.

## Authors Notes

1. The material in this novel is a work of fiction, but it is based on a great many facts. The description of the Legion of Christ and Regnum Christi – organizations founded by Marcial Maciel Delgado – is based on historical accounts and subsequent documentation and reports. Shocking but true. You can read more in the book Fr Marcial Maciel. Pedophile, Psychopath and Legion of Christ Founder by J. Pail Lennon. See also Vows of Silence: The Abuse of Power in the Papacy of John Paul II by Jason Berry and Gerald Renner, which was originally published in 2004 and updated in 2014. Other books on this topic include The Legion of Christ: A History by Gerald Renner and Jason Berry and A Priest's Tale: Autobiography of a Disgraced Priest by Fernando M. Gonzalez. As for the Vatican bank, Gerald Posner's account in God's Bankers: A History of Money and Power at the Vatican (2015) is well worth a read.

2. Homosexuality in the Catholic Curia has been well documented in the book In the Closet of the Vatican – Power, Homosexuality and Hypocrisy by Frederic Martel, published in 2015. Based on 1,500 in-person interviews, which included 41 cardinals, 52 bishops and monsignors, 45 apostolic nuncios and foreign ambassadors. It is very detailed and directly references some of the issues raised in this novel.

3. Money laundering is a truly global challenge. The estimated amount of money laundered globally in one year is 2 - 5% of global GDP, or US$800 billion - US$2 trillion in current dollars. Due to the clandestine nature of money laundering, it is difficult to estimate the total

278

amount of money that goes through the laundering cycle. The Group of Seven (G7) nations used the Financial Action Task Force on Money Laundering to put pressure on governments around the world to increase surveillance and monitoring of financial transactions and share this information between countries. Starting in 2002, governments worldwide upgraded money laundering laws and surveillance and monitoring systems of financial transactions. Anti-money laundering regulations have become a much larger burden for financial institutions and enforcement has stepped up significantly. The Financial Action Task Force (on Money Laundering) (FATF), with members from thirty-seven countries, has been active since 1987 and Britain has been a key player.

4. Bill Bryson did live in Kirby Malham but left to return to the United States in 1996 – three years before his appearance here. The Arvon Foundation does own Lumb House and runs writing workshops there (and it was Ted Hughes' home), but as far as I know, Bill Bryson was not one of their "instructors." For a witty examination of these kinds of workshops, see an excellent novel by Miranda France (2023), The Writing School.

5. Miss Hutchins, Sir John, Riya, the Valins, Sir Andrew Rabkin, Michael Major, and the other characters in this novel - other than musical performers, novelists, poets, and composers – are all fictional. They are based on fifty years of observing people, some who came to therapy when I was a practising counselling psychologist and others who were students. If you think I am capturing you as a character in this novel, you are mistaken.

6. Every effort has been made to ensure that references to menus, hotels and restaurants are accurate and appropriate. Things do change, however. Some liberties have been taken with dates. For example, the Kronos Quartet's CVD of Caravan did not appear until 2000.

7. I am most thankful to the Rivendell Retreat Society on Bowen Island, British Columbia, for letting me use Penny Lou Cottage – a true writer's retreat - in which the very rough 45,000-word manuscript I arrived on the Island with became the novel you have just read. This was in May 2023 – a month of peace, quiet, contemplation, reading, walking and serious, focused writing.